Marrying Mom

Olivia Goldsmith is the author of the international best-sellers *The First Wives Club*, also a major Hollywood film, *Bestseller, Flavour of the Month, Fashionably Late* and, with Amy Fine Collins, *Simple Isn't Easy*, a practical guide to stylish dressing. She is a native New Yorker who now lives in Florida.

Praise for Olivia Goldsmith:

Marrying Mom

'What a great feeling to fall into the capable hands of Olivia Goldsmith. The author of *The First Wives Club* and *Bestseller* always serves up believable characters in slightly outlandish situations in a mixture that makes highly entertaining reading . . . The resulting romantic twists and turns are funny, but better still is Goldsmith's sharp portrait of the maddening but lovable Phyllis . . . All pop novels ought to be as hard to put down as *Marrying Mom*.' *People*

'*Witty* . . . full of funny New York moments and read-for-the-big-screen charm . . . Perfect comic relief.'
New York Daily News

Bestseller

'Extremely satisfying.' *The New York Times Book Review*

'Like Jane Austen dealing blackjack . . . you keep licking your fingers and reaching for the next page as if it were another potato chip.' *Newsweek*

OLIVIA GOLDSMITH

MARRYING MOM

HarperCollinsPublishers

HarperCollins*Publishers*
77–85 Fulham Palace Road,
Hammersmith, London W6 8JB

This paperback edition 1998
Special overseas edition 1997
1 3 5 7 9 8 6 4 2

First published in Great Britain by
HarperCollins*Publishers* 1997

First published in the USA by
HarperCollins*Publishers* 1997

Copyright © Olivia Goldsmith 1997

The Author asserts the moral right to
be identified as the author of this work

ISBN 0 00 649988 0

Set in Life

Printed and bound in Great Britain by
Caledonian International Book Manufacturing Ltd, Glasgow

Thanks to:

Paul Smith for putting up with an insane schedule, and for giving me the house of my dreams.

Jim and Christopher Robinson for their understanding and sacrifice on behalf of this book.

Linda Grady, as fine a reader as she is a friend and writer.

Barbara Turner for her love, humor, and for giving me this plot in the first place. (Don't sue, sis.)

Paul Mahon because of all those trips to Montana, Ireland, Michigan, and the rest. Lucky I don't depend on you.

Jerry Young for never putting me on hold. What are you wearing, Jerry?

Sherry Lansing for sharing my vision, telling me jokes, and turning this book into a film.

Aida Mora for keeping me supplied with endless Diet Cokes and making things homey.

Allen Kirstein for encouragement when I needed it the most.

John Yunis for tempting me to look better than I ever have.

Flex (a.k.a. Angelo) for the streaks and blow job.

Gail Parent, whom I can't live without.

Chris Patusky, who tried to pick me up at a book signing. (Hope that trouble with the bar association clears up soon, Chris.)

Amy Bobrow for help with Wall Street lingo and with Matilda.

Harold Wise, the best, most caring internist in Manhattan. You were right about everything, Harold.

Diana Hellinger, the only girlfriend I have who will sing with me over the telephone.

Lorraine Kreahling for putting aside our project while this book consumed me; thanks for being my friend.

Amy Fine Collins for helping me with my ABCs. You know I'd always do it for you, girlfriend.

Mike Snyder for being one giant earlobe. You were so slow you hurt my whole family, but I love you.

John Botteri (a.k.a. Moe) for knowing exactly how many BTUs a girl writer needs.

Barry LaPoint for your artistic talent, integrity, and for knowing which of the hallway doors to change.

Laura Ziskin for kindly understanding and for giving this book up.

David Madden, even though you wouldn't marry me.

Robert Cort for giving me the really key advice about Mom's character. Wish this were an award, big guy.

Arlene Sorkin, girl screenwriter extraordinaire.

Andrew Fisher for his unmatchable expertise in dealing with the true professionals of the building trade.

Kelly Lange, because being Queen ain't easy.

Anthea Disney, a real woman, a real CEO, and a real pal.

Ruth Nathan, my inspiration in so many ways.

Lynn Goldberg, because I still worship you, Lynn. And by the way, when are you going to put me up on your wall?

Dwight Currie, superb book reader, bookseller, book writer, and bookkeeper (except for that last one).

Michael Kohlmann, still "the nice one" and still my friend.

Steve Rubin and Ed Town of Gallery North Star, Grafton, Vermont, for keeping me well fed and well hung.

Edgar Fabro at Copy Quest, because no one can duplicate his amazing talents.

Jody Post, because I miss you and I missed you.

Norman Currie at the Bettmann Archives for his inspirational help in filling the album.

"Old age is woman's hell."
—Ninon de Lenclos

One

*I*ra, I'm leaving you." It wasn't easy for Phyllis to give her husband of forty-seven years the news, but she was doing it. She had always told the truth. All her life people had called her "difficult" or "tough" or "insensitive," but actually she was just honest.

"I can't take it, Ira," she told him. "You know I never liked Florida. I came down here for you, because you wanted to." She paused. She didn't want to blame. It was a free country and Ira hadn't forced her. "Well, you'd always supported me," Phyllis admitted. "Let's face it: you earned the money, so I owed it to you. But it was your retirement, Ira, not mine. I wasn't ready to retire. But did you give me a choice?" Ira said nothing. Of course, she didn't expect him to. The fact was that in their forty-seven years of married life he'd rarely said much. Still, by some marital osmosis, she always knew what his position was on any given subject. Now she realized that the wave of disapproval that she expected to feel had not materialized. This meant that either Ira was sulking or that he wasn't there at all. She paused. Even for her, considered a loud mouth by everyone all her life, even for her it was hard to say this. But it had to be said. "You didn't pay enough attention to them, Ira. You needed me at the company, and I did what I had to do. But the children needed us. And I don't think they got enough of us, Ira. Things have gone wrong for them. Sharon with Barney . . . Susan unmarried . . . and Bruce!" Phyllis paused and bit her lip. There were some things best left unsaid. "I don't want to criticize you, but I don't think you were there for them, Ira. You paid for the best schools, but they didn't learn how to live. They don't know what's important. And I think they need their mother. I'm going up to take care of the children, Ira. I wasn't a good enough mother to them then, but I can try and make up for it now."

Phyllis sighed deeply. The sun was merciless, and she thought of the skin cancer that Ira had developed on his bald head. She should wear a hat, but she couldn't stand hats or sunglasses or any of the extra *chazerai* that most people schlepped around in Florida: sunscreen, lip balm, eye shades, visors. Who had the time? Florida was the place that looked like paradise but wound up deadly. "Ira, Thanksgiving was unbearable. Eating a turkey in the Rascal House yesterday and having the kids calling only out of a sense of obligation? What kind of holiday was that? It wasn't good for them and it wasn't good for me. It was depressing, Ira." She lowered her voice. Phyllis wasn't vain, but she lied about her age. "My seventieth birthday is on the twelfth, Ira. It scares me. Then there's Hanukkah, Christmas, and New Year's coming, I won't survive if I try to do it down here. Do you understand?"

Nothing. No response. Phyllis told herself she shouldn't be surprised. Always she talked, he listened. But at least at one time he had listened. In Florida, in the last several years, he seemed to have collapsed in on himself. His world was only as large as his chest cavity and the illness that resided in it. Phyllis had made sure he took his pills, watched his diet, and that he'd exercised. But conversation? A luxury. Phyllis sighed again. What did she expect?

Phyllis turned her back on Ira and wiped moisture out of her eyes. She wasn't a crier. It was ridiculous to get all emotional. She knew that and fiercely told herself to stop it. She turned back. "You won't be alone here," she said. "Iris Blumberg is just over there by the willow tree, and Max Feiglebaum isn't far away." She paused. "I know you don't have patience for Sylvia, but she'll visit every week to tidy up."

There wasn't anything more to say. They had had a good marriage, she and Ira. There were those who saw her as pushy, as too outgoing, as egocentric. Not Ira. And he'd been wrong because she was all those things. You couldn't reach the age of sixty-nine, she mused, without knowing a little bit about yourself.

Unless you were very pigheaded, or a man. Ira, a man, had never really understood her or learned a thing about himself. But then with men, how much was there to know?

With men, either they had a job or they didn't, they cheated or they didn't, they charmed you or they didn't. Ira had been an accountant before he retired, almost a decade ago. Ira was a good man. He worked and brought home his pay, didn't cheat, and didn't charm. But he had liked her. If he hadn't understood her, he had at least enjoyed her. And he'd given her three beautiful babies.

Phyllis thought of Susan, Bruce, and Sharon. Each had been so perfect, so gorgeous. Funny how babies grew up and became just as imperfect as any other adults.

She shook her head, dislodging the tangential thought. As she'd aged she hadn't, thank God, lost her memory. Instead, if anything, she remembered too much too often. "So anyway, Ira, I hope this doesn't come as a shock. You always knew I hated this place. Nobody down here but tourists, old Jews, and rednecks. I've got to leave you. It's for my mental health," she said, though she knew that Ira would hardly accept that as a legitimate excuse. "When did you become sane?" was one of the questions he'd frequently asked her. Despite his mild joke they both knew she was the voice of reason.

"I haven't told the children. I know they'll be upset. But I can't live only for them or you, Ira."

Phyllis stooped down and picked up a stone from the ground beside the grave. She walked up to his headstone and laid the pebble beside the others that still remained from previous visits she or the children had made. Who would visit the grave now? Just her friend, Sylvia Katz? The goyishe groundskeeper she always gave five dollars to when she came in? Whoever it was, she knew Ira wouldn't like it. "Ira, I have to," she said as she picked up her purse and prepared to go. "It'll kill me if I stay here much longer."

Virtually every morning for nine years and three months, Ira and Phyllis Geronomous had walked the strip of macadamized beachfront that was known throughout Dania, Florida, as "The Broadwalk." Now, since his death almost two years ago, Phyllis continued to walk it, more out of habit than desire. Today, Black Friday, the day after Thanksgiving, the beautiful weather did not match her mood, though she felt better after her talk with Ira. The sea, a Caribbean azure, winked at her as she made the turn from the shaded section of the path to the straightaway that led past the band shell, the cheap bathing suit and T-shirt boutiques, the snack shops, and greasy restaurants. In stark contrast, on the other side of the tarmac was a swath of flat pristine beach that met the aqua water. No one, not even the *meshuga* suntanners, was on the beach side yet. The Broadwalk was already peppered with pedestrians—dozens of people over sixty-five who found sleep impossible beyond 5 a.m. and did their morning constitutionals before the heat became too oppressive.

Phyllis didn't know why she was walking now. She had walked with Ira because he had to: with congestive heart failure you had to keep the circulation moving, the weight down, and the fluids out of your lungs. Ira wouldn't walk without her, so every morning they'd both gotten up and she'd done the three miles down to the parking lot and the three miles back, past the Howard Johnson's, past the palm trees and cheap motels, all the way to the California Dream Inn before quitting for the day.

Now she passed the Pinehearst and, as usual, Sylvia Katz was sitting out in front on her webbed aluminum lawn chair, waiting, with her ubiquitous huge black patent leather purse perched on her lap. Sylvia Katz was in her mid-seventies, maybe more, though she wouldn't admit it. She was *zaftig*, short, and her hair had thinned. She wore it teased and colored red—the unnatural red of those poisonous maraschino cherries that they put on top of the Chinese food in the bad restaurants down here. She was from Queens—Kew Gardens—and had spent the last fifteen years of her married life living here. She was neither smart nor witty, but she was loyal and patient and the best that Phyllis could do in the friendship department right now. Here, friends had died or dispersed in the diaspora of the aging. "Can I walk with you?" Sylvia asked, as she always did.

"It's a free country," Phyllis answered with a shrug, completing the morning ritual in their usual way.

Sylvia Katz pushed herself up from the chair and stepped past the concrete balustrade that separated Pinehearst Gardens from The Broadwalk hoi polloi. They walked in near silence for a moment, the only sound being the noise of Sylvia's sandals shuffling, and the swishing of her purse rubbing against her shorts. Over and over again Phyllis had begged Sylvia both to leave the purse behind and to get a pair of Reeboks just like everybody else. But Sylvia wouldn't do it. You couldn't tell with Sylvia whether it was that she hated change or that she couldn't spend the money. Phyllis shrugged. What did it matter if Sylvia schlepped the purse or dragged her feet? So it made her walk more slowly. Big deal. They weren't going anywhere.

"I told Ira," Phyllis announced.

"Do you think he was upset?" Sylvia asked.

"How could I know?" Phyllis heard her own voice betraying the irritation that Sylvia so often made her feel. "Even when he was alive, you couldn't tell if Ira was feeling anything. In the hospital, with his lungs filled with fluid, he didn't complain."

They were past the band shell, empty except for the sign that announced the swing-band concert that night. Once a week The Broadwalk was thronged with couples joined together by the lindy. Sylvia, whose husband had deserted her a few years earlier after over twenty-one years of marriage, came regularly and sat

9

watching, her patent leather purse firmly held on her lap. But no matter how often she invited Phyllis, Phyllis abstained. Sylvia never noticed and kept asking.

It wasn't that Phyllis didn't like the music, except maybe this Friday evening, when the sign said "The Mistletoes," the season's opening band, were playing a holiday medley. She needed chestnuts roasting like she needed a melanoma. Usually she loved music. Now, though, it made her too restless and sad. Somehow Sylvia could feel comfortable sitting on the sidelines, but for Phyllis, it was too painful knowing that she'd never dance again. People did dance on The Broadwalk, and then, in a blink of time, they were dead and gone. They might as well be under The Broadwalk, buried in the sand. Phyllis repressed a sigh. Ira had never been much of a dancer. Long ago, somehow, Phyllis had given it up. It was ridiculous at her age to care, but there was something about the music that got under her skin and didn't allow her to sit, blank and regretless, along with Sylvia.

"You comin' tonight?" Sylvia asked, as predictable as Republican bank scandals.

"I can't," Phyllis told her. "I'm having dinner in Buckingham Palace."

"Don't kid me," Sylvia said, but there was enough doubt in her voice that Phyllis knew she could.

"Betty is very unhappy," Phyllis continued. "All of her children have disappointed her. I said 'Betty, that's what they're for.' We're talking it over tonight. You know, they say that Edward is like my Bruce.

'Gay, schmay,' I said to her. 'Just help him find a nice *faigela* and settle down.' "

"Prince Edward is like your Bruce?" Sylvia asked, her voice lowering.

"Wake up and smell the nitroglycerin," Phyllis told her friend, who also had a heart condition.

"What a tragedy," Sylvia tsked. "And in such a family."

"It's in *my* family, too," Phyllis snapped. "What are we, belly lox? Nothing wrong with it." Plenty was wrong with it, in Phyllis's opinion, and with Susan and Sharon, too, but it was no one's job but hers to point it out.

If Phyllis ever took Sylvia seriously she'd be offended. But, luckily, she knew how ridiculous it would be to be offended by anything Sylvia said. The woman had a strong constitution, a good heart, and a weak mind.

"I heard the Queen Mother had a colostomy," Sylvia said in a lowered voice. "Like my Sid." For the decade before Sid left her, Sylvia had coped with not only her own heart condition but also Sid's colon cancer. "Can you imagine? All those garden parties." Phyllis ignored the non sequitur. Who knew how Sylvia's mind worked?

They had reached the end of The Broadwalk and, as always, Sylvia had to touch the post implanted in the macadam to stop vehicular traffic.

"What would happen if, just once, we walked to the end and you didn't hit the barrier?" Phyllis asked.

"Everybody touches the post," Sylvia said. "You have to touch the post."

"No you don't. I don't."

"You. You're different."

"*Nu*? Tell me something I don't know."

Phyllis sighed. Different was fine. It was lonely that was the problem. She didn't know how long she'd been lonely. Certainly way before Ira died. After a while, it became a fact of life and you just didn't notice it any more. That was the danger. It was like smelling gas: if you didn't pay attention to it, it could kill you. In Florida, Phyllis hadn't had a really good friend, one who understood her and got her jokes. Even Ira, long before he died, had stopped responding much. But nobody talked to their husbands. What was there to say after forty-seven years? "Do you still like my brisket?" "Do you think that I ought to shorten this skirt?" "Should we pull our troops out of Bosnia?"

Phyllis still had a lot to say, but who wanted to listen? And who had anything interesting to say back? Which was why she was now walking down The Broadwalk with Sylvia Katz. Sylvia was no Madame Curie, didn't understand half of what Phyllis was talking about, but at least she wasn't offended by Phyllis's wisecracks.

Most of the women that Phyllis knew *were* offended by her. She had to face it, she had a big mouth. She always had. And if she offended most of the women she met down here, they in turn bored her. They'd talk about recipes, grandchildren, shopping, and more recipes. They bored her stiff. Sylvia was a relief. No kids, no recipes, no aggravation.

Phyllis's own children interested her, but not just to brag about. They interested her because they were interesting, not because they were hers. Susan was brilliant, Bruce was remarkably witty, and Sharon . . . well, Sharon, she had to admit, favored her father's side of the family. Still, she loved them. Like Queen Betty must love her brood. It didn't mean she approved of their behavior, or that they approved of hers.

"This means you'll be with the kids for the holidays. Nice for you." She sounded wistful. "Nice for them." Sylvia paused. "Do they know you're going up?" she asked.

Phyllis was silent.

"You haven't told them, have you?" Sylvia asked accusingly.

"Not yet," Phyllis admitted.

"You have to. You have to," Sylvia said. Her own son had both refused a Thanksgiving invitation and not extended one to her. "If you don't tell them, I will."

"Don't you dare," Phyllis warned.

"When are you going to tell them?"

"Next Purim," Phyllis said, and opened the gate to Pinehearst for her friend.

Two

$\mathcal{Y}$ou're joking."

"You wish."

"Come on," Sig Geronomous said cavalierly. "It's just one of those empty threats. One of those nutty things she says that get us all jerked around for nothing. Like the time she corresponded with the Asian bride and wanted to import her for you."

"She means this," Sig's brother, Bruce, told her. "Todd, get over here and tell her that it's true." Bruce didn't live with Todd, but they had been spending a lot of time together. Whenever Sig asked if it was serious Bruce evaded the question.

"Bruce has the proof," Todd shouted into the receiver.

"How do you know?"

"Because she gave Mrs. Katz the rattan magazine rack," Bruce responded.

"The magazine rack? Oh my God!" Susan Geronomous—now known to her friends and business associates as Sigourney—accidentally dropped the telephone receiver. It crashed so hard against her granite countertop that her brother Bruce, at the other end of the phone, winced.

"What was that? Did you hurt yourself?"

"I wish." Sigourney had gotten control of the phone; now she just had to control herself. This couldn't really be happening . . . nothing was ever as bad as it seemed . . . absence made the heart grow fonder . . . too many cooks—she stopped. She was going crazy. This couldn't be true. Christmas and her mother both coming? She might as well pull out the razor blades now. Sig looked down appraisingly at her elegant wrist. "She just casually mentioned that she gave away the rattan magazine rack?"

"I'm way ahead of you," Bruce sang. "Mom didn't tell me. It's not a setup. It was Mrs. Katz who called."

"When?"

"Twenty minutes ago."

"Mom could have put her up to it."

"I already called the building manager. Confirmation. And there's a garage sale this week."

"A garage sale? She doesn't even have a garage, for God's sake."

"Yard sale, lawn sale, tag sale. Sigourney, don't play your word games now. It's happening. So, what are we going to do?"

Sigourney tried to regain some control. "What did

18

Mrs. Katz say when you talked to her? Exactly. Word for word."

"That Mom was leaving Florida for good. That she's packing up and moving to New York. She's getting a ticket today. She wants to arrive on Wednesday."

"Wednesday! That's only six days from now."

"Mmm. Good counting, Sig. That's why you earn the big bucks. Actually, it's five, since you don't officially count—"

"Don't be so anal, Bruce. And sarcasm is not necessary at this moment. We'll have more than we can handle starting Wednesday." Sigourney tapped the countertop. Her mother, living here in New York again. Calling her. Looking in her closets. Commenting. Criticizing. Oh God! Fear gripped Sig's chest like a Wonderbra. "This is the end of life as we know it, Bruce. How can we stop her?"

"Hmmm." He paused, ruminating. Bruce was smart. Maybe he'd have a solution. "How about plastic explosives in the cargo bay? We'd take down a lot of innocent lives, but we would know it was a small price to pay."

"Bruce!"

"Come on, Sig. It would be an act of kindness. People love tragedies at holiday time. It gives them something to watch on TV. Makes them feel better about the tragedy unfolding under their own Christmas trees."

"Amen, brother!" Todd yelled in the background.

Todd had been raised a Southern Baptist in Tulsa, Oklahoma, before he ran off to New York City to become an agnostic photographer.

"Bruce!" Sigourney forced herself to exhale while simultaneously staring up at the immaculate blue ceiling of her seventy-thousand-dollar kitchen. Her home, her beautifully designed, luxurious, and comfortable home, was her haven, her safe place where perfection reigned. It comforted her as nothing else did. She breathed deeply. Then her eyes focused on a tiny line. Was that a crack right in the corner? Was the glaze going already, despite Duarto's assurances that the fourteen hand-lacquered layers would last ten lifetimes? She had picked up the pen and jotted a note to herself to call him before she realized what she was doing. This news, this shattering news had come, *and she was writing notes to her decorator?* Where were her values, her priorities? It could only be denial kicking in. She'd better focus. "Did you speak to Sharon yet?" she asked her brother.

"You *are* losing it. I don't bother to call her with *good* news—not that I've had any of *that* lately." Bruce, at his end of the phone, eyed his shabby brownstone apartment. The two rooms, though neat and cozy, were cluttered not only with all his worldly goods but also with what remained of his entire business stock—the gay greeting card line he'd created and marketed until his partner had absconded with most of the money last year. And the season wasn't going as well as he'd hoped. It had really only just begun, but already stock had started being returned by Village shops. Queer Santa wasn't selling as he'd expected. Bruce sighed. Sig was buzzing in his ear. He adored his older sister, but she was sometimes so controlling, especially when she was frightened. He interrupted her chatter. "Sig, if I called Sharon, which I wouldn't, she'd just tell me how it was going to be even worse for her than for us, that it was always worse for her." Bruce sighed again, this time explosively. "I know it's the middle-child syndrome, but you'd think at thirty-seven she'd get over it."

Sharon was their disappointed and disappointing sister—four years younger than Sig, and only a year older than Bruce. But she looked twice his age. She had let herself go—it wasn't just her weight, it was her frosted hair that looked ten years out of date, the Talbots clothes in size sixteen that even a skinny Connecticut WASP couldn't get away with, and more than anything else it was the way her eyes and her mouth and her shoulders drooped in parallel, descending bell curves.

"We have to call Sharon," Sigourney said, ignoring her brother. "This is too big to handle on our own."

"Well, she's bigger than both of us," Bruce laughed. "Not that she'll be any use."

Sigourney knew all about it. Bruce had almost no patience for Sharon, but Sigourney felt sorry for her fat, whiny, frustrated, younger sister. Maybe it was because Sharri made her feel guilty. Maybe it was because Sig herself was so successful. Whatever the reason, she had no time now to listen to Bruce's usual sniping. "*I'll* call her," Sigourney said. "Can you meet here Saturday? I'm giving a pre-Christmas brunch at eleven for my A-list clients. Sunday I'm doing the B-list with the leftovers. But three on Saturday would be good for me."

"Well, don't put yourself out," Bruce said nastily. "What does that make us? C-list?"

Sig knew he was probably hurt because she hadn't invited him and Todd to either brunch. Bruce didn't realize how badly her own business had fallen off and she was too proud to tell him. She was also embarrassed about her necessary small economies, like using the catering firm for one party and making it do for two. But this wasn't the eighties anymore. And she couldn't afford to have Todd and Bruce acting up and alienating prospects and clients.

"I'll come," Bruce finally agreed, "but there's nothing we can do." He began to recite aloud in a singsong: "Roses are red / Chickens are white / If you think you can stop her / You're not very bright."

"No wonder your greeting card business is in trouble," was all Sig answered. "I'm hanging up and calling Sharon."

"Well, don't let Barney come," Bruce begged, defeated. Barney was not just Sharon's loser husband; he was also a blowhard. He was big and barrel-chested and balding. But what Sig and Bruce found intolerable was that he managed to lose every job he'd ever had while making Sharon feel like a failure. Barney was the kind of person who explained to heart surgeons at cocktail parties some new technique he'd read about in *Reader's Digest*. In short, he was an asshole.

Now it was Sig's turn to sigh. "I'll try to make it just us, but lately Sharon hasn't been driving. She gets those panic attacks when she has to cross a bridge."

"Oh, come on. She's a victim of faux agoraphobia. She's just too lazy to drive into the city. She's probably just trying to get a handicapped parking permit. Totally faux."

"Bruce! That's not true."

"Oh, Sig, Sig, Sig, Sig! Sometimes life could do with a little embellishment."

"My God! You sounded exactly like Mother then."

"I did not."

"You *did*."

"It's started," Bruce sang out.

Sig paused, biting back the need to tell him it was his fault. "You're right," she admitted. "Okay. It's Saturday at three and now I'll call Sharon."

"See ya. Wouldn't wanna be ya!" Bruce yodeled. Sig merely shook her head and hung up the phone.

Sig stood silently for a few moments in the center of her immaculate living room. She knew she shouldn't do it, but she was drawn irresistibly to the vanity in her bedroom. She looked around at the room and its beautiful decor. She'd have to sell the co-op, no doubt about it. She was behind in her maintenance payments and starting to get nasty looks from the co-op board president when she ran into him in the lobby.

Her client list had dropped, her commissions were down, and her own portfolio had taken a beating. Welcome to the nineties. Sig had done her best to downsize her expenses—she hadn't used her credit cards for months, had paid her phone bill and Con Ed on time, and had spent money only on the necessities. But it wasn't enough. Business had slowed to a trickle and even if she sold her stock now, she'd take a loss and have no possibility for the future. She'd just have to sell her apartment.

But this apartment was more than just equity: it was her haven. Maybe that was because she felt her mother had never made a home for her. As Phyllis had often said, "I'd be happy living out of a suitcase in a clean motel." The very thought made Sig shudder. Besides, the apartment was her visible sign of success, her security, and a place she could come after a long hard day of gambling with other people's money to lick her wounds. It was beautiful. It was perfect, and she'd have to face the fact that it was empty and she would have to sell it. The money would evaporate faster than good perfume out of an open flask and she would wind up destitute. Or worse: she'd wind up in an apartment in Fort Lee, New Jersey.

Sig looked into the mirror as she knew, irrevocably, what she would have to do. She didn't like what she saw. Was Bruce right? She wasn't just getting older, but also bitter? Were those new lines forming at the corner of her mouth? She stared more deeply into the mirror. And then her eyes flitted to the reflection in one pane of the three-sided glass. For a second something about the softness in the line of her jaw reminded her of . . . what? She was puckering, decaying, and withering. She was going the way of all flesh. Sig shuddered. But it wasn't just the age thing that gave her the shivers; she had looked like . . . her mother.

Sig moved her head but the trick of light, or the angle, was gone. Jesus, she would wind up alone. She wouldn't even have the comfort of three children to annoy and be annoyed by. Tears of self-pity and something else—a deeper sorrow—rose to her eyes. She was getting older, but she was also getting bitter. The thought of Phillip Norman made her sad. Sig had known he was no genius, but he was presentable, fairly successful—if a corporate lawyer could be considered that—and his warmth for her made up for some of her coolness. It was nice to be wanted, and Phillip seemed to want marriage and a child. She would have to at least compromise—she'd give up the idea of a soulmate for a friend, a partner, and a family. But she was starting to believe that Phillip was even less than a friend: he was an empty suit. He and all of the other empty suits and bad boys who had preceded him made her mouth tremble. She looked like shit and she felt worse.

It wasn't as if she hadn't been trying to find somebody, someone to settle down with, to marry. Even to have a family with, if it wasn't too late. Her mother acted as if it was Sig who was stopping it from happening. But the truth was there were no men who were interested. Despite her good haircut, her visible success, her careful makeup, her Armani suits—or maybe because of them—Sig couldn't remember the last time a new man had expressed any interest in her. The truth was, it wasn't like she had a choice except Phillip. Oh, she could have affairs with any of the more interesting but very married men she worked with, but she wasn't a Glenn Close/*Fatal Attraction* kind of girl. She didn't steal other women's husbands. And other than other women's husbands, who had looked at her lately? The Gristede's delivery boy? Her elevator operator? Women over thirty-five started to become invisible. She was losing it, and she was losing it fast.

She picked up a lipstick, about to paint a little color onto her lips when her hand froze in midair. Why bother, she thought. Why bother to paint it on. She was losing it—she had lost it. The bloom of youth, the promise of fecundity that attracted men, that even on some unconscious level promised them a breeder, was disappearing. Perhaps men her age wanted younger women not only for their looks but because of the hormonal message a young girl sent: that she could still carry their child. That she could demonstrate their virility to the world with her upright breasts and a bulging belly. Sig's periods were still regular. But how long would it last? She wasn't a breeder. The bloom of youth was gone, and she'd grow old alone.

She looked deeper into the mirror. Under her mother's brittle veneer, wasn't there a desperation? Wasn't there a gallantry that seemed to say to Sig that it was better to go down fighting, to be feisty and annoying, than to ever be perceived as pathetic and lonely?

Sig looked around once more at the bedroom and rose and wandered through all her perfect rooms. She wound up, as usual, in her kitchen. Her eyes immediately focused on the one flaw—the tiny crack in the lacquer finish. Had it grown? Perhaps she should have spent the money on smoothing her own wrinkles, in lacquering her own finish. Perhaps if she lost a few pounds more, did a little more time on the treadmill, and had her eyes done, she could attract someone more acceptable, more interesting, more human than Phillip Norman. Then again, maybe not. Sig reached for the door of her Subzero refrigerator, pulled open the freezer, and grabbed a pint container of Edy's low-fat double Dutch chocolate ice milk. She sat on the floor and, using a tablespoon, began to eat it all. She rarely gave herself over to this behavior, but the sweetness in her mouth was comforting. She understood how her sister had ballooned to over two hundred pounds. Thinking of Sharon, she realized she hadn't yet called her. Well, she'd call her later. After the Edy's was gone.

Three

*P*hyllis Geronomous. A ticket to New York," she announced. "One way. For a December fourth arrival."

"Do you have reservations?"

"Plenty of them, but I'm going anyway." The agent didn't look up from her keyboard or even respond to Phyllis's little joke. Phyllis shrugged. She knew this type. Old women were usually invisible to them.

They were in a tiny, tacky office, desks lined up facing each other, and in the center was a small white Dynel Christmas tree with tiny pink Christmas bulbs hanging down. The travel agent had been recommended by her son-in-law—she was the young woman who owned the agency. Barney had said, "She'll get you a deal. She owes me." Phyllis didn't like to think of what this annoying Floridian with the big hair could possibly owe Barney for, but she had to get a ticket somewhere. The clerk looked at her for the first time, as if she now knew something was expected but wasn't sure what. "So . . . you're going to The Big Apple?" she asked.

"It looks that way." She smiled sweetly. The only advantage to being an old dame was that if she smiled she could get away with murder.

The agent consulted her screen, then made a baby mouth. "You should have planned ahead. Do you know that a one-way ticket costs as much as a round trip?" She spoke in a condescending, louder voice, as if Phyllis were both stupid and hard of hearing.

"We're in peak season for the holidays. You can't meet the fourteen- or twenty-one-day advance ticket purchase deadline."

Tell me something I don't know, Phyllis thought, while the agent continued. Where was the help or break in price Barney had implied? Typical. Barney Big Mouth. Phyllis certainly wasn't going to ask this woman for any favors. "Anyway," the agent continued, "don't you want a round trip, for when you're coming back?"

"I'm never coming back!" Phyllis said vehemently. "I only moved down in the first place because Ira wanted to. But he's dead, so why stay?" Phyllis immediately realized she'd said too much. God, next she'd be telling strangers on buses her entire life story. The potential humiliation of loneliness was like a direct kick to her pride. She took a breath. She'd fight back with the only weapon she'd ever used—her tongue.

"Who needs to live in a place where everybody talks, but they're so deaf they can't listen? No one was born here, they just die here. Feh! Nothing has roots here, except the mangrove trees. I hate Florida!"

"*I* was born in Gainesville," the younger woman said. "I like Florida. Especially Miami."

Phyllis crossed her arms. "How can you like a city where the local rock band is called Dead German Tourists?" she asked.

The condescending younger woman recoiled. "Well, the violence *is* bad for my business . . ." she began.

"Not too good for the German tourists, either," Phyllis added. "But the survivors are enough to make you homicidal. And the retirees!" Phyllis rolled her eyes. "I didn't like any of these people when they lived up in New York and were important and pushy. Why the hell I should like them now, when they're just hanging around all day and still being pushy, is beyond me."

"Florida is a nice place for retirement. The weather's good and—"

"You call ninety-nine percent humidity *good* weather?" Phyllis asked. "Compared to what? Djakarta? You should see the fungus garden growing on my winter coat! And another thing: Who says that everyone the same age should hang out together? I don't want to be anywhere near these people. It's an age ghetto. This place isn't God's Waiting Room; it's Hell's Foyer. It's an elephant graveyard." Phyllis straightened herself up to her full height. "Well, I'm no elephant. I'm a New Yorker."

Coldly, the agent looked at her. "New York is a dangerous place, especially for an older lady alone." She was acting now as if Phyllis were incompetent, a doddering old wreck.

"You mean you think I'm incapacitated?"

"Uhh—no." The witch raised her brows. "Certainly not," she said, with the sincerity of a surgical nurse saying the procedure wouldn't hurt at all.

Why did every person under the age of fifty feel they could talk to an older woman as if she'd lost her marbles? Phyllis wondered. It made Phyllis feel more ornery than usual. "Look, just book me a seat. In first class. I'll get all the bad advice I need from my children."

Phyllis waited while the ticket printed out and took comfort in the idea that this girl would some day also be postmenopausal. In forty-five years she'd be plucking whiskers out of that recessive chin—if she could still see her chin, and had enough eye-hand coordination to hold a tweezers.

"Oh," the young woman cooed as she handed Phyllis the ticket. "Your *children* are up there. That's different. Well, I'm sure *they'll* be happy to see you."

"My eldest is a very successful stockbroker. She's got a gorgeous apartment on Central Park. And my youngest, my son, is an entrepreneur." Phyllis paused for a moment. She couldn't leave out Sharon. "My middle daughter has two adorable children."

"Which one will you be staying with?" the agent asked.

"Oh, I'm sure they'll all be fighting over *that*," Phyllis told the agent. "As soon as they know I'm coming."

"Don't they know?"

Phyllis shook her head. "Surprise is an essential part of the art of war." Mrs. Katz choked a little behind her. Phyllis turned her head. "Sylvia. Did you—"

"Do you want this?" the agent said, interrupting in a rude way.

Phyllis snatched the ticket from the agent and shook her head again. "Certainly. Just take the time from now on to show a little respect to your elders. Osteoporosis is in your future, too, you know." Phyllis got up from the chair, turned, and walked away.

Four

ho's going to pick Mom up at the airport on Wednesday?" Sharon asked. The three siblings were together at their elder sister's, but Sharon was doing most of the talking. She was a big woman, though her hands and feet were dainty—almost abnormally tiny. Her eyes, buried in her pudgy cheeks, were the same dark brown as the unfrosted parts of her hair and darted nervously from side to side. She'd already obsessed about the airport for two and a half hours.

Sig sighed. Between now and Wednesday she had a lot to cram into four days. She had to prepare for the marketing meeting, complete a newsletter, start her Christmas shopping on a nonexistent budget, and prepare Christmas cards for her clients, as well as coping now with the arrival of her mother. She always had to do everything, she thought, including making all the arrangements, dealing with their mother's minimal finances, and regularly lending money to both her siblings. Sometimes you just had to draw the line. She waited. She knew that Sharon, like nature itself, abhorred a vacuum. She'd break the silence, and once she did . . .

"I'm not going to do it," Sharon responded, filling the gap. Her voice sounded firm, though her chin wobbled. "I'm *not*," she repeated. The sureness was already gone, a whine beginning. Sharon was an expert in fine whines. Sig continued to wait. When she closed a large order she used this technique. "Don't you have to go over the Triborough Bridge?" Sharon asked anxiously, waiting for a response. There was none, except a groan from Bruce as he exhaled cigarette smoke. "I don't think I could do a three-borough bridge," Sharon said in a little-girl voice. Sig began to feel sorry for her. "Let Bruce get her."

Bruce snorted. He was a greenish color, but it didn't stop him from smoking, Sig thought, annoyed. One sibling ate. One smoked. Oh well.

Before Bruce could react further, Sig intervened. "Bruce says he can't. He's meeting with some new potential partner." He always was, and nothing ever came of it, but. . . . "I'll just send a car," Sig said wearily.

"You can't do that! Mom will talk about it for the next ten years."

"Look, Sharon, I can't go, Sig can't go, and you can't go. What do you suggest?" Bruce asked nastily.

Sharon ignored her brother. "Sig, she'll never step

into a limo. You know how she is about money. She'll try to get all of her luggage onto a Fugazy bus. And she'll have a stroke doing it. Then we'll all have to nurse her."

There was a long pause as all three siblings graphically imagined it.

"You're right. We'll all have to go," Sig said. She was feeling queasy. The brunch had not gone well and then Phillip had shocked her by—

"That's settled. Now what do we do with her once she's here?" Bruce asked, crushing out his cigarette in Sig's pristine Steuben crystal ashtray and lighting another.

"I have an idea." Sharon looked up from the sofa, which she was weighing down with her bulk. Despite her frightened eyes, she smiled hopefully at her two siblings. Bruce, sunk in his chair, was still recovering from a big Friday night. The upcoming holidays, the low reorders, and the news about his mother's imminent arrival had pushed him to overdo it.

Sig, overwhelmed by it all, stood up and began fussily picking up tiny specks off the rug, moving the holly-decorated candles and napkins around and wiping microscopic smears from the cleared-up remains of her client brunch. She had to keep things in order for her B-list brunch tomorrow. Neither Sig nor Bruce even looked over at Sharon, but Sig—in a voice that sounded less than interested—at last asked, "So?"

"Mommy, can I have some juice?" Jessie interrupted as she rubbed Sig's white cashmere throw compulsively against her cheek. Despite Sig's request to the contrary, Sharon had brought Barney and her daughter, though the former wasn't minding the latter as Sharon had promised.

"Here's my idea," Sharon said, ignoring her relentless daughter. "We put Mom in a home."

"Yeah. Right," Bruce said with disgust.

"Sharon, no home would take her. She's not physically incapacitated," Sigourney pointed out. "She isn't sick or crippled . . ."

". . . Except emotionally," Bruce agreed. "Anyway, there's not a pen that could hold her. She'd start food riots. The Big House. Mom's Wallace Beery in drag. She'd tunnel her way out with her dentures."

There was a pause. "We could tell them she's mentally unstable," Sharon suggested.

"Hey. It just might work," Bruce said, opening his eyes to narrow slits. "We take her to some high-security retirement home and say she has senile dementia."

"She's *always* been demented, Bruce. It has nothing to do with her age," Sigourney reminded him. "Anyway, she knows what day of the week it is. And who the president is." Sigourney laughed bitterly. "When they ask her *that* one, they'll get a fifteen-minute tirade!"

"Mommy, can I have some juice?" Jessie asked again.

"Barney, would you give Jessie a drink?" Sharon nearly shrieked. Both Sig and Bruce recoiled and winced. Barney had planted his own bulk in the kitchen and was simultaneously scarfing down every bit of the leftovers and watching the Rams game. Bruce clutched at his head. Sharon didn't notice, nor did she move off the sofa. She certainly didn't lower the volume. "Jessie, be patient or you'll have to go sit in the thinking chair in the corner," she warned in a little-girl voice. Jessie hung her head, then went to hide behind Sig's eighty-dollar-a-yard Scalamandre silk curtains, taking the throw with her. "What if we say she's delusional?" Sharon continued desperately. "We could say she's not our mother—she only thinks she is."

For the first time Bruce sat up straight and fully opened his eyes. "Why Sharon, I'm proud of you. That's a truly devious idea. I like that in a person." He paused. "*Gaslight*. Mom as a small, Jewish Ingrid Bergman. We all play Charles Boyer. 'But Auntie Phyllis, you know you have no children!' Then we start hiding her hat in the closet."

"I hope you're having a good time with this nonsense," Sig said. "But Mom doesn't have a hat, you're out of the closet, and this nightmare begins in three days. Don't encourage Sharon, Bruce." Sig turned to her younger sister. "Sharri, no home would take Mom, and even if they did, she can't afford it. I can't afford it. Do you know what the DeWitt charges? Twenty thousand a month."

"Well, she doesn't have to be on East Seventy-ninth Street," Barney said, finally entering with the juice. His bare belly hung out under his Rams T-shirt. Despite his own girth he still criticized Sharon's weight. "She doesn't need anything that fancy. She's no friggin' duchess."

"Shut up, Barney," Sig and Bruce told him simultaneously.

"Just put her in a mental institution," Barney said as he was about to hand the brimming glass to Jessie. "A place for the criminally insane. That's where she belongs anyway. She's crazy."

"She's *not* crazy, Barney," Sig began in a voice calibrated to be understood even by four-year-olds. "She's not crazy: she's hostile. To you. There is a difference."

"Well, I say she's crazy."

Bruce raised his brows at his brother-in-law and looked over at Sharon. "Maybe it's time for Barney to go sit in the thinking chair in the corner?" he said in a little-girl voice. Without a word, Barney turned and walked toward the kitchen. "Ah, that's better," Bruce said, closing his eyes. "Now I can die in peace."

"Bruce, stop it. Have you got any ideas?" Sig asked, watching Jessie and the juice nervously. Was her niece wearing a hole in the cashmere? And why did she worry herself about material things when her whole life was coming apart?

"Well, I've been thinking. Mom is a kind of negative Auntie Mame." He paused. "Eureka! That's it: she's the Anti-Mame. Not to be confused with the Antichrist, although in the South I understand she has been." He paused. "What to do, what to do? Maybe we could spray her gold and sell her as a standing lamp at the Twenty-sixth Street flea market. She's very fifties."

"Would you get serious?" Sig snapped. Bruce wasn't stupid. It was just that he was always joking, right until he went bankrupt. She thought of a way to focus him. "Mrs. Katz called me, too. Apparently Mom told her she was planning to be at the Chelsea."

"Oh my God!" Bruce cried and nearly dropped his cigarette. "That's only three blocks from my apartment!"

"Isn't that where Sid Vicious and all those rock stars died of overdoses?" Sharon asked.

Bruce nodded, starting to feel well and truly panicked. "We should be so lucky. What would she die of? An overdose of Provera? The only way *that* stuff could kill you is if a carton of it fell on your head."

Sigourney ignored the two of them. She would have to handle her mother and the holidays and the end of her relationship with Phillip all at once. "Would both of you stop with the jokes and hysteria and try, for just a minute, to get a grip?"

Bruce looked up at his older sister through blood-shot eyes. "Only if *you'll* stop being so superior!" He clutched at his aching head. "You know, the minute Mom gets here she's going to start calling you 'Susan' again and you're going to lose it. She'll call you 'Susan' in front of all your brunch-eating, bond-dealing friends. And she'll follow you to the bathroom after you eat to make sure you don't vomit. You'll balloon back up to a hundred and seventy pounds in no time."

"Pthew. Phtew." Jessie said as she sprayed juice all over the carpet and drapes. "Pthew! This has stuff in it!"

"Yes, sweetie. It's called 'pulp.' It's part of the orange," Sharon explained serenely.

"It's fresh-squeezed," Sig said through clenched teeth, attempting to avoid a cerebral hemorrhage. "Barney, would you bring some paper towels and club soda in here?" she called, managing not to scream. "I'll wipe off your face and take away the juice," she said to her niece.

Jessie began to wail. Then, to Sig's astonishment, so did Jessie's mother. Sig and her brother looked at Sharon and then at one another in astonishment. Sig raised her brows in the international gesture for 'what gives?' Bruce shrugged in the answering symbol, 'who knows?' Even Jessie stopped crying and looked at her mother. Sig forgot about the stains and gingerly perched beside Sharon on the sofa. "What is it, Sharri?"

"I know you want Mom to come live with us. That's what this is about. I know it. But she can't. She just can't!" Sharon sobbed. "We don't have a place to put her. We don't have a car for her to drive. Barney is using the spare room as his office until he gets a new job and, anyway, it would just be too much for me."

Sharon continued sobbing, and picked up the corner

of the cashmere throw to wipe her eyes. "I know you're going to try and make me, but I won't. I just can't. I can't let her live with Jessie and Travis," she whimpered. She fumbled in her voluminous purse for her inhaler. When she was upset she reached for her asthma medicine. "Last time she did we had to have six double sessions with the family therapist. Do you know what that costs?" Sharon wiped her nose on the throw, and Sig winced. "Travis was having nightmares every night. He thinks 'Nana' is a curse word. And Jessie went mute."

"Well, *that* would be a relief," Bruce muttered. "Worth every penny."

Barney reentered the living room. It was too late. Jessie had cleaned her mouth and tongue with the other end of the white cashmere throw. Sharon's sobs grew louder and uncontrollable. Sig now divided her concern equally between her sister and her afghan. She patted Sharon's bloated shoulder, and gently handed her a paper towel.

"Sharri, we don't expect that. We know it would ruin your life."

"Not that it isn't already ruined . . ." Bruce added. Sharon's wails increased.

Sig threw a now-look-what-you've-done look at Bruce. "We're not trying to trick you into taking Mom home with you. First of all, it wouldn't be fair. Secondly, Mom wouldn't go. She doesn't like Westchester." Sig figured it wasn't necessary to add that Phyllis also didn't like Barney. "Thirdly, it wouldn't really solve our problem. When she wasn't nagging and interfering in your life, she'd come into town and ruin ours." Sharri looked up. Slowly, her tears abated. "Listen," Sig continued, "we have to find a permanent solution. A way to really neutralize her and separate her from us once and for all. And I think I have the way to do it. It's got to be done right away. It's a fill or kill."

"Oh my God! You want us to murder her," Sharon gasped. She clapped her hands over Jessie's ears to protect her. "You're going to make us help you do it, aren't you? We'll all go to prison."

"Nope. Murder's out," Bruce said. "Not on moral grounds, mind you. It's just that the woman wrecked the first thirty years of my life. I'm not going to spend the second thirty in jail for her." He shuddered. "Can you imagine me in prison? God, every night would be prom night. I'll bet Todd wouldn't even visit." He looked seriously at Sigourney. "With all of those shady clients of yours, don't *you* know someone who will bump her off and keep us out of it?"

Sigourney rolled her eyes. Couldn't Bruce ever be serious and couldn't Sharon ever make sense? "We can't *kill* her," Sigourney explained through clenched and beautifully bonded teeth. Sometimes Sharon was a complete ditz. "First of all, she's our mother and, more importantly, I have no intention of taking up residence in the Menendez Brothers' Wing at the nearest correctional facility. Fill or kill is just market talk for completing an order right away or dropping it. You have to help me with this. This is an immediate fill." She looked at her younger siblings sternly, the way she used to do when they were kids and she forced them to play Monopoly until she landed on Boardwalk *and* Park Place and had hotels on both. "We need a plan, a strategy, and I've got one. But we'll have to work together to get it to happen." Finally, for the first time, silence reigned and Sig had everyone's complete attention. That was just the way she liked it.

Her mind had been working at lightning speed, doing what she did best, when she was trading: pulling together a wide and diverse bunch of information and coming up with a cohesive, realistic program. She could deal with their weaknesses and play to their strengths. She knew she could motivate them, and maybe, for once, they could all work together. She saw, as the Iron Duke must have seen the Waterloo battle plan, the roles that each of them could play in not just winning this battle but ending the war. As it always happened when she was trading, she grew calm and it felt as if time stopped. She knew she could cover the short.

"Sharon, aside from more money coming in, you need something to do. You're bright, and you used to be a great librarian. We can use your skills." Sharon opened her small eyes as wide as she could. "Bruce, you need an investor for your rapidly failing business. And you also have a sense of style second to none. I need some new clients. And we all need Mom distracted so that she won't be driving us totally nuts."

She paused again for the drama of it. "I have a way to accomplish it all."

Bruce cocked his head. "How?"

"We marry her off."

"We *what*?" Sharon, Bruce, and Barney asked simultaneously.

"We marry her off. Preferably to a wealthy guy with bad health and no heirs."

"Ahh," Bruce said, light dawning. "The old Anna Nicole Smith ploy."

"I prefer to call it 'Operation Geezer Quest,' " Sig announced with dignity. "If we work together, it could happen." She warmed to the sale, just the way she did when she was pushing OTC equity or TFI bonds. "We set Mom up like a jewel in a velvet box. We dress her right. Bruce, that's your job. We put her in a good hotel—no, not just good, but the best. I'll take care of that. And then we present her to the prospects. Finding them is your job, Sharon. If we work it right it's a short sell—we get someone to go for it before Mom's price goes down."

"But what if it doesn't work?" Bruce asked.

"Then we got a street-side buy-in," Sig said, rolling her eyes. "I lose a lot of money covering the short."

"But what about Daddy?" Sharon asked. They all turned to look at her.

"Sharon, Dad's dead," Bruce reminded her.

"I know that! But that doesn't mean he would like it. And what does she want with an old guy? She never even took care of us. Why would she want to take care of some old geezer?" Sharon's eyes filled. "They're sick and they usually don't smell very good."

"Not for *her* to take care of *him*. For *him* to take care of *her*," Sig explained. "We want 'em sick. We have to marry off Mom to somebody really old and really wealthy. Somebody who likes us—likes us a *lot*. He can introduce me to some rich, powerful clients. He can give Barney a job, and pay for Jessie's and Travis's private school. He could even bail out Bruce's semibankrupt business."

"He'd have to be deaf, dumb, and blind," Bruce said.

Sigourney nodded. "That would be good," she agreed. She began counting off on her fingers. "Deaf, dumb, blind, old, and rich."

"Oh, come off it, Sig," Sharon almost sneered. "*You're* only forty-one. You're thin, you're successful. You have a weird first name, you're beautiful, and *you* can't get a decent date. Phillip Norman is a jerk. He doesn't even appreciate you. Men want young, beautiful, fresh girls. How in the world are we supposed to find a rich man for Mom?"

Sig recoiled. Phillip Norman had come to her A-list brunch and afterwards, as she cleaned up the mess and waited for Bruce and Sharon, he had told Sig that though he truly liked her he thought it was important for her to know that he didn't believe there was a future in their relationship. Sig hadn't known whether to laugh or cry. Phillip was such a compromise for her, such a corporate drone. She'd been with him mainly because of his enthusiasm for her. To find that he wasn't avid was almost a joke, but one that had an unpleasant irony to it. How low would she sink? Could *she* find another man anywhere? Next she'd be sleeping with Eldin the painter.

"Right," Bruce agreed. "If *I* haven't found one, why should *she* get one? And even if we *could* get ahold of such a commodity, how could we possibly get Mom to date him? You know what she's like." He shrugged. "To know her is to be permanently irritated."

Sigourney pulled herself together. It was now or never. She tried to do her best Andy Hardy imitation. "Oh, come on, kids. I'm not saying it's easy, but we're not licked yet. You haven't lost all your librarian skills, Sharri. You can do the research, finding the geezers. And Brucie, you still have all those dresses in your closet." He grimaced at her. "Okay. We'll buy costumes! But we can use your makeup. I'll write the script and direct the rehearsals. And Barney . . ." She paused, momentarily losing her enthusiasm. "Well, we'll find *something* you can handle. So, come on, kids. Let's put on a show!"

She dropped the fake energy and her tone became cold and as frightening as she could manage. "Because if we don't, let's face it: our lives will become even worse than they are now."

Five

$\mathcal{A}$lthough it was seventy-eight degrees and sunny, the Miami airport was incongruously decked out in fake firs and Christmas tinsel. Sylvia Katz, forlornly schlepping her oversized purse, looked at Phyllis and shook her head. "First class? It's such a bad idea. *And* a waste of money," she said.

"What the hell." Phyllis shrugged. "I've never flown first class in my life. And that travel agent of my son-in-law's looked at me with respect."

"For wasting money, she respects you?"

"Oh, life can always use some embellishment. If I play my cards right, I'll never fly again. Might as well go out with a bang, right, Sylvia?"

"God forbid. Don't even joke." Sylvia paused. "You sure you won't change your mind? I'll give you back the magazine rack."

"Tempting, but no cigar."

"Cigars?" Sylvia said. "What do cigars have to do with this?"

Phyllis leaned forward and kissed Sylvia on the cheek. She'd never known anyone as literal as Sylvia. Nine-tenths of what Phyllis said went right over Sylvia's overpermed head. "You're in a world of your own, Sylvia," Phyllis told her friend. "That's probably why you can stand me. I don't get on your nerves because you don't have any."

"Nerves? Who cares about nerves? I won't have any *friends* now." A tear began to run down Sylvia's very wrinkled cheek.

Phyllis fished into her jacket pocket and pulled out a key chain. "Keys to the Buick," she said. "Stay off I-95 and don't get carjacked, if you can help it."

"You're giving me your car? Your car?"

"I won't need it in New York. No one has cars in New York. It's a civilized place. We have taxis."

"Your *car*?"

"Sylvia, stop repeating yourself. You sound like a demented toucan." Phyllis reached out, took Mrs. Katz's plump and wrinkled hand and put the keys in them. "A little Christmas present. From me to you."

"But you already gave me so much. The magazine rack, the plants . . ." Sylvia took out a crumpled handkerchief and noisily blew her nose.

"Sylvia, who uses handkerchiefs anymore?" Phyllis asked and looked at the wet cloth distastefully. "What are you going to do with it now?"

"Put it in my purse."

"Feh! You'll get mucus all over your wallet. Get with the times and get yourself some Kleenex."

"Don't you think you should call the children?" Sylvia asked. "Tell them."

"You mean warn them. No. Why should I? So they'll argue with me?" She paused. "Sylvia, did you interfere?"

Sylvia cast down her eyes guiltily. Phyllis didn't need to ask any further and let her friend off the hook.

"You still giving me your car?" Sylvia asked.

"Yes. And I won't put any of them out, Sylvia. I'll stay at a hotel. I'll get my own place. It will make a nice surprise." Phyllis wasn't altogether sure that "nice" was the word any of her three children would use, but it was a free country.

"I'm going to miss you, Phyllis."

"I know."

"If it doesn't work out, you can come back down and stay with me any time."

"I know."

The fat woman fumbled in her purse. "I only got you a little something. A token." She handed Phyllis a small box.

"I know. A woman who hasn't picked up a check for more than seven years is not going to suddenly begin handing out Harry Winston." Phyllis took the little package and opened it. "Oh. Handkerchiefs. What have I done without them?"

"What will I do without *you*?" Sylvia sighed, the sarcasm lost on her.

"Play a lot of canasta. The girls will let you back into the game now that I'm not around to insult them."

"They never should have banned you," Mrs. Katz said with fresh indignation.

"Sylvia. It was four years ago. Forget about it. Play canasta. Meld. May you draw many red threes. Go to Loehmann's, schlep around the Saw Grass Mall. You'll be fine." Phyllis had never been good with emotions. What was the point? Most things she deflected with a wisecrack. The rest she ignored.

Mrs. Katz mopped at her eyes. "I'm going to miss you."

"You're repeating yourself, Sylvia. I have to go." The two women hugged one another briefly, and then Phyllis turned and walked with the crowd, moving toward the security checkpoint and the waiting flights.

Phyllis passed under a big sign that said: "Come Back to Miami Soon. We'll Miss You." "Fat chance," she answered out loud to herself, her voice caustic. "I'm getting out alive."

Sig sat at her dining room table, a tumbler of Chianti beside her. She was secretively filling in the real estate broker's form to put her apartment up for sale. She didn't know if she could renegotiate her home equity loan or if she could get a hiatus on her mortgage. But while she was trying both of those strategies it was best to take this frightening step. She was not in a good mood. She'd actually considered calling Phillip last night before she'd regained her dignity and sanity.

"This isn't easy," Sharon said from her seat at the other end of the table. She had spread its lacquered surface with dozens of files as well as her laptop and printer. "I don't know why I always get the hardest job." Before Sig had a chance to launch into just how difficult it was for her to conceive of and finance Operation Geezer Quest, the doorbell chimed. Before Sig could even rise, Bruce had turned the lock with his key and had come in and collapsed onto the love seat under the dining room window.

"I'm busy doing the research." They both looked at Sig.

"Yeah, and I'm busy working to pay for this entire sting operation," she reminded them. Each of them looked resentfully at their siblings. There was a pause that could have gone either way: they could all disintegrate into endless childish bickering or move on. Bruce decided to make a heroic effort.

"So, how is the research coming?"

Sharon, with some difficulty because of her bulk, got up, found her huge canvas sack, and pulled out even more armfuls of files, magazines, and clippings. Sig thought she might go mad.

"Okay. Operation Geezer Quest. Cross-referenced in different categories." Sharon began to sort colored folders, laying them in various piles on the coffee table. "What I have here are all unmarried men in the tristate metropolitan area, seventy or older, with a net worth of more than fifty million." She looked up at Bruce and Sig with a worried expression. "I didn't know if I should make the cutoff fifty million or a hundred million. But there weren't many at a hundred, so I arbitrarily picked fifty. I did keep an initial reference list so I can go back if you want me to."

"I think you made the right decision, Sharon," Bruce told her.

Sharon merely nodded into her categorized stack. "I sorted them by geographical location, religious affiliation, previous marriages . . ." She looked up. "I separated the widowed from the divorced. I wasn't sure, but I thought it might make a difference down the road. Among the divorced I listed the settlements, if any. I also categorized them by whether or not they require a prenuptial. Lastly, I listed their philanthropic histories. I figured we wanted to find the generous ones."

Sig poured the last of the coffee into the bone china service. She might order takeout, but she ate off porcelain. Sharon pulled out a list and handed it to Bruce and Sig as a justification. "Okay, here's my initial analysis. Bernard Krinz's on the list. So is John Glendon Stanford and Robert Himmelfarb. I thought those three would make a good first cut. They're all here in New York." She paused. "Well, Himmelfarb is out in Sands Point, but he socializes in Manhattan."

Sig looked over Sharon's findings. "Good targets," she agreed.

"This is where having an anal compulsive as a sister finally pays off," Bruce said.

Sharon's face crumpled like an empty beer can against a jock's forehead. "I worked very hard on this. You don't have to be so critical."

"Sharri, he's *not* being critical," Sig assured her. "It's Bruce's way of saying he thinks this is good."

Sharri looked at her brother. "You do? You think it's good?"

"I think it's superb! Sharri, it's wonderful."

"Honestly?"

Bruce put up a hand in a crossing-guard stop sign. "Sharon, shut up. You always go too far. No more praise. It's good, so now let's get to work."

Sig called out for more coffee—she never made her own but ordered it instead from the Greek joint at the corner. Mostly in silence, together the Sibs pored through Sharon's findings. They devoured the dish, whistling or exclaiming every now and then at the numbers of homes, numbers of ex-wives, and numerous offshore accounts.

"Sharri, this is *really* outstanding," Sig finally said. "You've done an excellent job." Sharon glowed from the praise.

Bruce looked at her appraisingly. "You know, Sharon, I need market research like this for my company."

"Sharon, why don't *you* get a job? Forget Barney's downsized career," Sig said. "You certainly need the money."

"Oh, I couldn't do that. Libraries aren't hiring."
Sharon shrugged. "Anyway, Barney is the one who
needs to boost his self-esteem."

"Just call her Cleopatra, Queen of Denial." Bruce
shrugged.

"You don't need a librarian's job, Sharri. You
could do this." Sig waved a sheaf of paper. "This is
great market research. Really thorough."

Sharon just shook her head. "Who'd hire me?"

"You know what I've got here?" Bruce asked. The
two others shook their heads. "I've got Mr. Right."

"I don't remember that name," Sharon said.

"Du-uuh! I'm not using it literally, Sharon." Bruce
opened the file. "This guy lives right here in New
York, he's loaded, he's a widower, *and* he gives a lot
of money to charity."

"Who is he?" Sig wanted to know.

"Bernard E. Krinz."

"The architect?" Sig asked.

"Yeah." Bruce rolled his eyes upward and got what
Sharon called his "movie look." "Hey, it could be just
like Patricia Neal and Gary Cooper in *The
Fountainhead.* Except for the sex scene," Bruce shuddered. "Boy, look at this." Bruce held up a page from
the file. "Well, maybe not exactly. The 'E' stands for
Egbert. His mother really hated *him*."

"Phyllis Krinz. Eeuw!" Sig said.

"You won't say that when you look at his P&L."
Bruce handed the folder to his sisters. Both of them
raised their eyebrows, deeply impressed.

"Well, what's in a name?" Sharon shrugged.

"Plenty," Bruce said. "Rothschild is good. Rockefeller is good. Gates is *very* good."

"Names! Don't talk to me about names! 'Susan!' Does it get any less original than that?" Sig asked angrily. "Is there any name more dated, more boring, more stereotypically dull than Susan?"

"Well, actually, 'Bruce' does seem rather like a self-fulfilling prophecy. She made me a *faigela*, wouldn't you say?" he asked.

Sharon looked up. "Oh, what do you two have to complain about? I was named for a woman who stuck her hand up Lamb Chop's ass to make a living."

Chastened, Sharri's sister and brother looked at one another and nodded. "She's got a point," Sig admitted.

"Let me see," Bruce ruminated. He waved the file. "If we pick our mark, how do we get Mom to meet him?" Bruce asked.

"Let's figure out what events he's planning to be at. These people all have public lives. They attend openings, theater, they go to dinners. Especially the charitable ones," Sig said. "I know all the events my firm helps underwrite and I think I can get access to seating arrangements. We have our target and we get next to it. Then we get a ticket for Mom to go, and make sure she meets him and he likes her."

"Yeah. How do we manage that last part?" Bruce asked. "You can bring a horse to water, but—"

"Obviously, one of us has to take her to the event, be sure we've got her near the mark, and make it happen."

"Not me," Bruce said. "It will be bad enough getting humiliated in a department store, let alone some—"

"Oh, I'd *like* to go to a party," Sharon volunteered.

"Not *you*," Bruce added. "Sig, you go with Phillip Norman."

Sig nearly blushed. She didn't have the strength to admit she'd been dissed by Phillip. "I don't think so," she said as casually as she could. "Look, this is going to be an expensive proposition," Sig told them. "The clothes, the tickets, a limo. Bruce, I think you and I should both go and make sure that we at least get Mom in front of the target." Sig turned to Sharon. "Sharon, we need you as the secret weapon. This was great work so far. But now you have to research the next phase."

"What's the next phase? I can't do anything else."

"Yes you can. Just find out the next big charity events in New York. I'll see which one my firm helps to sponsor and if any of these three clowns is going to attend. Then you dig out everything extra you can on our first target."

She handed the three folders back to Sharon. "Needless to say, Mr. Phelps, if anything goes wrong with this mission we will disavow all knowledge of—"

Bruce interrupted her. "You're right. This *is* Mission Impossible."

Sig put down the folder she held. "Well, one thing I know for sure: you can't catch fish without bait. Sharon's done her job and I'm doing mine. We'll see what you can do with Mom when she gets here."

Six

At La Guardia airport all three Sibs waited nervously. A group of people was coming out of the jetway entrance like nothing so much as cattle moving down the slaughter chute. Then, behind them, strode Phyllis. "It's amazing," Bruce said sotto voce. "She's like Keyser Söze in *Usual Suspects*. She limps among them without revealing her lethal talents."

"Shut up," Sig warned. "Here she comes. She'll hear you."

"Try to look happy to see her," Sharon said, but neither Sig nor Bruce were listening. "Hi, Mom," Sharon sang out in a falsely cheerful voice.

Phyllis walked up to the three of them. "How did you know I was coming?"

"Mrs. Katz called."

"Figures. She can't keep anything to herself." Phyllis nodded. "So? No flowers?" she asked. Then she looked directly at Sharon and said, "You must have gained another twenty pounds, Sharri." She looked her daughter over while Sharon shrank from her gaze. "I always gained weight when I was sexually frustrated. Has Barney become completely impotent?" she asked. Then she kissed her fat daughter, who recoiled.

"Let the games begin!" Bruce declared.

Phyllis turned to her son. "So, how's the gay greeting card business? Have you gone *mahula* yet?" She pecked Bruce on the cheek. Then she waved her hand in the air. "My God! You're wearing more perfume than I am!"

"At least it's *good* perfume."

Lastly Phyllis turned appraisingly to Sig. "A lot of people think red and black go together, Susan." She shrugged. "Don't ask me why."

"Maybe because they're a classic." Sig smiled.

"Or maybe because they're a cliché?" Phyllis responded and shrugged again. "But hey, if you *want* to look like a drum majorette . . . burr-rump-a-bum-bum." Phyllis winked at Sig, then glanced around at the cosmopolitan bustle of the airport. Here the Christmas *chazerei* looked good: tinsel, wreaths, red ribbons, and white snow—well, gray snow—out the window. "Let's get over to baggage claim before some jerk walks away with my luggage."

Numbly, the three shell-shocked Sibs began to walk beside her. She smiled expansively. "It's great to be in New York again! Talking to Floridians was like

chewing on avocado: everyone down there is soft. Up
here people are like bagels: when you chew on them
your jaw gets some exercise. I had a lovely conversation on the plane."

"Can you imagine being stuck next to Mom?"

"Oh my God," Sharon breathed. "I'm getting claus-
trophobic just thinking of it. Where's my inhaler?"

"He asked for my phone number," Phyllis added in
a self-satisfied tone.

"What was he selling?" Bruce asked, puffing on his
Marlboro despite the No Smoking signs.

"What difference does it make? She doesn't have
any money," Sig reminded him.

"Be like that," Phyllis sniffed. "He was very nice."

Bruce sighed deeply. "It's started," he said in a
singsong. "Sharri is fat / Mom is no fun / Sig is
unmarried / And I'm a bad son."

Phyllis turned and looked at him and his cigarette
disapprovingly. She waved her liver-spotted hand in
front of his face. "You know, you're killing both of us
with that smoke."

"Not fast enough," Bruce muttered.

Phyllis pretended not to hear and speeded up,
heading toward baggage claim, looking ready to chew
out everyone. Her three stunned children followed.

"Unbelievable. No matter how often I'm with her,
in between sightings I forget what it's like," said
Bruce.

"That's what they say about UFOs," Sig reminded
him. "Yet doubters still persist."

"No wonder I'm fat," Sharon mumbled resentfully.

"No wonder I'm unmarried," Sig added.

"No wonder I'm gay."

"*Bruce, you're gay?*" Sig asked, pretending shock. Bruce looked at her murderously.

"Forget Operation Geezer Quest. Let's just kill her," Sharon suggested, blood in her eye. "And I *didn't* gain twenty pounds. Fifteen, tops."

"Twenty," their mother called back from way ahead of them.

"God, she still has her faculties," Bruce commented.

"Not for long," Sig threatened. "Come on. Let's get her to your place and brief her."

"My place? Why my place?" Bruce almost squeaked. "We're closer to *your* neighborhood," he told Sig.

"Yeah, but there's no room for her to stay over at your apartment. Plus there's Todd. He'll move her right along."

Despite the crowds, Phyllis had spotted her bags right away and dived for them. She was still fast, for an old woman. In minutes they were standing in the cold outside of baggage claim, waiting for Todd to pick them up in his van. Even in her winter coat, Phyllis shivered. Sig tapped her foot, irritated and impatient. They had to indoctrinate their mother ASAP, get her to cooperate, and get her into the Pierre Hotel suite Sig had already reserved. But it wouldn't be an easy sell.

"Can't we do something else?" Bruce asked.

"No."

"Why?"

"Why? Because I say so, that's why," Sig told Bruce.

Phyllis laughed. "You sound just like me," she said to her daughter.

"I do not," Sig retorted.

"Do too." Bruce and Sharon confirmed with a nod. Just then, thank God, Todd drove up with his van. It took them almost fifteen precious minutes to load all the assorted crap into the battered vehicle that Bruce used for card deliveries.

"Do we need anything else?" Todd asked cheerfully when they were all settled in at last.

"Just Valium and a baseball bat," Sig said through her teeth.

Seven

orget it. I'm not even considering it," Phyllis
told her children. They were sitting in Bruce's
apartment, crowded into the front room of his
tiny brownstone flat. Boxes of greeting cards towered
above them, threatening to collapse, just as Bruce's
business was. Phyllis paid no attention to either the
disorder or her children's arguments.

"Mom, you don't understand. It's not that we
don't want you here or staying with us," Sig lied, "it's
just that you don't understand the realities in New
York anymore. It's not as safe as it used to be. And
it's not as cheap."

"Since when is a hotel cheap?" Phyllis asked.

"Not cheap, but safe. New York has changed,"
Bruce said. He was desperate to have her out of his
already crowded space.

"Don't worry about me," Phyllis said. "I can take
care of myself. I always have. I don't plan to be a

burden on any of you." She paused. It was hard for her to admit her mistakes to anyone, much less her children. "Listen," she said, "I haven't come for a visit. And I haven't come for myself. I've come for you. I know that your father and I were so busy with the business that I didn't give you all the attention that you needed. If I had . . ." She shrugged her shoulders. "Well, things might be different."

"Mom, you—"

Phyllis held up her hand. "I couldn't stand those women at the PTA. I wasn't a Brownie leader or a den mother. I didn't help you with your homework. And I'd like to make up for that now. I'm here for the duration," she said as bravely as she knew how.

"The duration of what?" Sig asked. Her mother had been in Manhattan for only two hours and it already felt like a month to Sig.

Sharon let out a whimper, while Sig thought she heard her brother groan. "You mean you're serious about living up here permanently?" Sig asked.

"Well, at least until you straighten out your lives. I'm your mother. I'm here to help. And I'm *not* staying at some expensive hotel." She patted her purse. "You don't have to worry about anything. I have a little put away, and my Social Security check. And I still get some of Ira's pension money. I'll be fine."

Sig smacked her forehead. Despite how often she'd begged her mother, she'd never gotten into TFIs or any other bonds. "Your Social Security check is six hundred and sixty-three dollars monthly," Sig said.

"Daddy's pension is . . . what? Three hundred? Four hundred more?"

"Three eighty, but it's all tax-free."

Bruce covered his eyes with his hands. Sharon looked away. It was only Sig, as always, who had to continue relentlessly. "Great. So you have less than a thousand a month to live on here in Manhattan, the most expensive city in the world."

"No, Sig, I think Hong Kong and Tokyo now rank as slightly more expensive," Sharon corrected.

"Yes, Sharon, but Mom isn't thinking of living in Hong Kong or Tokyo," Sig said through gritted teeth.

"In my dreams," Bruce said under his breath.

"I heard that, Bruce," his mother snapped. "Susan, a thousand dollars is still a lot of money. And I do have a little something put aside," she repeated.

Sig shook her head bitterly. If her mother had only let her put some money into Paine Webber's Select Ten Portfolio, her yield could be twice as high. But no. "Mom, you just don't get it. Do you know what the rental on a small studio apartment is here? A very small studio apartment?"

"I'm not so out of touch, Susan. I'm willing to pay four fifty or five hundred if I have to."

Bruce laughed out loud. "A *parking spot* for a car in midtown is four hundred dollars, Mom," he laughed.

"Don't be ridiculous," his mother snapped and put down her teacup. Todd had served them and then discreetly disappeared into the tiny bedroom. "I may be old, but I'm not an idiot." She shook her head. "Four hundred dollars for a parking space? You think I just got off the boat?"

"No, you came from the Planet of the Senior Citizens. You believe in early bird specials and movie discounts. But now you have to live here in a really strange place—among humans on planet Earth."

"Worse than that: among New Yorkers in Manhattan," Sig said, and handed a folded newspaper to her mother. "In Manhattan we don't have early bird specials at dinnertime or discounts for senior citizens. Except during the day at the movies, when you only have to pay four fifty."

"Four fifty?" Phyllis cried. "In Florida we pay three dollars. What do regular people have to pay?"

"Eight fifty."

"Next you'll be telling me that tokens are a buck," Phyllis laughed.

Bruce rolled his eyes. "A subway ride will cost you a buck and a half, Mom. And that's if you *don't* get robbed."

"Meanwhile, we don't have senior housing. Read it and weep," Sig directed, pointing to the newspaper. "I've circled a few of the cheaper apartment ads for you."

For a few moments silence reigned while Phyllis perused the paper. Then she looked up at her children. "So I'll live in Queens," she said. "Manhattan was only my first choice. Queens is nice, and it's just a subway ride away." She paused.

Sig, prepared, handed Phyllis another newspaper with another group of circled ads. "Queens," she said smugly.

Phyllis realized again that it had never been easy to love her daughter. She scanned the listings, one after another, then threw the paper down. "All right. So I'll get a little job. A part-time job."

Wordlessly, Sig handed Phyllis yet another newspaper section, this one the classifieds. But nothing was circled here. "Ivy League college graduates are making minimum wage at fast-food joints, Mom," Sig explained. "Kids with MBAs will work for Reeboks. What, exactly, did you have in mind?"

Shaken, though too valiant to admit it, Phyllis stood up, brushed off her skirt, and tried to look nonchalant. "Look, I'll work it out. Just help me get my things over to the Chelsea Hotel and then I'll see. A career will develop."

"Photos develop, Mom. Careers are built."

"Anyway, Mom, you can't stay at the Chelsea," Bruce said. "Number one, you can't afford it and *b*, it's not safe for an old lady."

"I'm *not* an old lady," Phyllis barked. "I may be an old dame, or an old babe, or an old woman, but I'm certainly not an old lady, and don't you friggin' forget it."

"Slip of the tongue," Bruce apologized, reaching for a cigarette.

Now it was Sharon's turn to take a deep breath and pick up a butter cookie. "Do you think the éclairs

are any good?" she asked. No one else had eaten anything with their coffee, despite the array of cookies
and pastries that Todd had brought out. Everyone
ignored her. They always ignored her, she thought
resentfully.

"You don't need anything extra on your hips anyway." Phyllis took a sip of her coffee and settled back
into her chair. She shook her head. "You know, I
believe in this ecological movement. I have a theory:
couples should only reproduce themselves. If they
have three children they get to kill one." She paused.
"So what's all of this really about anyway? I smell a
rat. Which one of you is getting ready to set me up?"

Sharon gasped, from surprise or asthma or both.
"Mom, it's nothing like—"

"Oh, I get it. You're just trying to get me back on
that airplane to Florida, aren't you?"

"No, Mother," Sig said as reassuringly as she possibly could. "Actually, we're trying to get you into the
Pierre."

The lobby of the Pierre was always attractive and elegant, but at Christmas it had a special, discreet holiday decor that added extra glisten to the gilded wood
and sparkling ormolu. There were no white Dynel
Christmas trees here, Phyllis noted. Still, it wasn't
until Phyllis got upstairs to suite 1604 that she looked
around and let out an ear-piercing whistle. "This is
where you think I should stay?" Phyllis asked. "Marie

Antoinette would be uncomfortable here. It's too big.
Too fancy-schmancy."

"Sometimes life can use some embellishment," Sig
said wickedly.

"Yeah. Well, if I'd brought my tiara, I'd feel right
at home," Phyllis told her, looking at the grand living
room with a fireplace, the damask drapes framing a
view of Central Park, the ebony baby grand piano and
the plush carpet. Some kind of vase—it looked
Chinese to Phyllis—had been placed on a side table
and it was filled with lilies, more lilies than Phyllis
had seen at the last three funerals she'd been to. She
opened one of the doors and found a bedroom, complete with canopy bed. Another door led to a smaller
room with the sofa and shelves of books.

"You think I need all this to get a date?" Phyllis
asked. "How much does this all cost?"

"I got the corporate rate," Sig lied. "Anyway, I look
at it as a loss leader. Like when they have a special at
the supermarket and sell something below its normal
cost, so they get you to buy other things."

"What are you talking about?" Phyllis asked.
"Have you turned into the Mayflower Madam here?"
So far all of the pickup and conversation couldn't
have gone worse, Sig thought. If we were an Israeli
SWAT team, all the hostages would be dead. Sig had
begun to pitch the idea of remarriage to what could
be charitably described as a total lack of enthusiasm
on Phyllis's part.

"Screw that," Phyllis said. She was as enthusiastic

as a cow at a barbecue. "I need a man like a fish needs a bicycle," she said.

"I never did understand what that meant," Bruce commented.

"You're not a woman," Sig muttered bitterly, and thought of Phillip Norman.

Phyllis hadn't quite agreed on the idea of dating yet, but she was trying to listen to her children. That had been one of the problems when they were growing up. She hadn't listened.

"I thought you already agreed to try this," Sig said, exasperated.

Phyllis sighed. "Look, a woman needs a man for sex or money. . . . I've had the first and I still have the second: ergo I don't need a man," Phyllis said.

Sig ignored her. "So back to this marriage plan. You see why we think it would be nice for you? No matter how much money you have, it would make the financial burden easier. Not just on you, but on us, too."

"Have I asked for a penny? For one penny?" Phyllis demanded.

"That's not the point. You need some security. And you need companionship. You need attention, and time. The three of us are so busy. It would be nice for you to have someone in your life who—"

"Cut the crap. You want me to marry for money and get out of your hair. But I'm not that kind of a girl."

"You haven't been a *girl* in sixty years, Mom."

"Oh, you know what I mean! I never mixed money in with it. You know, I could have had a stage career if I was willing to play hanky-panky for profit."

"Hanky-panky?" Bruce yodeled. "*Hanky-panky*?" He leaned back to laugh.

Phyllis ignored him. "Anyway," she said with some dignity, "I've never been attracted to a wealthy man in my life. They're all so arrogant. They're so controlling."

"Unlike anyone else in this room," Bruce muttered.

"We're not saying you should marry someone you don't like," Sharon said, trying to be helpful. "You could like him *and* he could also be rich."

"I was already married. Been there, done that."

"Exactly. You were married to Daddy, and you liked it. So why not get married again?"

"When I married your father, we married for life. Everyone did. Only movie stars got divorced, and even when they did, there was a scandal. Not that I think there's anything wrong with divorce," Phyllis added and looked pointedly at Sharon. "Some people need one. I wouldn't want to discourage it." Sharon, choosing to ignore Phyllis, picked a luscious, chocolate-covered strawberry and put half of it into her mouth. "Nowadays things are different," Phyllis continued. "Nowadays every woman should either stay single or make four marriages."

"*Four*?" Sig asked. Four weddings? She hadn't even had one. Her mother was as unpredictable as an Oklahoma twister, and almost as disorienting. "Four weddings and a funeral," she said sarcastically.

"Four," Phyllis repeated with the maddening assurance she always had about everything. "Let's face it: the first is always a mistake." Phyllis smiled at Sharon again and lifted her shoulders in a shrug. "You marry a Barney," she said to Sharon. "Or, in my case, I marry an Ira. Who knows anything?"

"Mom! What was wrong with Daddy?" Sharon bleated, her mouth full of the other half of the strawberry.

"He was a man. Other than that, nothing. Not for a first marriage. A first marriage teaches you how disappointing a man is."

"Thanks, Mom. No wonder I've had such gender confusion," Bruce said.

"Oh, don't take it so personally," Phyllis told him.

"So what should women marry again for?" Sig couldn't stop herself from asking.

"The second is for love. Ha! At least that's what they think it is for at the time." Phyllis shook her head. "You gotta work that stuff out of your system, or else you're doomed. Everyone with brains finally gives up on it." She looked at Bruce. "Except for you. You just keep chasing rainbows." She gestured with her chin toward Todd, who was taking pictures from the balcony.

The criticism slid off Bruce's well-moisturized back. "What about number three?" Bruce asked. His mother occasionally fascinated him, like O. J.'s ride in the Bronco. You knew it would end in tragedy, but you couldn't tear your eyes away.

Phyllis sat back in her chair. "The third marriage

should be for L.F.S.—lifetime financial security. Somebody who will take care of you and make sure you won't ever be living on Social Security."

Sig felt mesmerized, a snake before the snake charmer. "And what's the fourth one for?"

"Companionship." Phyllis smiled, almost wistfully. "After all, a Sylvia Katz only goes so far."

"Well, all this just proves our point: you do need to get another husband. You're three short."

"It's too late for me. I was talking about you. I don't want a husband! I want more grandchildren."

"You have two already," Sharon reminded her. "Isn't that enough?"

"Yes, Sharon. You've delivered," Phyllis said, then lowered her voice. "It's the smart ones who never breed," Phyllis said bitterly, under her breath.

Bruce and Sig exchanged looks. "Not this again," Sig muttered.

"I thought you finally gave up on me, Mom," Bruce told her. "I mean once I came out."

"Once you came out! You made such a drama out of it. Like I didn't already know! Who used to sneak my mascara? And what other fourteen-year-old boy knew the name of every shoe designer in France?"

"You knew?" Bruce asked, truly shocked. His mother nodded.

"That's why your greeting-card business is going nowhere. Gay men don't need funny 'I've come out of the closet' announcement cards. Or queer Santas for Christmas. And lesbians don't need *anything* funny."

Bruce sank into a chair. "I have to take this in. I'm so confused I can't think straight."

"You never could, Bruce."

"But you were always nagging me to get married."

Phyllis lowered her voice. "Yes. Because I want you to be settled down. Pick someone and make a commitment." She jerked her head toward Todd snapping pictures of Central Park. "He seems nice. Did I ever say it had to be a girl?" Phyllis stood up. "Gender, shmender. Look at your sisters. Definitely *not* a recommendation for my sex." She raised her hand in a placating way to both Sig and Sharon. "Don't blame yourselves. You did the best you could for brunettes," she told them.

Then she leaned toward Bruce and put her hand on his knee. "I screwed up with them," she admitted sotto voce. "What's his name again?"

"Todd."

"Todd? You sure he's Jewish?"

"Yes, he's Jewish, but he's also too young and probably too dumb. He's a visual kind of guy. He looks a lot like David Hemmings in *Blow-Up*," Bruce sniffed. "Not to be confused with the remake. Travolta's adorable, but DePalma can't compare with Antonioni."

"Nothing wrong with young and dumb. They make good wives. Better than I was. You serious about him?"

"Ma, would you leave me alone? I like him. He's nice. But he needs his own space."

Phyllis shook her head. "I ought to rent a loft in New York for all the men who need more space," Phyllis said. "You and your sister Susan have run into at least a dozen of them. But *you* know how to have fun. Now, though, it's time to settle down. Find a nice decorator who cooks. Stop living out of takeout boxes. Adopt a nice Chinese baby. You know?"

"Well, if you're so hot for marriage, why won't you get married?" Sig asked, totally exasperated. "Why aren't you cooperating?"

"Darling, I was married. I drove your father crazy for forty-seven years. Then he died. I think that's enough. Now it's *your* turn to drive somebody crazy."

They had come to a stalemate. Sig, as always, tried to think fast to come up with an approach—any approach—that might work.

"I want you children to know: I'm here for you. I'm going to make up for all the times I didn't stay home with you when you were sick. I'm going to make up for all the PTA meetings and the Girl Scout meetings I missed. I'm going to make up for—"

"Mom," Bruce said. "I understand you have regrets. I think all parents do. But you can make it up to us by going back to Florida."

Phyllis tried hard not to react. After all, Bruce was deeply hurt. Ira hadn't paid enough attention to him. Or maybe she hadn't. Or maybe she'd paid too much. Whatever it was, hadn't she or Ira made him into what he was? She turned to Sig.

"Mom," Sig said, "this is very important to me."

"And to me," Bruce added. Sharon was silent, but she was watching Phyllis intently, as if her life depended on it.

Then, suddenly, Phyllis realized what this was all about. She'd been on the right track. The children *did* need a mother, but that wasn't all. They needed a father, too. This was their cry for help, and this time she had to recognize it. She wouldn't fail them again the way she had before, or the way her mother and father had failed her.

But what would Ira think? In her whole life, Phyllis had never had any man but Ira. Wouldn't Ira have been hurt? And would any man but Ira have her? She considered the idea and bit her lip.

Maybe, just maybe, if she could serve as whatever they called it—a rolling model or something—then Sig could find a decent man, Bruce would finally settle down, and Sharon would leave that *shlub* Barney. Phyllis wasn't sure she could make it happen, but at least she could try. "I'll consider it," Phyllis said.

"So you'll cooperate? You'll meet some of these men we've searched out. You'll be nice to them?"

"*Nice?*" Phyllis asked. "I don't think we said anything about being *nice*."

"You're right. That would be too much to expect. But you won't immediately pull a Lorena Bobbitt? You'll encourage them, as best you can?"

Phyllis sighed. "Garage space here is really four hundred a month?" She paused, ruminating. "If I hadn't given Sylvia Katz my Buick, I could have lived in the car." She stared for a while out the window onto the park. "Maybe I'll call Sylvia."

"Are you going to do it?" Sig asked after the silence had lengthened.

"Please, Mom," Sharon begged.

"With sugar on top," Bruce added.

God, when was the last time her children had been united on *anything*? This was important, deeply important to all three of them. And if a man would make them happy, if a surrogate father would do the job, who was she—or Ira for that matter—to object? Phyllis at last nodded.

"Then you'll do it?" Sig asked.

"Does the Pope write bestsellers?" Phyllis asked.

Eight

*B*ruce was regarding his mother critically, as he always did. But this time there was a purpose. Sig had given Bruce some cash, a budget, and authorization to use her department store charges. Today was the day the transformation was to begin.

Bruce and his mother had met at the Pierre and the two of them were walking down Fifth Avenue past Tiffany's, the Plaza, and the Sherry Netherland. All the doorways and windows were dressed up in elegant New York Christmas decor—silk ribbons, real balsam, and ever-so-subtle dustings of artificial snow. It was only the crowd that looked bad. Bruce observed them in parkas, sweatpants, and ugly, lumpy winter gear and shuddered. His mother was as bad as any of them. Heterosexuals—they didn't know a thing about style. "We start with the hair."

"My hair? What's wrong with my hair?"

"Only everything," Bruce told his mother calmly.

"The color. The cut. The . . ." he shuddered, "the perm. Why do all old women think 'blond' and 'perm'? We need a genius for this." He lifted a strand. "This is worse than the Hindenburg disaster. And you call that a part? Moses couldn't fix this. We need to get to an emergency room."

"Mount Sinai?" Phyllis asked sarcastically, because of the Moses wisecrack, but Bruce ignored her little joke.

"Flex. The Einstein of hair color."

"Flex? His mother named him Flex?"

"His real name is Angelo. Flex is his professional name."

"A hairdresser with a *nom des cheveaux*? Forget about it."

"You're going. *If* we can get an appointment."

"Bruce, if I can get an appointment with a genius, I'm not going to talk about coiffures. I've been dying my hair myself for twenty years and I already know how."

"You're always the expert. You know more about hair color than Flex, the style coordinator for Dramatics for Hair."

"Well . . ."

Bruce, always quick to give up his anger, took his mother's arm in an affectionate way. "Come on, Mom, cooperate. You're as stiff as Charlton Heston in *Ben Hur*. I know it's against your religion, but just this once, break a commandment."

"Excuse me. Isn't there one about honoring thy father and thy mother?"

"Yes, but not my mother's hairstyle. Come on, girl-friend. I'm taking you to Columbus Avenue."

Columbus Avenue had been a blur of those new kind of boutiques, ones that Phyllis never went into, that seemed to either be crammed full of an overwhelming selection of insane choices or stripped down to empty, displaying only three black T-shirts each costing four hundred bucks. There was construction on the street, and piles of dirty snow, and Christmas crowds of young people all making their way easily through the chaos and cold. Phyllis hated to admit it, even to herself, but the temperature and the people were all a lot cooler than she had remembered. When was the last time she'd been in New York in the winter? The bustling and pushing and the temperature sapped her strength. After moving through three blocks of it, she was grateful to have Bruce take her arm and lead her into a warm haven.

Well, a kind of haven. The beauty parlor wasn't anything like the ones Phyllis was used to. There were no rows of women sitting in their own bell-shaped dryers. Instead, the music was blaring so loudly that Phyllis could hear nothing else. The very strange thing was that she also couldn't hear the music. It was that loud, or it was the way the singers—if you could call them that—sang. Skinny kids were running up and down the long, narrow shop wearing black and white outfits, clients were constantly coming in, conversing in shouts, being seated, and getting washed and blow-dried. Each workstation was framed with colored Christmas garlands that swayed whenever the gunlike hair dryers were on. Lights, those little white Christmas tree ones, were blinking all over. And that was aside from the hot pink and blue neon that out-lined the reception desk and waiting area. It wasn't just her. The place, she decided, would definitely throw an epileptic into a seizure.

But it wasn't the conversations or lights that were so disorienting: it was the damn blaring noise over the radio, or hi-fi, or whatever they called it. It made a buzz in her ears and a kind of confusion in her brain. Phyllis didn't like it. After all, she prided her-self on being alert. She wasn't one of those dotty old ladies—a Sylvia Katz—who barely knew what was going on. Yet she'd been robed and shampooed and coated with chemicals and rinsed and conditioned and she still couldn't hear what the loud music was about. She stopped thinking and concentrated on the words.

"Did that singer just say 'Hot tramp, I love you so'?" she asked.

Bruce, who had been deep in a shouted conversa-tion with Flex, looked up. He cocked his head and lis-tened effortlessly for a moment. "Yeah. It's Bowie. 'Rebel, Rebel.' "

"You like Bowie?" Flex asked Phyllis.

"Who is she? Is she new?"

The two guys laughed. "Mom, he's a really famous

rock star. He's been around forever. You know, Ground Control to Major Tom." Phyllis hadn't a clue, but she nodded. She wondered if this was what it would feel like if the Alzheimer's kicked in. She was tired. She had to admit to herself that, despite her temperament and her intentions, she didn't have the stamina that she used to.

Well, she was almost seventy, she told herself. What did she expect? These kids—no one in the beauty parlor seemed older than thirty—these kids were listening to their Frank Sinatra and using their energy just the way she had used up hers. Nothing to regret. Nothing unusual.

The music changed to a rap tune that Phyllis tried to hear. She actually thought it was "Jingle Bells," but it was such a different beat that she wasn't even sure if that was what she was hearing. She sighed. "Just a little longer," Flex said kindly. "Are you happy with the color?" Phyllis shrugged. She couldn't see in the mirror, though it covered the wall in front of her from ceiling to counter, but she wasn't going to ask to put her glasses on again because Flex had taken them off when her hair was washed and Bruce wouldn't give them back. He'd made that very clear. She squinted at the wall.

"Very nice," she said, feeling a little defeated by it all. Flex squeezed her shoulder kindly. He was really a very nice boy: his name wasn't Flex. It was Angelo, and all the other kids there had weird names that weren't their real ones—Ice and Storm and Electric and Heater. Why, Phyllis wondered, did children change their names? Why did Susan insist on being called Sigourney? It hurt her. It was an ugly name. Susan was so pretty. Why would someone want to be called Sig, or Flex, or Heater? You were given a name by your mother. After all, it wasn't easy to give birth, and naming seemed the least a mother could expect in return for a life she had created. Phyllis sighed again and felt all of her sixty-nine years.

Flex tapped her shoulder gently, as if in response to her sigh. "All done," he said. "What do you think?" She looked toward the mirror, but could see nothing.

"Unbelievable," Bruce said. "Flex, you're a genius." Then he handed her glasses back to Phyllis. A woman stared out at her from the mirror, but—for a moment, in her fatigue and disorientation—Phyllis didn't recognize herself.

"My God," she said. "Not bad for a woman in her sixties."

"Yeah. And great for one about to be seventy."

"Seventy? Really?" Flex asked.

"Sixty-nine," Phyllis snapped. Seventy frightened her. She avoided their eyes and instead focused on her image in the mirror.

Her hair had been completely re-created. Instead of the permed, blondish mound that she wore, hers was now a thick, straight, silvery crown. She shook her head, just to clear it. Her hair moved around her face, leaving little wisps against her cheeks, where the ends curled, just slightly, onto her face. She stared, and almost dropped her jaw. Light bangs covered the deep wrinkles on her forehead and somehow the color or the cut made her skin seem brighter.

Behind her glasses, her eyes were nearly popping out. You could still see her chicken neck and she still looked like an old lady, but not so old and more like . . . a lady. Phyllis blinked behind her lenses.

"You don't like it?" Flex/Angelo asked in a voice full of concern.

The boy really cared about his work, she realized, just as she once had. But she was still speechless. She stared again at her image in the mirror and tilted her head to one side. Her hair moved, each strand, in a kind of waterfall. She was trying to define what this change had done, exactly. It wasn't that she was younger looking, but she looked . . . She paused. Phyllis looked the way rich women looked when they got older. She had never been beautiful, and she wasn't beautiful now, but she was transformed nonetheless.

"Come on, Mom, what do you think?" Bruce questioned.

"Not bad," Phyllis told him.

"Bergdorf's, Bruce? Are you crazy? Isn't that fortune we spent on my hair enough?" Of all the department stores in New York, Bergdorf Goodman was the most elegant. And now, with only twenty shopping days before Christmas, the place was thronged with exquisitely dressed clientele. It was definitely not the Saw Grass Mall.

"You need something to wear, Mom."

"I *have* something to wear. I have lots of things to wear. Look through all my luggage."

"I did, Mom. Frightening. I didn't know they still made Naugahyde jackets. You have nothing. Not a single decent thing. This is not Collins Avenue."

"What am I missing?" Phyllis asked.

"For one thing, you have no sportswear."

"Sportswear? Why do I need sportswear? Do I look like Andre Agassi?"

Bruce stopped next to the Plaza fountain and looked at his mother coldly. "Don't you know it's not appropriate to wear your old cocktail dresses for early morning grocery shopping?"

"Why not? Recycling is the modern thing to do, isn't it? Anyway, if I *do* need something why can't we go to Loehmann's?"

"Because, Mother, right now Loehmann's only has the things that didn't look good on anybody at Bergdorf *last* season." He paused and glanced beyond the fountain toward the Plaza Hotel. "This is the very spot where Barbra Streisand ran into Bob Redford in *The Way We Were*," he said with a sigh. "So poignant."

"Poignant? He was a putz and she was an idiot not to notice it."

Bruce dragged Phyllis past the Salvation Army band playing carols and through the revolving door.

The Christmas season was upon them. Bruce threw five dollars of Sig's money into the pot. As he hustled his mother up the escalator, he looked her over. "You know, Mom, now that we got rid of that atrocious haircut, aside from your horrible makeup and frightening clothes, you're really not bad looking."

"Thank you, darling," she said coldly. "I can't tell you how much your approval means to me."

Bruce took another step up the escalator to give him some distance and squinted his eyes. "I'm looking at Phyllis Geronomous," he hummed, "but I'm seeing Carolina Herrera."

They stepped off the escalator onto the designer floor. Phyllis surveyed one of the mannequins dressed in yards of tulle and silk jersey. "Nipples? The dummies have nipples now?"

"Big deal," Bruce shrugged and took her by her upper arm.

Phyllis pulled it away and stopped to regard the dummies distastefully. "Listen, if you're going to get anatomically correct, how about potbellies or saddlebags?" she asked bitterly as she pointed to the mannequins' legs. "How about varicose veins and hammertoes and bunions?"

"God! Spare me!" Bruce cried. All he needed was for Phyllis to pull what he always thought of as her "Bella Abzug" in the middle of Designer Formal Wear.

But Phyllis merely shook her head. "America hates the reality of what women truly are," she said sadly.

"No they don't. Look at movie stars. Look at models. Women are making more money, they're more visible . . ." He took her arm again and began to move her to the designer sections.

"Get a grip! Men control everything and don't you forget it. They own the magazines that women edit and write in and read. They own every channel on television. They pick a few genetically female mutants to shill for them and mortify the rest of us. They hate aging women. They hate sagging and drooping and menopause. Old bellies. Old thighs. Men, no matter how old, how bald, how fat, think they're great. Unlike women, they don't have a biological clock. So they don't know what the hell time it is. They deny death."

Bruce had taken her arm and—with difficulty—was able to move her away from the mannequin and lead her through a maze of garments. They approached a rack of clothes. "This could be nice," Bruce said, trying to lift the tone and lifting up a hanger holding a black satin suit. "Satin is big this year."

"Nah. Too dull. I like more drama."

"It's a Karen Kahn. It's not dull, Mom. It's classy."

A thin, young saleswoman approached them. "Maybe I could help?"

Bruce smiled at her. "I think we're looking for a dinner suit. Something in black satin, perhaps." He looked down at his mother's slightly bulging stomach. "With a peplum," he added.

Marrying Mom

—o—

"I have just the thing," the saleswoman chirped. She went to another rack and lifted up a beaded jet jacket and dress. "Escada."

"Black. Why black?" Phyllis asked. "Nobody died. At least not yet. What's wrong with color, here? Let's be festive."

"Oh great. You probably want something red and green. You want to look like a psychopathic Christmas elf?" Bruce complained. He pushed the Escada suit in front of her. Phyllis looked at the price tag.

"Oh my God, Bruce. This is more than your father's entire annual pension check."

Bruce put his hands on his hips. "Why do you always go for the price tag first? Since I'm a kid, whatever I wanted, first it was 'how much'! You haven't even *looked* at the dress."

The saleslady turned from one to the other, seeing her quick sale evaporate. "I'll let the two of you work it out," she said. "Talk among yourselves."

"That's what's wrong with you!" Bruce went on. "It was never the quality, always the price. When I was eleven and I wanted those two perfect Izod shirts, you bought me a dozen from J.C. Penney."

"Bruce, I could buy an entire condo in Del Ray for this!"

"Yeah, but you'd feel like shit in a condo in Del Ray. In this, you'll feel like Greer Garson in *Mrs. Miniver*. You'll feel like a queen."

"Isn't one queen enough in any family?" Phyllis sighed.

Bruce pursed his lips and put his hand on his hips. "Mother, are you going to cooperate?"

"*No.*" Phyllis seemed impervious. Bruce paused and actually tapped his foot. "Bruce, I am not going to try on a dress that costs forty-seven hundred dollars. I'm not going to do it."

Bruce looked up to the ceiling as if the writing on the wall wasn't crystal clear. "Okay," he said. "I'll try again, Mom. I don't think you understand the concept yet. You see, to attract money you have to look like you already have it. Don't think of this as spending money, think of it as an investment in our future."

"My future isn't long enough to amortize a forty-seven-hundred-dollar dress."

"Yeah, but *my* future is, and I'm going into bankruptcy court if something doesn't change." He looked at her, his face serious for the first time. "Mom, this company means something to me. It really does. I got three kids working for me, all out of my apartment. I got so far with the company. I was doing so well. And then that son of a bitch—"

Phyllis looked at him with a scolding expression. "You took out bank loans? You're paying interest?"

"Well . . . loans. Not from a bank, exactly. Banks wouldn't lend after Bill absconded. I had to borrow from a guy named Lefty. He has a *lot* of interest in this."

"But no principles, I bet," Phyllis tsked and shook her head. "Bruce, Bruce, Bruce." Giving in, at last, she followed Bruce to the dressing room.

The interior of the dressing room on Bergdorf's third floor was as disarrayed as the inside of a schizophrenic's mind. A three-thousand-dollar sequined jacket lay crumpled on the floor. An Italian silk evening stole and matching turquoise gown hung disconsolately from a single hanger clasp, its four-figure price tag dangling. And the floor and the hooks were littered with enough rejects to rival Bruce's own suitor list. A faux leopard strapless sheath with matching bolero was thrown over one of the two tiny upholstered chairs, while Bruce sat on the other one, calm and resplendent.

Phyllis, exhausted, was struggling into yet another dress, this one in red accented by gold trim and buttons. She looked in the mirror. "Dowdy, dowdy, dowdy. Holy Baby Jesus! Am I supposed to be doing a Nancy Reagan impersonation?"

Bruce looked her over from head to foot, ignoring her comments completely. He turned to the saleswoman. "You know," he said. "For once she's not all wrong. It's a little too St. John. Too many buttons. I want something sleeker. Don't think Adolfo—think Lacroix as done by Calvin Klein."

The saleslady stood stock-still for a long moment.

"What language are you talking in?" Phyllis inquired. Bruce just sat there and the saleswoman didn't respond either. They seemed to be communicating on some deeper level.

"I think I know *exactly* what you mean," the saleswoman told him.

"That'll be a first," Phyllis said, sitting down on the other tiny chair, waiting for the next phase of her transformation.

"Mission accomplished! God! I'm exhausted," Bruce said to his sisters as he collapsed onto a fauteuil and dumped a collection of glossy shopping bags around him. He lit a cigarette.

"God! How much did you spend?" Sig asked nervously.

"Don't worry. You can afford it."

"Where's Mom?" Sharon asked.

"She said she wanted a drink. She's in the bar."

"Mom wanted a drink? She doesn't drink," Sharon reminded her brother.

"I told you not to leave her alone," Sig added.

"She's not a child," Bruce said defensively. "Anyway, she's just here in the hotel."

"Drinking alone? Do you think she's been drinking alone down in Florida?"

"Alcoholism? Are you worried Mom's a lush? Hah! That's the least of our problems. I wish she *would* drink. It might take her edge off. Nothing like a nice gin and tonic at four or five o'clock to give one that false sense of well-being. If you could describe what was wrong with Mom, we could join some kind of support group. You know, like Adult Children of Alcoholics."

"Yeah. That might be a comfort," Sig said bitterly. "But first we have to diagnose her. How about 'Adult Children of Extremely Annoying, Stubborn, and Sarcastic Mothers Who Come Back Home to Live?' "

"A little long, but we could use an acronym," Bruce laughed. "You have no idea what I went through at Bergdorf's."

"Never mind Bergdorf's, where's Mom now?" Sharon whined. "You've lost Mom."

"Look, if you don't like the way I'm doing my job, *you* do it."

"*I'm* busy doing the research."

They both looked at Sig, as if she'd been tack-free.

"Yeah, and I'm busy working to pay for this entire sting operation," she reminded them. Each of them looked resentfully at their siblings. It was all so familiar. Sig had a sense of déjà vu. There was a pause that could have gone either way: they could all disintegrate into endless childish bickering or move on. This time it was Sig who decided to make a heroic effort. "Let's go find Mom," she said, and they did.

Nine

Sig had worked behind the scenes since the Sibs had found a candidate. She had wangled three tickets to the Winter Wonderland Ball, held at the Plaza Hotel. Her firm had a table, but Sig had managed—through more than a dozen phone calls to people who were not altogether happy to hear from her—to get the seats moved to table eleven, the table that Bernard Krinz would be sitting at. That is, if he attended. During the holidays, a high point of the social season in New York, lots of people bought tickets but preferred to spend the season in the Caribbean. Sig would like to herself, and in the glory days of the eighties she had. But that was then and this was definitely the nineties.

Now, the day before the Wonderland Ball, all they had to do was indoctrinate Phyllis and then introduce her to Bernard or another rich, eligible old coot. Drag the guy to the Pierre, set the wheels in motion and hope that Cupid's bow would not misfire. They had to cast a spell, project the illusion that Phyllis Geronomous was a wealthy, stylish, charming, and available woman. It was a long shot, but Sig had long been used to playing the odds. It wasn't a bull market for rich widowers, so they'd have to make the most of this opportunity.

Sig got to the Pierre before work on Friday morning. She was almost wet through from the sleet that had been falling. She only hoped it hadn't spoiled the dress she had schlepped along with all her other accoutrements. She found that Bruce wasn't yet there with Todd, but that her sister had just arrived by train from Westchester.

Sharon took out a bag almost as large as she was. It wasn't full of formal wear. Instead it held research data. She began riffling through file folders. She finally pulled out a large one and snapped it open. "His name is Bernard Krinz. The architect," she explained to her mother. "Well, he started out as an architect. Then he became a developer. He built the Thompson building on East Fifty-fifth. He was the one that built the new wing for the museum; you know, the one that everyone talked about? He's done headquarters buildings for close to a dozen of the Fortune 100. We have pictures of them right here. Anyway, before all this he already had family money. As if that's not enough, his wife died eight years ago and left him more. They had no children, and he's never remarried." Sharon moved her finger down her

notes. "Net worth in excess of fifty million dollars."
She pulled out a clipping and handed it to Sig.
"Here's his picture."

Sig looked at the photo. As Bruce might say in his
movie mode, definitely *not* Gary Cooper in *The
Fountainhead*. But then Mom was no Patricia Neal.
"Your architect, Mr. Right," she said and handed the
picture on to her mother. Phyllis eyed the wizened
face, the bald pate, the narrow eyes.

"Looks like Frank Lloyd Wrong to me. Feh! Forget
about it."

"Mother! You promised you were going to try.
You haven't even met him."

"I don't need to."

"The next possibility would be John Glendon
Stanford. He's about eighty-eight years old. But I
couldn't get a picture of him," Sharon told them.

"That's perfect. One foot in the grave and the
other on a banana peel. We can all imagine what he
looks like," Bruce said from the doorway. He and
Todd had arrived, schlepping makeup, hair dryers,
brushes, and God knows what else. They were going
to do a dry run.

Sharon ignored her brother. "And last but not least
is Robert Himmelfarb. He's younger than Stanford,
but his net worth is lower."

"Well, if I really have to . . ." Phyllis began.

"You want us settled?" Bruce interrupted. "I need
a father's influence."

"And more grandchildren? Don't you want that?"

Sig joined in, jumping on the guilt bandwagon. Sometimes Bruce was shrewd. "You weren't there for us when we were kids. You go to the dinner and get a date with this guy now," Sig said.

Phyllis sighed. "What do I have to do?"

"Pull out the portfolio," Sig commanded. The spell was working and the preparation had to begin.

"To review, what's a corbel?" Bruce asked.

Phyllis crossed her eyes. "A cross between a corner and a dumbbell."

"Come on, Mom. Concentrate." Sharon had been prepping Phyllis all morning on architectural terms. "A corbel is a piece of stone or wood projecting from a wall and supporting a cornice or arch."

"Okay. If you say so," Phyllis shrugged.

"What's a dentil?"

"A female dentist? Or maybe the cousin of a corbel?"

"Mom! How are you going to impress Mr. Krinz if you're architecturally illiterate?"

"With my expensive haircut," Phyllis said.

"What's Bauhaus?" Sharon continued relentlessly.

"Corbels and dentils and Bauhaus with noodles, these are a few of my favorite things," Phyllis sang, parodying Maria in *The Sound of Music*. Sharon didn't even crack a smile. It was an endless mystery to Phyllis how she could have raised a daughter so completely devoid of humor.

"Would you stop it! Would you stop it and just concentrate!" Sharon moaned, exasperated. "Here's a portfolio of his buildings. Would you just study those at least?"

"Buildings? They look like melting ice cream."

"Another thing. Krinz loves the opera. He's a fanatic."

"Forget about it, I'm not doing opera," Phyllis said sternly.

"Now you know what I've been going through." Bruce said as he and Todd emptied their bags. Phyllis made sure to smile in a positive way at the boy. He was sweet. What did it matter if he wasn't successful? He'd make a nice wife for Bruce, and photography could become his hobby. "Time for a dress rehearsal," Bruce called. "And Todd is going to help."

It was Saturday evening, and almost zero hour. Sig paced nervously, waiting for her mother to appear. Sharon sat on the sofa, eating cashews by the handful. We shouldn't have done it, Sig thought. It's ridiculous. I'm wasting time and money. "Are you almost done?" she yelled into the bathroom for what seemed like the fiftieth time.

"Almost," Todd sang out. Sig smoothed down the skirt of her dress. With all this pacing her feet would ache and she'd be a wrinkled mess before they even got to the party.

"I don't know why I can't come," Sharon said

resentfully as she popped another handful of cashews into her mouth. They must be at least a thousand calories, Sig thought. Sharon was impossible. Sig looked at her watch. "We'll be late," she called.

"Fashionably late," Bruce said and stepped into the room, turning toward the dressing-room door. "Ta-da!" he announced.

"Oh my God."

Phyllis Geronomous emerged from the dressing room of the bedroom suite. Sig stared, her eyes popping, Susan Sarandon style. Sharon actually allowed her jaw to drop. "Are you my mother?" she asked.

Phyllis did a slow pirouette. "I'm ready for my close-up, Mr. DeMille," she told them as Todd snapped her picture. The sateen coat with the matching sheath dress under it was in an indeterminate color, somewhere between lavender and gray. As she spun, the costly fabric's subtle sheen flashed in a most unflashy way. Phyllis's once-blond, frizzy hair was now coifed in the simple elegant bob and virtually all silver. Her makeup, immaculately applied, seemed nonexistent. Instead, her skin looked nourished with a sheen that rivaled the one on her dress. And instead of her usual turquoise eye makeup and clashing blue-red lipstick, there was only a hint of purplish shadow above her eyes, a shadow so natural that it enhanced the deep-set hood of her eyelids and could almost have been mistaken for her natural color—if she had any.

Her lips glistened, though the color there again seemed no more than the blush of a healthy mouth.

Around her neck a large—very large—double strand of gray pearls covered some of the still-visible ravages of time. The only glitter was reflected off the diamanté clasp of the necklace, worn chicly to the side, and the matching earrings, which twinkled at her cheekbones.

"Oh my God!" Sig repeated. She managed to tear her eyes off the vision and looked at Bruce, proudly preening behind Phyllis. "You're a genius," she told her brother. He blushed, but Sig was too fascinated with her mother to notice.

Phyllis's legs were encased in some silken but magical mesh that managed to pick up the gleam of the coat and dress while also covering her varicose veins. The shoes were the finishing touch. Feminine, strappy sandals, they were ladylike, clearly expensive, and sexy all at once.

"Are those Blahniks?" Sig breathed. Six hundred dollars a pair.

"They're cripplers," Phyllis admitted. "I feel like Lady Astor's pet horse."

Bruce got the movie look. "It's just like the Ascot scene in *My Fair Lady*," he breathed. "You know, when Audrey Hepburn looks beautiful, but she still speaks like a guttersnipe."

"Nice way to talk about your mother," Phyllis complained genially and walked across the room to the table on which her evening bag lay.

Even in her gait some Pygmalion-like transformation had taken place. Was it the shoes? Sig wondered.

Or did Phyllis walk differently because she felt differently? Phyllis almost . . . glided. "Can you do that for me?" Sig asked Bruce. "I could meet a decent man if you'd do that for me."

Bruce nodded enthusiastically.

"What about me?" Sharon asked, coming out of her trance.

"Impossible," Bruce told her. "I'm an artist, not a magician."

"Bruce, be nice." Phyllis warned. She turned from the table, purse in hand. Phyllis looked her eldest daughter over.

"So severe, and your skirt should be shorter," Phyllis said, staring at Sig. "Never wear a white top and black bottoms to an affair," she told Sig. "You'll be mistaken for the help."

Sig looked down at her black and white Moschino Cheap & Chic. God, sometimes she felt like strangling her mother!

"Okay. Now what?" Phyllis asked.

"Now we take Cinderella to the ball and she meets the prince," Bruce said.

Ten

My maiden name was Steen. Can you imagine? Phyllis Steen."

The architect didn't crack a smile. "One of the Cincinnati Steens? I built a home for them. They were in shipping."

"No, the Bushwick Steens. They were just in trouble."

"Excuse me?" Bernard Krinz said. He looked puzzled. Phyllis rolled her eyes.

"It was a joke, Bernie."

"Bernard," he said.

Sig shifted in her chair. The Winter Wonderland Ball had transformed the already beautiful Grand Ballroom at the Plaza into a Viennese Christmas card. The chandeliers were hung with faux icicles, and the tables were set with tiny Blue Danubes, complete with weensy ice-skaters. The band was playing nothing but waltzes. But nothing else was going right. Sig was sitting on the other side of the architect, their mark, and she could already tell that dinner was not progressing as she'd hoped. They had arrived at the Plaza, taken their seats, and made sure to arrange it so that Phyllis sat beside Krinz, who had come unescorted. But the conversation so far had been a collection of missed jokes, gaffes, and general cross-purposes.

"So, Bernie, have you decided to take early retirement?" Phyllis asked as Sig winced.

"Bernard," Krinz corrected again. "I prefer to be called Bernard."

"Why?" Phyllis asked. "Let's face it, Bernie isn't great, but Bernard! It's hardly the name a woman would call out in the throes of passion."

Bernard Krinz deliberately turned to Sig, who tried to salvage what she could. "My mother admires your work so much," Sig said. Krinz didn't even blink. "She has a really large portfolio," she gabbled, desperate to say something. "My brother's best friend is doing a photography book about some of your buildings." She meant to talk about how Phyllis had collected photos of all of Krinz's buildings, but her Wall Street background got in the way. Krinz misunderstood and turned immediately back to Phyllis.

"Oh. Do you dabble in the market? I'm absolutely fascinated by it."

"Dabble? No. I buy what I need and I get the hell out."

"So you're a plunger!"

"Are we talking shopping or are we talking plumbing?" Phyllis asked, momentarily confused.

"I'm talking about your portfolio."

Phyllis shrugged. "Oh that. The kids filled it. For research. I don't even know what's in there."

"Really? I'm not sure that's a good idea. You obviously have a sense of taste in style. Is that dress by Lacroix? They don't come cheap." He paused. "You know, many people think that those of us in the practical arts can't be practical ourselves. But I take pride in the profitable little investments I've made. I don't claim to be a professional, but I'd be happy to take a look at your portfolio, if you'd like me to."

"Forget about it," Phyllis said, and then Bruce, at her other side, jabbed her sharply under the perfectly cut armhole of her sheath. He bent across her and turned to Krinz.

"You know, Mother would really love that. We've said to her, over and over again, that she should show more interest in the market."

"When did you say that? You're the one who always makes me throw out my coupons."

"Throw out your coupons?" Bernard said, really disturbed. "My dear, you *do* need some kind of assistance."

"That's what my kids say: 'You need help.' "

Across the table a handsome older man laughed. He was probably seventy if he was a day, but he had a glowing tan, a head of mostly thick white hair, blue eyes, a noble profile, and, Sig noted, a very blond young woman with him who looked as if she was in her teens. Phyllis narrowed her eyes and stared at him and his very youthful companion. "I hope she's your daughter," Phyllis said loudly.

"She's not," the man taunted.

"Do you know one another?" Bernard asked. Phyllis shook her head. "Permit me." Bernard did the introductions. "This is Paul Cushing. We go way back. I built a corporate headquarters building for him. They may do another." He cleared his throat. "Paul, this is Phyllis Steen."

Paul Cushing laughed. "Somehow I already guessed that."

"You see! What a name. No wonder I married the first person who asked me!" Phyllis said. "I *had* to get married. Not for that reason. For a different name. Not that 'Geronomous' is any bargain. Sounds like I'm about to parachute-jump. Who knew then that you could go down to City Hall and change your birth certificate for twenty-five dollars?" She looked across at Cushing with contempt. "Have you seen that young lady's birth certificate?" she asked.

Sig felt as if she were about to explode, but, luckily, Bernard Krinz tried to smooth the situation. "Mr. Cushing is the ex-president and chairman of Whetherall Industries." He lowered his voice discreetly. "He's also a widower."

"Well, I'm Phyllis Geronomous," she told Cushing.

"Ex-president of the Turnbury Island Ladies Canasta Club. Widow of Ira Geronomous. And who's your little friend?"

The girl beside Paul Cushing looked up. She giggled. "I'm Wendy. Wendy . . ."

"Just Wendy," Paul Cushing said, cutting her off and obviously rising to Phyllis's bait.

"Oh. First names only, huh?" Phyllis asked acidly.

"Need-to-know basis," Paul Cushing told her serenely.

"What are you, the Man from UNCLE?" Phyllis looked the pretty young girl over. "I just hope she's over eighteen, or you're in trouble, mister."

"Mother," Sig said, as a wide but insincere smile spread across her face. "I think Mr. Krinz wanted to tell you something."

"What's *your* name?" Paul Cushing asked Sig.

"Sigourney Geronomous."

"She's too old for you," Phyllis spit out. "She's only half your age."

"I'm sorry, Mr. Cushing," Sig said, "my mother . . ."

"Your mother is charming," Paul Cushing interrupted smoothly. He was *very* handsome, Sig thought, despite his age, and the wrinkles around his blue eyes made him more attractive. Her own were already making her consider an eye job. Life was so unfair.

"Mother is outspoken."

"I admire that in a woman," Paul Cushing said. He looked at his young companion. "My granddaughter does, too." Wendy giggled again. "What is it you do, Miss Geronomous? Or is it Mrs.?" he said to Sig.

Sig saw Wendy glance at her left hand. She didn't wear a wedding band, obviously, but on her fortieth birthday in a fit of despair, she had splurged and bought herself a fabulous emerald. She had realized then that no one else was going to buy one for her. She looked at it as an investment rather than just an indulgence. But it was an investment she could relish. She loved the ring and lost herself for a moment in extreme depths. "Miss," she said. "And I'm a broker."

"Well, it's my lucky day. I'm in the process of looking for a new apartment."

"I'm not that kind of broker." The man turned her off. Residential real estate brokers were morons. Didn't he know that? Sig did her best to make general conversation. She spoke about the Bonnard show she'd recently seen and a bit about market trends. She drew Wendy, the young girl, out about her figure skating. She tried hard to hint, from time to time, that her mother loved to dance, that she spent the season in Palm Beach doing it, but there were no takers.

During all of this, Bernard Krinz and Bruce had been conversing. At last he was helping out, Sig thought with some relief as their coffee was served. Then, just as she was beginning to relax, the oddest thing happened. A stranger approached the table and, finally, it was he who asked Phyllis to dance. "I'd love to, Monty," she said. Bruce and Sig looked at each other in surprise. The old man was short and tubby. His dinner jacket looked like it was from some other era.

"Who is *he*?" Sig asked her mother as Phyllis stood up.

"Oh, he's Monty. Monty Dunleathe. The guy I told you about. The one I met on the plane."

Phyllis started to walk off with the codger. "The guy she met on the plane?" Bruce asked. "What guy?" Sig stood up and put her hand out in a gesture of unknowingness. A fat matron in an expensive beaded dress pushed past the table and put an empty glass in Sig's outstretched hand.

"See?" Phyllis said, her voice raised with satisfaction as she reached the dance floor. "She thought you were the hired help."

Before Sig could react, Paul Cushing addressed Sig. "I was about to ask your mother to dance, but it seems that someone beat me to it. Since my granddaughter doesn't waltz, could I interest you?"

He was asking something about dancing. Sig was flustered. She put down the glass. "Me?" she asked.

Bruce nudged her. "Get his number," Bruce whispered. "A backup for Mom. We're going to need it."

"I'd love to," Sig smiled at Mr. Cushing. But she felt a strange reluctance. Cushing was smiling back, making his way to her. "We don't want him for Mom," Sig hissed at Bruce. "We've already got Bernie."

"I don't think that's going to work out," Bruce told her as she walked away.

"Don't be so negative," Sig criticized.

"I'm *not* negative," Bruce answered. "It's just that I'm certain." Paul joined Sig and took her hand.

"How can you be certain?" Sig asked Bruce over her shoulder as Paul Cushing led her away.

Bruce smiled. "Because Bernard just asked me to dance."

Eleven

I told you it was stupid," Sharon said as she lifted a toasted bagel with too much cream cheese to her mouth. The Sibs were eating in a diner close to Grand Central Station, for Sharon's convenience, since she'd taken the train in from Westchester for a progress report after the ball the night before. The station was thronged with suburban Christmas shoppers; it was a nasty place to meet since it was also inconvenient for Bruce and Sig *and* the food was bad. "You can't handle Mom as if she was a normal person," Sharon went on. "She *isn't* normal. I can't believe the two of you didn't expose her to some other guys. Who else was there?"

"*You* try to manage a rodeo," Sig snapped. "We're ruined." What was the use. Why complain or explain? They'd always thought of her as a money-bags, an endless font of financial flow. "I think it's time for us to pack this project in. I must have been crazy. I've spent God knows what at the Pierre already." She looked at Bruce bitterly. "That's not counting designer dresses or Blahnik shoes, thank you very much." She'd have to try to explain to them, even though it hurt her pride, the kind of financial shape she was in. She took a deep breath. "You know, since Black Monday things have been . . . well, dark gray. It's not the eighties any more. I have fewer and fewer investors. I'm making money for everybody, thank God, but I have fewer people to make money for. That means fewer commissions."

"Yeah, yeah, we know all about it," Bruce said dismissively.

"Listen to me, you ignorant pooftah," Sig said, her teeth clenched. "It wasn't necessary to charge up eight thousand dollars to dress Mom up. It's not like she appreciated it. I can't bankroll this thing much longer. I'm going to have to pack her up out of that suite by Christmas. Where is she going to go then? *Your* house, Bruce?" Sig asked nastily. He recoiled. Sharon actually snickered at his discomfort.

"Your house?" Sig asked Sharon, who visibly shriveled and looked away. "We had a perfect target," Sig said. "Bernard Krinz. I spent three hundred bucks a plate just to get into that stupid party and sit beside him. I figured we *might* meet a fallback— Sharon, you might look up that Paul Cushing guy— but to find that *Mother* found a fallback, inappropriate as he was, well, that tears it. The guy was a loser, but at least he was heterosexual," Sig said. "He wasn't as damned inappropriate as Bernard was, Sharon."

Bruce sighed. "Sharon, didn't you know that Bernie was gay? Wasn't that on the Internet or in the *Who's Who* or something?"

"If he was married once before, he could be married once again," Sharon said defensively.

"But not to Mom. Not to our Mom," Sig said bitterly. "She didn't even try to cooperate for thirty seconds. We got her the haircut, the clothes. Even the shoes. And then she pissed Bernard off . . ."

"Bernie," Bruce corrected.

Sig shot her brother a murderous look. "She pissed *Bernard* off from the very beginning. Plus she antagonized Paul Cushing. And then, even if we could cast around for another candidate, she wasted the rest of our evening *and* my money by dancing with some jerkoff in a suit that predated the War of 1812." She paused and rubbed her head. "I'm pulling the plug on this," Sig said. "It's hopeless."

"Paul Cushing?" Sharon asked. "Wasn't he chairman of Whetherall?"

"It doesn't matter if he was the president of the Czechoslovakia," Bruce said. "She accused him of statutory rape. You know, her usual dinner banter. He *didn't* like Mom," Bruce sighed. "He could join the club. It's a large and distinguished group."

"Oh, I don't know, Bruce. I thought she piqued his interest," Sig said.

"Can't you get in touch with reality?" Bruce asked Sig.

"Can't you be helpful and productive and practical? All those things I have to be," Sig snapped back.

"Oh, do I hear the martyr marimbas being played?" Bruce asked and began to mime Carmen Miranda while he sang to the tune of "Mañana." "My name is Sig the eldest, and my life is very bad. My mother treats me difficult, and I am very sad. I have to pay out money; it's money all the time. Nobody really likes me because martyrdom's my crime."

Sig glared across the Formica table at Bruce, who put down the salt and pepper shakers he'd been using as castanets. To Bruce and Sharri's complete surprise, tears welled up in Sig's eyes and began to roll over her lids and down her carefully Renova-ed cheeks. Then she burst into loud, wet sobs. "What are we going to do?" she asked. "Mom can't stay on at the Pierre for long and she can't live in some hovel." Sig sniffed and tried to control herself. "It's not fair to the neighborhood. And I can't afford an apartment for her. None of us want her living with us. This isn't working," she sobbed.

In a moment, both Bruce and Sharon had moved to either side of Sig. Sharon offered her Kleenex. Bruce patted her hand. "I just can't do it anymore." Sig continued to sob. "I'm up to my neck in debt. My commissions have dropped off to almost nothing. I haven't dared to use my Platinum American Express because I can't pay a bill at the end of the month. I'm going to have to sell my apartment and auction off my emerald." She took Sharon's Kleenex, put it up to her nose, and hiccuped.

Sharon and Bruce looked at each other in one of their few moments of bonding. "Broke. Yeah, right!" Bruce whispered. They'd been hearing Sig complain about money all their lives.

"We know how hard you're trying," Sharon soothed. "We appreciate what you're trying to do. I'm sorry about Bernard."

"That was in the days when men didn't come out of the closet," Bruce said. "He's out now. He's *way* out in front."

"Mom could cooperate just a little bit, just a little bit," Sig said angrily, brushing away at her eyes and her ruined eye makeup. "She could have *tried* with Bernard, for chrissake. She didn't have to make herself Enemy of the People."

"She should have, she could have, but she won't. That's our Mom," said Bruce.

"On top of everything else, to spend most of the evening chatting to some minor director of a charity! Some loser in a dinner jacket that I saw Leslie Howard wear in 1939 . . ."

"What was his name?" Sharon asked. "Monty what?"

"God, I don't know. It sounded like a game show host or a hairdresser," Bruce added.

Sig wiped her eyes and seemed to regain possession of herself. "Montague Dunleathe," she said.

"Mom's Prince Charming. They could have danced all night. Look, I can't bankroll Operation Geezer Quest based on these results. But check the Dunleathe guy out, Sharon. And check on Paul Cushing." Sig looked over at her younger sister and just shrugged. "Bruce, you salvaged Bernard as best you could. Call him on some pretext or other. Anyway, Mom didn't do what we wanted, but we'll give it one more shot. After that, I swear to God, I'll wash my hands of her."

Phyllis opened her eyes, didn't know where she was, and for a moment had to recollect herself. The few times before, when she'd woken up disoriented, it had frightened her. But this morning—it was the morning—she felt not the slightest anxiety.

Where was she? It felt like a puzzle to play with more than it felt like a diamond. The bed was enormous and the sheets were so smooth—she stretched her arms over her head as she tried to recall what she'd been dreaming and where she was. Something about dancing, and the song that still ran through her head was that old rock 'n' roll one that Bruce and his friends used to sing about: being under the broadwalk down by the sea. It was all so very pleasant.

Then she awoke fully. It wasn't a dream. She'd been dancing all night with Monty, the man she'd met on the plane. Unlike Ira, Monty was a *very* good dancer. Phyllis shut her eyes for a moment. Her legs hurt her—there was no doubt about it—but she didn't care. Her feet hurt, too. Maybe that was a blister on the left heel? But Phyllis smiled. So? She'd put on a Band-Aid and take a couple of Motrin. It was worth it. She wasn't under The Broadwalk yet.

Her eyes swept across the vast white expanse of the bed. Then she remembered: the suite at the Pierre, the charity ball . . . the whole *megillah*. She pulled up the sheets to cover her shoulder. What size was this bed, anyway? It was bigger than any she'd ever seen. Was it bigger than a California King size? Maybe it was a Pierre Prince. Was a Pierre Prince more important than a California King? Who knew? There was room for all of Coxey's Army in there with her. She rolled over, ignoring the pain in her right hip. She looked at the clock on the bedside table. It was early yet. If she had been in Florida she'd be about to begin the schlep along the beachfront with Sylvia. She smiled. Today, instead, she'd bundle up, walk along Fifth Avenue and look in all the store windows to see the Christmas displays before everybody else was up and out. She'd wrap herself warmly and she'd wear the new brown leather gloves she'd managed to buy herself at Bergdorf's. But first, maybe, she'd just pull up the blanket and sleep for a minute . . .

When the buzzer rang, Phyllis sat up. Who could that be? The chambermaid never came this early. And certainly the children wouldn't be up yet. She'd already learned that New York was a late-rising town on the weekends. Phyllis gingerly swiveled her legs out of bed, grabbed the robe that the hotel had thoughtfully spread across the foot of the bed, and moved toward the door of the suite. The bell rang again before she could get to it, then there was a knocking. Forgetting to even look through the peephole, Phyllis threw the door open angrily. "What! What?" she asked, and then, as the door swung back she saw a huge bunch of flowers, taller than most bridal *chuppahs,* with Sylvia Katz standing behind them, in the hallway of the Pierre, dressed in a wrinkled green polyester jogging suit. The jacket was half unzipped and Phyllis could see part of the "I Love New York" logo on Sylvia's T-shirt.

"You up yet?" Sylvia asked.

"I don't think so," Phyllis told her. "I think I'm having a bad dream."

"Very nice. No 'hello' *and* you call me a nightmare," Sylvia said, unperturbed, as she stepped in past Phyllis. She was carrying her patent leather purse and an Eckerd's shopping bag. Sylvia left the flowers in the hall, but she set the bag down on the coffee table, appropriated a silk-covered club chair, and sat in it, her purse primly perched on her lap. "There," she said.

Phyllis carried in the flowers and turned to her friend. "When did you get here?" Phyllis asked. "How did you get here so early?"

"I took the last plane last night. I got in at eleven forty-five, but I didn't want to bother you."

"So where did you go?"

"I didn't go, I stayed. I stayed at the airport."

"At the airport motel? At La Guardia?" Phyllis was shocked. Sylvia didn't spend money like that.

"No. What motel? At the airport. I had a chair."

"You spent all night sitting up in a chair at the airport?"

Sylvia Katz shrugged. Phyllis thought, with something close to a pang of guilt, of her huge comfortable bed. "You should have called," she said.

"I did. You were out. So I stayed at the airport. It was fine."

"But what are you doing here?"

"I had to get away," Sylvia said.

"Away? Away from what?"

"I couldn't stand the pressure I was getting."

"What pressure? Who was bothering you?"

"Ira. Your husband. You know how he can be sometimes. All I would hear him say when I'd visit was, 'Sylvia, New York is a lonely and dangerous place.'"

"Ira can't talk. He's dead."

Sylvia waved her hand. "You know what I mean."

"I'm not in any danger and I'm not exactly alone."

Sylvia rose from the chair, as if it was the webbed aluminum one at the Pinehearst. She walked slowly toward the bedroom door. She motioned with her head to the partially opened bedroom door. "Don't tell me you're . . . you know."

"Of course not. Not yet anyway."

"Are you even thinking about it? Feh!"

"I'm thinking about it."

"Feh." Sylvia repeated and then looked around the suite. "This is some place," she said.

Phyllis nodded, as if she were used to it. "The kids insisted," she said. "You want a tour?"

"I wouldn't say no," Sylvia told her.

Phyllis opened the door to the bedroom, showed Sylvia the gorgeous bed, the huge closets, the four telephones, and the palatial marble and mirrored bath. "So why are you really here?" Phyllis asked as Sylvia rummaged through the bath products and shampoos on the vanity.

Sylvia looked into the mirror and then down at her T-shirt, protruding stomach, and the sandals she was still wearing (though now they were complemented—if that was the right word—by a pair of thick red socks). "I didn't want to spend the holiday alone," Sylvia admitted very quietly. "Not again."

"But I thought the children were coming in from Cincinnati?"

"They were. Then they weren't. My daughter-in-law got sick."

"Hah! If you believe that, I have a dental bridge I want to sell you."

"You having dental problems again?" the literal Sylvia asked with concern.

Poor Sylvia, Phyllis thought. Her daughter-in-law hated her and her son allowed it.

"Should I go back?" Sylvia asked in a small voice. "I don't want to horn in."

"Of course not. You're welcome. The children will love to see you." Hoo-haa! Now there was a fib of significant proportions, Phyllis thought, but no one should have to spend the holidays alone. "Sylvia, come out of the bathroom. Sit on the couch, or maybe you want to lie down in bed." Sylvia shook her head and went to the straight-backed chair that flanked the tea table.

"This is fine," she said, sitting down stiffly.

"You want some breakfast?"

"No. I had a bagel at the airport. I don't want to be any trouble to you, Phyllis. I could go stay someplace else."

"Where?" Phyllis asked. "At a hotel? You know how expensive New York hotels are? Anyway, everything's booked for Christmas." Sylvia must be truly desperate if she was actually offering to spend money. "Look," Phyllis said. "I'm calling room service. I'm getting myself some French toast and I'm getting you some, too. Plus coffee and fresh-squeezed grapefruit juice. It's better here than in Florida. I don't know how they do it." Phyllis picked up the phone.

"Can I help you, Mrs. Geronomous?" a voice asked. It was amazing how the hotel staff knew her name and everything about her. She'd only been there for five days.

"Breakfast for two," Phyllis said, a little self-consciously. As if she had something to hide. As if . . .

"My girlfriend came to visit," she explained. The room-service clerk made no comment.

"Isn't that expensive?" Sylvia asked. "Room service and all? At Howard Johnson's they charge you an extra $2.50. Just to take it up the elevator."

Phyllis merely shook her head. "They don't charge that here," she said. No, they didn't charge extra because the prices were already astronomical. She would pay for this herself. Susan didn't have to pay for everything. But for the moment, looking at Sylvia's glum but gallant face, Phyllis didn't care if she spent her whole month's check. "Sylvia, sometimes life needs some embellishment," Phyllis said. "After all, this is your first trip to Manhattan in years, isn't it?" she asked. Sylvia had lived in Queens, but she wasn't much of a cosmopolitan. "You never came into the city, did you?"

"Yes," Sylvia said. "I was here with my sister right after the war."

For Sylvia there was only one war: World War II. Forget Korea or Vietnam or even Desert Storm. "Well, things have changed a little since then. The war is over," Phyllis told her and picked up the phone again.

"Yes, Mrs. Geronomous?" the kind voice asked. "Is there something else?"

"Please," Phyllis said. "A bottle of champagne. We're having a party."

Twelve

Date: December 9, 1996
From: Sharon@missioncontrol.com
Subject: Operation Geezer Quest
To: Sig <Sis@sigmonde.com>
Sig, I haven't finished all the backup,
but Montague Dunleathe was listed as
one of the ten richest men in Great
Britain, according to Forbes
International 1981 Yearbook. Born in
Glasgow in 1921. A canny Scot. He made
most of his money in airlines back in
the seventies. He owns most of
Montana. He was married for twenty-six
years to one of the Guinness
heiresses, but she died in '89. No
children . . .

T he E-mail message went on, but Sig didn't need to. It was unbelievable. Somehow, Phyllis had managed to meet and attract a rich geezer. Sig shrugged. Go know.

Sig had been feeling grim this Monday morning, as she had most Monday mornings the last few months. The market was jumpy, and so was she. One of the guys in the cage had bitten her head off, and she'd found that a restricted security had been accidentally (and illegally) transferred out of one of her clients' positions. It would take her and a clerk an entire morning to straighten that out with a net gain of zero, but here, here on her terminal screen was the first really Merry Christmas greeting she'd received this season. She turned away from the screen and punched Bruce's number into her speakerphone. "Houston?" she asked when he picked up. "We have liftoff."

"Have you been having another one of those private Tom Hanks film festivals, sister mine?" Bruce asked. "He's happily married, Siggy. Forget *Apollo 13*." Bruce groaned. "God, I should have known better than to trust Sharon. Do you know how many hours I spent trying to pull Mom together for that ball on Saturday night? And then Bernard just wanted to try on her dress. Do you know the crazy old queen has called me three times since last night?"

"Forget Bernard. We've got a hot one."

"I know he's hot, but he's hot for me! And I'm not into older men."

"Bruce, I'm talking about Montague Dunleathe. He's richer than God and he's going out with Mom."

"You're kidding me. Well, it won't do any good. She'll wreck it."

"I'm going to double with her."

"You're *what*?"

"I'm going to double with her. That way I can try to control her—well, at least as much as I can."

"Ha! Good luck. Control a tsunami, why don't you."

"What the hell is a tsunami?"

"A Japanese tidal wave, Sig. Amazing! You *don't* know everything." He paused. "All right. I'll come up to the hotel early. And you can try your double-date control. But it's hopeless. Anyway, I'm glad I'm the one with the easy job; you know, turning a sow's ear . . ."

"Bruce! She is your mother."

"I mean it in the nicest possible way." A thought occurred to him. "Anyway, who are you going to bring? You haven't had a date since Bob Dole was in puberty."

Sig decided to take the high road and ignore the comment. "I'm going with Phillip," she told her brother. She'd broken it off with Phillip when he'd told her that they had no future. It would be a blow to her pride to ask him to see her, but she needed an escort and she had no one else.

"Dead man walking."

"Bruce, just button it and be at the Pierre by three."

—o—

——

It was a quarter to eight and the Pierre suite looked like a tsunami had hit it: the bedroom was a beach strewn with the flotsam and jetsam of rejected wardrobe items. The bathroom was an impressionist painting, one makeup color melding into another all over the vanity and onto the floor. Sig, dressed in a severe navy sheath, was busy trying to straighten out the living room and simultaneously listen to her brother and her mother fighting in the bathroom. "I'm *not* putting on those goddamn Barbara Bush pearls again," Phyllis was saying. "I'll look like Nathan Lane in *Birdcage*."

"As long as you don't look like Gene Hackman, you're ahead of the game," Bruce told her.

Sig tried to clean up around Mrs. Katz, who sat placidly while she did so. What was the old bird thinking of ? How long did she plan to hang around? "This must be Susan, and that must be Bruce," she had said, looking at Todd, who was more effeminate. "And that, of course, is Sharon," she said.

"The fat one," Sharon responded glumly.

Sig was spending almost a king's ransom—and the room looked worse than an adolescent's dorm. Sig kicked a Bergdorf's bag under the sofa with a vicious swipe. The afternoon had been three hours of constant argument. First Phyllis had wanted to go as she was; then she'd agreed to get dressed up, but she wouldn't double with Sig. Finally Sig had prevailed, but then Phyllis wouldn't let Bruce renovate her face and hair. "He met me plain, on the plane," she said. "He likes me like that." Bruce had finally ended the discussion by threatening to jump out the window. Sig picked up half an armful of newspapers, opened a closet, and chucked them inside violently. Then she threw her mother's schlep bag, pilled cardigan, and assorted debris behind the floor-length curtain. Nothing with Phyllis was ever normal, easy, or painless.

Even this stroke of luck with Montague Dunleathe seemed about to go down the drain. They had to make Phyllis appear financially secure, attractive, and at least minimally pleasant. An impossible task, Sig realized. Bruce wasn't negative, he was realistic.

Sig looked around at the suite. The hundred-and-sixty-dollar flower arrangement from Renny was breathtaking. Sig added more water and picked up the card. *"You fascinated me. I'd like to get to know you better. Paul Cushing."* Her mother fascinated a man like Paul Cushing? Sig opened her eyes wider, moved past the arrangement to the sofa, and plumped up the pillows. Then she pulled magazines out of her bag. *Town & Country, Forbes, Fortune,* and the British *Country Life.* She arranged them casually on the coffee table and lowboy. Then she took out a copy of the *Wall Street Journal,* folded it to the NASDAQ page, and left it lying over the arm of a club chair.

At last everything looked perfect, including Phyllis. She entered the room, arrayed in a silvery beige St. Laurent pantsuit, a Hermés scarf tucked in at the throat of the jacket. Sig nearly shuddered thinking of what all *that* had cost her, but she had to admit her mother looked casually elegant. It was Bruce who looked like the wreck of the Hesperus, or whatever the hell the boat was that Phyllis always talked about.

"Is she soup yet?" Bruce asked. Sig nodded. "Thank God," Bruce said, and fell back into the bedroom, sprawling across the bed. "Bring me a blood transfusion."

"Mom, I have to talk to you," Sig said brusquely. Sig took her mother into the bathroom, now filled with Phyllis's new wardrobe and a few of Mrs. Katz's *shmatas*. "Enough is enough. She's not supposed to stay here," Sig was telling her mother.

"What do you mean 'supposed to'? She's staying. She doesn't have any other place in New York to stay."

"Mom, New York is full of hotels."

"I have a perfectly good room here."

Sig tried to restrain the overwhelming urge to kickbox her mother in the spleen. She was edgy, no doubt about it. The clock was ticking and, though things looked promising with Monty, Sig would not be able to front this gig for much longer. To have Mrs. Katz here, always sitting calmly on a straight-backed chair in the living room, her purse on her lap as if she were riding the bus, was not conducive to romance. Her mother needed a duenna like Sig needed a credit check. Sig took a deep breath. "The room here is for you," she explained as if she were talking to someone significantly younger than Jessie.

"Oh, the bed is enormous. I wouldn't even know she was there, if it wasn't for her snoring."

"She's sleeping in the same bed with you?" Sig asked, her voice betraying the horror of it all. All that old female flesh, the fallen rumps, the veined and knobbied legs, the arthritic hands. Sig shuddered. Someday she would . . . "Mom, tell her to get her own hotel room. If you're going to sleep with anyone here it should be a man. This is a love nest, not an old age home."

"Oh, excuse me, Miss Schprintz. Just because you're paying the bill you'll decide who can come and who can go? Sylvia may not set the world on fire, but she's the only friend I had who doesn't get offended by my jokes. She always included me in everything, even though nobody wanted me and I didn't want to go. She's a good friend. You have no right . . ."

Sigourney was doing a quick mental calculation. If she didn't have to give her mother much walking-around money, she might be able to float this thing until the new year. She'd go back to the Sylvia Katz issue later.

"How's Monty?" she asked, her voice as casual as she could manage. How do you question your mother about the seriousness of her intentions? Did he get to first base? Second? Sig shuddered again. The idea of the two physical ruins uniting was more nightmarish than Sylvia Katz beside her mother in bed. Perhaps, Sig thought, it would be better if people just expired at fifty—no muss, no fuss, no bother. The bottom line was Monty certainly wasn't going to get too far with Sylvia Katz snoring in the bedroom.

"Look," Sig said, "this isn't Mrs. Katz's home. It's not even your home. For God's sake, it's not my home. This is a place that we're using to . . ."

"Oh, Susan, Susan, Susan. What am I going to do with you? Life needs a little embellishment sometimes. Think of Mrs. Katz as that. How could I tell Sylvia to go stay in some motel on West Fifty-fifth Street? She's my friend, Susan. And she's not messing up my chances with Monty, believe me." Phyllis stood up, went to the dresser, and consulted the mirror above it. "He knew what I looked like before my makeover. He likes me as I am, warts, perm, friends, and all.

"Anyway, I'm doing my part: I've seen Monty twice since the ball. We had brunch and we've gone Christmas shopping." Phyllis looked at Sig. "We got something for you," she said. Phyllis needed to show that Monty was going to be a good father to Sig.

"I don't need a present, except a proposal for you from Monty," Sig snapped.

"Look, I don't see men asking you to marry them,"

Phyllis said sharply. "I'm doing the best I can. I'm always the one who has to do everything." Phyllis sat down and crossed her legs. For a moment Sig had a feeling that Mendel may have been right: Phyllis sounded exactly like her and she could hear it.

"I'll go out with Monty because I like him, not just for you. But he'd be a good influence. He knows his business and responsibility." She stood up. "I need to get my bag," she said and turned and walked into the bedroom.

The buzzer rang and Sig closed the door on her brother. "I'll get it," Sig said. Phyllis nodded and moved toward the couch.

"Don't sit down!" yelled Bruce from the bedroom. "You'll wrinkle the pants!"

"Such a nag," Phyllis said.

"Look who's talking!" Bruce yelled.

"Stop it, both of you," Sig told them, feeling, as usual, like the only adult in the room. Sig glanced at herself in the mirror and straightened the back of her hair where the cowlick pushed it up. Then she opened the door.

Montague Dunleathe stood before her, rising on the balls of his feet. He put out his hand and shook hers heartily. "Hello, hello," he said, his accent thick but charming.

Sig invited him in and hoped he noticed the room and all the trouble she'd gone to. But it seemed that Montague Dunleathe only had eyes for her mother. "Phyllis, you look good enough to eat."

"Please. Let's not get into that kind of talk so early," Phyllis told him. Sig wondered if she was going to faint or, alternatively, strangle her mother. She could hear a smothered whoop from Bruce in the bedroom. She'd strangle him too while she was at it. But Monty seemed delighted by Phyllis's ridiculous humor. He sat down and chuckled.

"That reminds me," he said, "what's old and wrinkled and smells like ginger?" He waited, and when neither of the women answered, he laughed. "Fred Astaire's face," he told them, and he literally slapped his own knee.

Sig heard another smothered whoop from the bedroom and thought again of fratricide. She was grateful when the buzzer rang again. She ushered Phillip into the room. He was a tall, thin man with a sharp suit and a dull sense of humor. "This is Phillip Norman," she said, introducing him to Monty.

"My name's *not* Norman," Monty said.

Phillip didn't smile at the lame joke. "No," he began to explain. "Norman is my surname."

"So, you've been knighted. It's Sir Norman?" Monty asked.

"No," Phillip began, "it's just Phillip Norman."

"My name's not Norman," Monty repeated, and this time Phyllis cackled. So did Bruce in the bedroom.

Phillip looked toward the door. "That's just Mrs. Rochester," said Sig. "We keep her in the other wing with Jane Eyre. Pay no attention." Sig looked at her watch. "We're going to be late if we don't leave now. And this being the holiday season and the city is jammed, we'll lose it if we don't show up on time," she told them and led her party out into the night.

"Why would you bury all the lawyers a thousand feet underground?" Monty was asking.

Phyllis leaned closer to him. "Why?" she asked.

"Because underneath it all, they're nice guys."

Phillip Norman, who was a corporate lawyer at AT&T, attempted a smile. "Who are you with again?" Monty asked, grinning wickedly. "Wasn't it Dewey, Cheetem, and Howe?"

Phyllis barked a laugh. "No, I think it was Pipedown & Beenice."

Monty roared. "How about some more champagne?" he asked.

They were on the West Side, at Cafe Luxembourg, which was a little bit noisier and a little more raucous than Sig was used to. But she had to admit, it had its advantages. The first was that she wasn't totally embarrassed by the conversation of her mother and Monty, and the second was that if Phillip decided to talk, no one could hear him. Lastly, no one she knew would see her here with him, and that was salving to her pride. Dinner was almost done, coffee had been served, and Sig was getting to feel as if the whole charade might be worth it.

"No more for me," Sig said as Monty tried to pour

the last of the champagne. "Some of us have to work in the morning." She could hardly believe it, but her mother and Monty seemed to be getting on like an asylum on fire. In a way it made sense. They were equally bizarre.

"None for me," Phyllis agreed. "I'll have a terrible headache in the morning."

"It's not the champagne that'll give you the headache. It's the lack of sexual release," Monty told her.

"Somehow I don't think that's one of my problems," Phyllis said, but she had a gleam in her eye that made Sig nervous and Monty bold.

"Not to put too fine a point on it, the solution to your problems is in my pants," he told Phyllis.

"Listen, honey, I may need love, but I don't need a laugh," Phyllis replied with restraint. "Why do men think *anyone* cares about their penises besides their urologist?"

"I rest my confidence on public opinion," Monty leered. "Do you know what a rattlesnake and a two-inch willy have in common?"

Phyllis shrugged.

"Nobody wants to fuck with them," Monty said and laughed uproariously again.

Phyllis couldn't help laughing back, but then she composed herself and compressed her lips. "Personally, I have no further interest in ever seeing any man's three-piece set again."

But the rejection only seemed to incite Monty. "No

one has said no to me in almost thirty years," he admitted.

"Get used to it," Phyllis told him, but Sig could tell that Phyllis was actually rather charmed by this crass, wild Scot.

Sig wondered how long their luck would hold.

Thirteen

The first night of Hanukkah had come and gone. Since they were young, the Sibs hadn't paid much attention to the holiday, but now that Travis and Jessie were around they'd gone back to buying gifts. It was too bad, Sig thought, that Hanukkah, which came on different dates each year, never came *after* Christmas—when Sig could take advantage of the marked-down prices. Tonight, she'd decided she was going to show her apartment to Cornelia Warren, a broker, then do some shopping for modest gifts, check in on her mother, and finally wind up at her firm's despised-but-necessary-to-attend Christmas dinner party. It was always an endurance test, but this year guaranteed to be a trial by fire. As usual, it was held downtown at one of those wood-lined, steak-serving, Dewar's-scotch kind of places—the places that Sig detested.

She left work early, rushed home, showered,

dressed, and blow-dried her hair. Then she got three hundred dollars from the cash machine near her corner and went out into the December twilight with the determination to get things done.

Forty minutes later Sig weaved out of FAO Schwarz, empty-handed and more than a little bit queasy. She'd seen a basket filled with a momma cat and three kittens and very nearly bought it for Travis, until she looked at the price tag and realized it was two hundred and seventy dollars! Jessie was into Barbies, but she already had so many of them that the only one Sig was sure might fill the bill was the special edition Holiday Barbie. Sig wasn't spending a hundred and twenty-five dollars on a plastic doll. Who had this kind of money? Who were these people? The store was full and Sig, a delicate tinge of green highlighting her complexion, left with her three hundred dollars intact but her pride in tatters.

Somehow it seemed natural to walk the two blocks to the Pierre. Just to check on her mother, she told herself. But she knew she herself needed comfort and reassurance as much as she needed to suss out the situation. Her mother wasn't a warm, cuddling type, but she was rock solid, and right now Sig needed something solid. She had calmed herself down by the time she got up to the suite. It was just as well, because Phyllis—as usual—was too self-absorbed to notice much.

"What are you doing tonight?" Sig asked, perhaps a little wistfully.

"Oh, Monty's coming over. Maybe we'll go out to dinner, or maybe we'll call down for something."

Sig hoped they went out; room-service dinners at the Pierre could easily hit three hundred bucks, and that was without wine. "So what are *you* doing?" Sig asked Mrs. Katz pointedly.

"Oh, I guess I'll just stay in, too. I have some reading to do." The old woman pulled a rolled-up copy of *Modern Maturity* from out of her sweater pocket. For the second time in less than a minute, Sig seriously considered the option of strangling a postmenopausal woman to death.

Christ, she should have invited Mrs. Katz to her firm's dinner as her escort, just to get her out of the way! How on earth was Monty supposed to get close to Mom with Sylvia Katz always underfoot? Didn't Sylvia have any tact at all? "Perhaps we could meet downstairs for drinks later?" Sig hinted to her mother. If she could get Monty and her mother into the bar, things might happen. And in the meantime maybe Mrs. Katz would go to bed and leave the coast clear.

"I don't usually drink that late," Mrs. Katz told Sig. She lowered her voice, "If I do I have to get up in the middle of the night. Or *you* know."

Sig didn't want to know. Sig didn't even want to think about it. When would she hit the adult-diaper phase of life? God, she was getting morbid. It was the

holidays; they always did this to her. She glanced at
her watch. Now she was almost late for the damned
dinner. "I won't be out late. Enjoy your evening with
Monty," she said pointedly to her mom.

"We will," Mrs. Katz sang out.

Sig had tried, successfully, to avoid her boss all night,
but that was only half of her challenge. If she gave
Bill a chance, he'd give her another talk about how
she wasn't pitching, how she hadn't ACATed an
account in four months, and how, in the end, there
would be no Christmas bonus this year. Sig couldn't
bear to hear it. But now, alternatively, she was having
to sit and listen to the braggadocio of the other brokers at her table. Brokers were a lot like fishermen:
they always had to tell how big their catch was. And
they all had a tendency to lie. The lie served two pur-
poses: it made these guys feel better about themselves
in this bad year and it made the other guy feel worse.

Sig knew for a fact most of them were lying. The
wire operators posted all new accounts and Sig
checked them weekly. Sig knew she wasn't the only
one not pulling her weight, but for her—older than
many of the others, the only woman, and one who
had always been a real rainmaker—there seemed to
be a lot more at stake.

She managed to get through most of the meal by
talking animatedly to some sales assistant from Staten
Island and smiling widely around the table from time

to time. She hoped to give the impression that she was just too happy to pay any attention to anyone else. She sighed with relief when dessert was served and she made an immediate exit.

In the taxi she could relax and drop the act. She couldn't help but wonder what her mother was doing right at that moment. It had to be better than her evening.

Sig arrived at the Pierre after fighting the post-theater traffic. She walked through the beautiful rotunda and proceeded into the Café bar. She looked at her watch. With the long cab ride uptown it was already half past eleven. Probably too late to call upstairs, but Sig thought perhaps she'd try. It was ridiculous, but Sig wanted, longed for, the comfort of . . .

"Hello. What are you doing here?" Sig looked up into the very blue eyes of an older man. It took her only a moment to recognize him—it was Mr. Cushing from the Winter Wonderland Ball.

"What are *you* doing here?" Sig asked.

"Chaperoning Wendy," Paul said. "But you didn't answer my question."

Sig laughed. "Well, I'm sort of chaperoning my mother. I think she told you she's staying here," she explained. She thought of the flowers he had sent. "But I guess you knew that." Somehow, looking at Paul Cushing she thought, for a moment, she could tell at least a small part of the truth. "I'm a little concerned about that character she met at the party the other night."

Paul smiled again. "You can't be too careful nowadays," he agreed. "Mothers and granddaughters need to be protected." He lowered his voice. "Would you like me to check him out for you? I have a service that does that."

"Really?" Sig asked. "Is that a bit paranoid of you?"

Paul shrugged. "Perhaps," he said. "But when my son and daughter-in-law died, I was left with no one but Wendy. I'm probably overprotective, but she is an heiress, and it isn't easy for anyone raising a teenager nowadays."

Sig nodded. "I don't think it was ever easy. Not that that's a comfort to you." She paused. "I'm sorry to hear about your son and daughter-in-law."

Paul shrugged. "He drank and drove. I'll always feel guilty that I couldn't ever stop him." He shrugged again. "I'm grateful Wendy survived." They both fell silent. "Hey, how about a drink?" he asked.

He was a nice man, Sig thought. If he wasn't so old she'd even . . . but actually he was a perfect father figure. "Would you like to come upstairs for that drink?" Sig asked on the spur of the moment. If Phyllis had antagonized him, he seemed to like that—or be amused by it. Maybe he was bored—or a masochist. Hey, you never know.

"I'd like that," he said. "I have to admit I really admire the closeness of your family. It's rare to see people who enjoy being together the way you all do."

Sig just smiled. "Oh yes," she said, and reminded herself that discretion was the better part of valor. Then inspiration hit. "How would you like to come to my mother's birthday party the day after tomorrow?"

"Certainly. Can I bring Wendy? I like her to see families together."

"Of course."

He handed her his card. Sig and Paul Cushing strode over to the elevator and Sig pressed the button. The doors immediately rolled open and they went up to the suite. She had taken out her key and was as quiet as she could be in opening the door. She didn't need to disturb her mother if Monty had already gone home. But from the foyer she saw a light on. Sig could hear voices coming from the living room. As she came closer to the doorway she heard her mother's voice. "Oh, nice meld. It's a natural."

"You said it was possible with a hand and foot," added a husky voice.

"Yeah, but you could get minimum points if it's concealed," she heard Mrs. Katz say.

Sig tiptoed into the living room, Paul Cushing following. Then she froze. "You can't do that. The frozen discard pile has a wild card," a voice rebuked Mrs. Katz. There, at the table where room service usually lay its tray, sat her mother, Monty, Bernard Krinz, and Mrs. Katz. The scary part was that in the middle of the table lay a pile of garments and shoes, while Monty was naked from the waist up. It took Sig another moment to realize that Mrs. Katz was worse than naked: she had taken off her own shoes and stockings, which lay on the table, along with her lumpy sweater, her glasses, and her dress. She sat there in a voluminous nylon slip and you could see that she was buckled into some kind of frightening foundation garment under that. Sig averted her eyes from the straps and zippers and screamed. "It isn't just the cards that are wild in this room," she yelled.

"Oh my God!" Mrs. Katz said, her hand fluttering to her huge and sagging chest. "You scared me."

"What in the world are you doing?" Sig demanded of the four miscreants.

"We're playing strip canasta," Monty explained pleasantly. "I've lost my shirt to your mother."

Sig looked past Monty's chest, matted with white hair, and over to her mother, who sat coolly with her cards arrayed in front of her. She hadn't even lost an earring. None of the garments and accessories on the table belonged to her. Thank God! But what did Paul Cushing think? The idea of these superannuated delinquents misbehaving made Sig feel crazy. She wasn't sure if she should laugh or cry, but whichever she chose, she knew she didn't like it. "Who started this?" she asked accusingly.

Mrs. Katz looked up at her calmly. She actually seemed to have *more* clothes on rather than less, now that her heavy corset and long-line brassiere with all their structural underpinnings showed. No wonder her husband Sid left her: she seemed to have as much metal supporting her as the Tappan Zee Bridge. "It was my idea to play canasta," Mrs. Katz said modestly, as if she should get credit instead of blame. "We needed a fourth, so we called Bernard." She hiccuped. There were three empty whisky sour glasses in front of her. Had she been drinking?

"And who suggested this gambling part?" Sig asked.

"Well," her mother said calmly, "Sylvia never likes to gamble for money, so Monty suggested we play it like strip poker. Since he's never played canasta before and he doesn't wear jewelry, we gave him a handicap."

"I've got my Cartier cuff links riding on this hand," Bernard said, with more enthusiasm than he'd shown during the whole Winter Wonderland evening. "I haven't played canasta since my mother died."

Sig turned to Monty. "You talked them into playing strip canasta?" she asked, her voice rising in disbelief. "What's next? Spin the bottle? Truth or dare?"

"How do you play those?" Monty asked, obviously interested. "I don't think we had them in Glasgow." Sig averted her eyes from Monty's chest. His neck hung like a wattle from under his chin and joined his chest at some place that she didn't care to see. His jowls were imperfectly shaved, his eyebrows wilder than Brooke Shields's in a twister. Growing old was a terrible thing. It was a disgusting disintegration, a humiliation of the flesh.

Sig promised herself she would double up on her aerobics and lose three pounds. She would not ever let her flesh sag, her skin bag, her step drag. She would rather die first. She looked across at her mother.

"How was *your* evening?" Phyllis asked.

Fourteen

Sylvia Katz lay mounded on the Chesterfield sofa, nursing a glass of Maalox and holding a plastic bag of ice against her forehead. Phyllis couldn't help but smile, though she tried to suppress it. The wages of sin were costly for Sylvia, but the improvement to her personality that alcohol brought was, at least from Phyllis's point of view, well worth it. Sylvia had shown another side of herself the night before and Phyllis had certainly enjoyed it. She suspected that Monty and Bernard Krinz had enjoyed it even more. "You better think of getting up soon. Sig and Sharon are coming over to pick you up for the birthday party preparations. They want to make a big deal out of it." Sylvia slid the ice back onto her forehead. "So," Phyllis asked, a wicked grin beginning to spread across her face, "would you like some scrambled eggs and cheese for lunch? Or maybe some eggs benedict. The hollandaise is delicious."

"*Oy gevalt.* I must be coming down with the flu," Sylvia said. "Even toast would . . ." She shuddered.

"Maybe it's morning sickness," Phyllis laughed.

"Such a joker."

"Who's joking? That was some night you had last night. Three whisky sours."

"I don't remember everything, but I think Monty and I were losing."

"I think the two of you melded," Phyllis said.

"Don't be disgusting. Anyway, he's your boyfriend."

Phyllis shrugged. It was odd: Monty was bald and unattractive. He certainly drank too much, and his nose was veined with blood vessels to prove it. He was short and had a potbelly. But when he had taken off his shirt, Phyllis had felt a certain . . . Well, she couldn't exactly put a name on it, not even for herself. His chest was furred with grizzled white hair. His breasts were almost the size of hers. Yet Phyllis hadn't been able to stop thinking of what it might feel like to have her own torso pressed against his.

"Excuse me. It's none of my business, but . . ."

Whenever Sylvia was about to make something her business, something which she had no business to make her business, she prefaced it with those words. Phyllis smiled. Amazing how she could be endlessly patient with the bluntness and stupidity of Sylvia, yet totally intolerant of even the slightest dumbness from Susan or Sharon. Why was that?

Sylvia cleared her throat with a noise that sounded like the one her dishwasher used to make, just before it went on the fritz. "If you keep seeing him, this Monty, especially only late at night, do you know what he's going to think?"

"That I'm a vampire?" Phyllis asked.

"Joking. Always joking. Well, I want to tell you this, and I mean it: he's going to start to think that you're asking for it, and then you'll be sorry. It'll end in tears."

"Asking for it?" Phyllis wondered if Sylvia had somehow overheard the children's plans for Monty. "Asking for what?" Phyllis asked.

"You know," Sylvia lowered her voice. "S, E, X," she spelled.

"Yeah, and then what?" Phyllis asked.

"Then what? Then he might want you to do it. You know, Oscar Bernstein wanted Natalie Schwartz to do it with him after they went out the first month. She told me. She was horrified. First he stuck his tongue in her mouth. Then he asked her to . . ." Sylvia lowered her voice again and leaned forward. She had to sip her Maalox again to gather strength. "He wanted her to kiss his dickie bird," she whispered. Sylvia let herself fall back on the sofa. "Ecch!" she gargled.

"Listen, Sylvia, Monty's already stuck his tongue in my mouth."

"See! See how I knew about this! Oh my God! You have to stop it now. He's not like Bernard.

Bernard is a perfect gentleman. But that Monty . . . I think he spiked our drinks."

"Really?" Phyllis asked.

But Sylvia was really taking this seriously. "It's not too late. Nip it in the bud." Sylvia straightened up, clutching her purse to her bosom. "Lunches. Daytime. Nothing in the dark. Otherwise they get ideas, these men."

Phyllis shook her head. "I'm the one with ideas, Sylvia. I *liked* it when he kissed me."

"With a tongue? He kissed you with a tongue and you *liked* it? Come on. Don't be crazy. Do you eat snails, and other *traif,* too? I'm warning you, Phyllis, you're playing with matches. What are you going to do when he wants to go to bed with you?"

"Go to bed?" Phyllis laughed. "I should live so long. Sylvia, I *want* to have sex with him. I like him." As she said it, Phyllis realized it was true.

"I liked Sid," Sylvia admitted. "That didn't mean I enjoyed . . . you know."

Phyllis paused again. She knew she wasn't like a lot of women she had known, but now, here, with Sylvia Katz, the gap widened into a chasm. "So what exactly are you telling me? That you didn't like sex with your husband?"

"Who could like it? His thing—it was purple. And the rest of it was wrinkled and it hung and shook like President Nixon's jowls." Sylvia shuddered and finished the Maalox. "Remember how his jowls would tremble when he talked? Just for that they should have impeached him. Every time I looked at the president I thought of Sid and his . . ." Sylvia winced. "Why would a man want to show that to anyone? There's a reason they call them private parts."

Phyllis thought about Monty and the way he put his hands on her shoulder and her back when he moved her around the dance floor. He was a very good dancer. She'd always felt that that was an indication of . . . possibilities. Not that she'd ever tested her theory. She'd never slept with anyone except Ira. But the thought had entered her mind. Not often. But once, when they had vacationed with Kitty and Norman Steinberg and she'd thought Norman was . . . well, interested.

Ira had never been a good dancer, but he'd stopped dancing altogether long before his heart disease. And once he got the diagnosis, there was no more hanky-panky. When had he been diagnosed? Phyllis wondered, for a moment, when the last time she'd had intercourse with Ira had been. Certainly not in this decade. She wasn't sure if it had been in the eighties, either.

As best as she could figure, it would have been in Lake George the summer of 1979. If she had known it would be the last time, she would have paid more attention. Phyllis sighed, remembering the sun coming in the hotel window, Ira on top of her. She used to like it when Ira would hold her breasts. By then they were already sagging, but he didn't seem to mind. His touch had always been very gentle, tender.

When she was younger she'd worn her hair long, and Ira would take out the pins slowly so that her hair fell down to her waist. If he wasn't very imaginative or creative he had at least been affectionate.

Phyllis shook her head. Now her breasts were down to her waist and her hair was short. She wondered what Monty, no pinup himself, would think about her body. And what she'd think of his. She knew what she looked like, and the news wasn't good. But somehow, when she'd seen his hairy chest and when he'd held her up against him, when his hand on her lower back moved her commandingly around the dance floor, she felt a shiver in the old places. Phyllis blushed. She was about to turn seventy. It was ridiculous to think this way, to feel this way at her age, she told herself. But it felt very good.

Phyllis looked at her friend Sylvia across a divide almost as wide as death itself. She knew it was laughable for her to have these feelings, but the tips of her breasts tingled in a way she hadn't even wanted to remember. And down there, there . . . well, she felt alive again. Maybe it was the old way and she just didn't remember. Like riding a bicycle, it seemed, you never forgot. Then the fact that she'd never learned to ride a bike occurred to her and she smiled. She liked the feeling she had, and it was sad that Sylvia didn't. After all, what were these areas of feeling on her body but life itself, concentrated into three intense points?

Sylvia was talking again. Phyllis forced herself to focus. Sylvia was in the middle of a lecture. "Not only that, but you know it isn't safe anymore," Mrs. Katz said. "You have to worry about what could happen."

"What's going to happen? Morning sickness like you've got? I'm going to get pregnant?"

"Very funny," Sylvia snapped. "No. I mean you could get the AIDS. You could die."

Phyllis looked directly into Sylvia's eyes. "I'm about to turn seventy. I'm going to do that anyway, Sylvia," she said. "But I think I'd like to live a little more first."

Sharon and Sig arrived at the Pierre to pick Mrs. Katz up and take her over to Sig's apartment to help with setting up for tomorrow. This way Sig could be certain that Mrs. Katz was safely out of the way later, and with any luck Sig could convince the elderly woman to stay over, giving Phyllis and Monty some much needed privacy. She had volunteered to bake one of her special angel food birthday cakes, and Sig had accepted the offer. It wasn't that she didn't want to spend the money on a professional cake, and she did want to break in her oven, since she had never used it. Sharon was her stolid self, only waiting to see if she could get through Hanukkah and Christmas without disappointing the children too badly, or throwing Barney out of her house.

"Ready to go?" Sig asked. Monty was due to arrive and take Phyllis out yet again.

"Pssstt," Mrs. Katz said as she was putting on her

coat in the suite foyer. "He's not a nice man. He tried to get fresh with your mother," she whispered. "It was a good thing I was here."

"What do you mean, fresh?" Sig asked, with her heart lifting but her stomach churning.

"I heard a noise. I was almost sleeping, but I heard a noise. So I came out of the bedroom and they were here on the sofa and he was trying to . . ." Mrs. Katz stopped. "He was getting fresh," she reiterated.

At that moment Phyllis stepped into the foyer dressed in a knit suit and matching toque. Sig raised her eyebrows. "I know," Phyllis said with a shrug. "The hat. Bruce made me." Sig wondered how much the hat cost and wondered if it would look equally good on her. "Bruce insisted. And Monty said he likes hats."

He was fresh with her mother and her mother wanted to please him? This *did* sound promising, Sig thought.

"It's adorable," Mrs. Katz said about the hat. "So are you."

"You see why I keep her around?" Phyllis asked.

Just then there was a knock at the door. "He's early," Sig said, "that's a good sign."

"It can't be Monty. He didn't ring up. It must be one of the chambermaids."

When Sig went to the door and opened it, she found her brother, Todd, and Bernard Krinz before her. For a moment Sig was disoriented. Bruce hadn't seen Krinz since the benefit fiasco, had he? And what was Krinz doing here now? Todd seemed to wonder too, because he was holding on to Bruce in a possessive way. Bruce smiled and pecked him on the cheek.

"Hi," Bruce said casually, walking past Sigourney, with both Todd and Bernard in tow. "Hello, Sylvia. Hi, Mom," Bruce said. "Tilt the hat." He approached his mother, kissed her on the cheek, and then angled the toque so that it was the perfect enhancement. The foyer was getting crowded. Bruce breezed into the living room. Once he sat down, they'd never get out. Then he threw himself onto the sofa.

What the fuck was going on? Sig wondered. "Bruce, could I talk to you for a moment?" she asked as she glided toward the bedroom door.

"Oh God. I can't get up now. I'm exhausted."

"*Now,*" Sig said in the voice she used to use to wake him up on schooldays—the voice she used before she got the pot of cold water. Her glare levitated him off the couch. When the door was closed between them and the living room Sig started in. "What the hell is going on? What did you bring *him* over here for?"

"Oh, he called. He invited me to a book signing he was doing and I bought one and invited him over for a drink."

"Are you insane?" Sig asked. "Monty is due here in ten minutes and you're bringing Bernard back? I'm trying to get a proposal out of Monty, not another old-age orgy."

"Lighten up. Lighten up, Sig." Bruce threw himself onto the bed. "This is not brain surgery here. It's only dating. Anyway, the guy says he might want to get into my card company."

"What else of yours might he want to get into?" Sig asked. "You are incorrigible. You are such a little flirt. There's no excuse for your behavior. Jeopardizing this whole thing for . . ."

"Hey Sig, we're not talking about a cancer cure. It's not like *you* need the money." Sig felt like strangling him right there on the bed. "Anyway, *I* need the money. And Krinz isn't such a bad guy, for an old pooftah." Too furious to talk, Sig turned and stomped into the living room where she found her mother being helped into her coat by Monty.

"*Tempus fugit,*" he was saying. "I'm taking your mom to a little concert."

"The opera?" Bernard asked longingly.

"No."

"The San Francisco Orchestra at Carnegie Hall?" Bernard asked.

"No. Warren Zevon down in the Village."

"Have a good time," Sylvia said brightly.

Monty raised his eyebrows and leered at her. "You have a good time, too," he said. "Who sleeps with cats?" he asked in a teasing voice, obviously repeating a joke between them.

"Mrs. Katz," Sylvia giggled.

"And sometimes Mrs. Nussbaum," Monty reminded her and laughed.

Fifteen

Sharon, Barney, Jessie, and Travis were gathered in Sig's apartment. Sharon and Sig were busy putting out the final touches for the big do. Todd was in a napkin-folding frenzy, ready to perform origami miracles of the season. He seemed to be in some kind of a snit. Well, why not? Sig was. It was Phyllis's birthday—her seventieth, though she kept insisting she was only sixty-nine. In previous years Sig would have sent her mom a check and a card, but since she was here in New York and since her romance with Monty had blossomed, Sig and Bruce and Sharon were hoping that a family gathering might force Monty's hand, while getting a ring on their mother's.

Despite the bustle, Sig became aware that it was unusually quiet. Where were the kids? "Who's watching your children?" she asked Barney. Mrs. Katz was still diddling with the birthday cake and

Barney seemed totally uninvolved. Sig pushed past them.

"Oh my God! They're throwing things over the railing." Sig imagined poor Travis making a very quick trip down thirty-two stories. Sig brushed against her sister on her way by, strode across the festive dining room, through the immaculate living room, and out onto the tiny terrace. Travis had just launched a linen cocktail napkin out into space and Jessie was about to pitch a crystal champagne flute.

"Freeze," Sig told the two children in a voice that stopped both of them dead. "Give me back that glass, Jessie," Sig told her niece.

Mutely, Jessie shook her head and clasped the flute behind her.

"Jessie," Sig asked in her sweetest voice, "have you ever been spanked so very hard that your tushie turned red?"

Jessie shook her head again.

"Today might be the day. Now give the glass to your Auntie Sig."

Jessie thrust the Baccarat crystal at Sig, who smiled and took it gently from her hand. "Good choice, Jessie," Sig said approvingly. "Your tushie is safe for one more day. Now go inside and behave or you and your brother won't get your Hanukkah presents from Auntie." The two kids preceded her into the apartment. "Barney, where are you?" Sig yelled. Barney came out of the kitchen, an olive martini in one hand and a clutch of hors d'oeuvres in the other.

"Everything under control?" Sig asked him in a pleasant voice.

Barney nodded. That morning Sharon had told Sig that a bank was going to foreclose on their home next month if they couldn't raise some money. Barney didn't seem concerned. Sig leaned close to him, despite his intoxicating aroma. "Keep one eye on the children, Barney, or I'll pluck out your other one and put it in your goddamn martini. Next to the olive."

Sig pushed past Barney into the kitchen. Mrs. Katz was putting the final touches on her angel food cake, a fantasy complete with a portrait of Phyllis, "Happy Birthday," and a wreath of pastry posies encircling it all. Monty seemed to dote on Phyllis and, with any luck, this family gathering would be the opportunity to show off their loving family and put the pressure on him to make the move. More problematic was Phyllis. Despite the grand inquisition that the Sibs continually attempted, Phyllis hadn't told them anything about the way she felt. But what else was new? Who knew what she would do in the face of a proposal? There was no doubt she enjoyed Monty, but she still persisted in doing nothing but wisecracking at him and ducking all their questions.

"Please, Mrs. Katz," Sig begged. "Please finish that up."

"Good doesn't mean fast," Mrs. Katz said.

Sig was called out to the dining room, where Sharon was overseeing the table and deeply confused. "How many for dinner?" she asked. It had

been hard to find anyone appropriate to invite.
Phyllis had been feuding with her sister for thirty-five
years, so their aunt and uncle were out of the question. She'd never spoken to her in-laws, Ira's side of
the family. Sig had resorted to inviting Phillip
Norman. She'd also invited Bernard Krinz. What the
hell. And then Sig had remembered Paul Cushing
and her invitation to him and his granddaughter. To
her delight, he'd accepted. With a little luck, he
might also be attentive to Phyllis and push Monty
over the edge into a proposal. It seemed that
Bernard's presence had some kind of effect like that
on Todd, who was more attentive to Bruce than Sig
had ever seen. Anyway, if Cushing didn't work as a
ploy, Monty could be dumped, and Paul Cushing
looked like a very good next candidate.

Bruce was helping his mother prepare for the festivi-
ties. Preparing her toilette wasn't getting any easier.
"So? How's it going with Todd?" she asked as she
twitched and fidgeted while he attempted to do her
makeup.

Bruce sighed. "It isn't easy being gay in the
nineties."

"Hey, it's easier than being gay in the fifties.
And you think straight people don't also have
problems? You think Monty is perfect? Do you think
I should tell him I'm really going to be seventy? I
mean . . ."

"No, he's not perfect. Definitely don't tell him your true age. I never tell anyone mine. I don't think it matters to him. But don't take chances. He's very rich."

"Rich, schmitch. Brucie, he's nice to me. He makes me laugh. He's kind. Okay, he wouldn't know a kreplach from a doorknob, but he's a good person."

"So? Will you marry him?"

"He hasn't asked me," Phyllis said coyly.

"But if he does?"

"Well, I think he loves me . . ."

"Nobody loves me that I love back," Bruce admitted. "Not even you."

"Bruce Geronomous! How can you say that? Don't you know that I love you? Of course I do. You think I put on control top pantyhose just to get a rich husband? I did it to please *you*."

"You did?"

"Yes. Because you've always liked slim. Audrey Hepburn. You with those movies. How many times did you watch Audrey Hepburn in *Charade*? Let's face it, you liked her better than me."

Bruce nodded. "I loved her. She would have been perfect for me if she was a guy."

Phyllis took Bruce's face in her hands. "Honey, nobody is perfect for anybody. Not Ira. Not Monty. Not this Todd. Not even Audrey Hepburn, she should rest in peace."

"So you won't marry Monty? You don't believe in true love?"

"No, Bruce. I believe in true compromise. Be nice to Todd. Don't tease him. It sounds like he's nice to you."

The party was in full swing. Well, perhaps it would be more accurate to say half swing, but it was as swinging as it was going to get, Sig realized. Phyllis had sung her favorite song while doing an imitation of Bea Lillie. One of the problems was that virtually nobody remembered Bea Lillie, so even a good imitation—which Phyllis's probably was—was wasted. But the song, "There Are Fairies at the Bottom of the Garden" went over really well with Todd, Bruce, Bernard, and the children. And Monty, as he always did, laughed hard and smacked his thighs.

Monty had convinced Mrs. Katz to have another lethal whisky sour and she'd become as frisky as a mating whale. "And who are you?" Sylvia Katz asked, turning to Paul Cushing. "Do you come down to Florida much?" Paul admitted that he didn't. "Where's your wife?" Sylvia asked archly.

"Sylvia, forget about it," Phyllis told her, taking her by the arm and pulling her back into Monty's presence.

Sylvia put out her hand. "You know, the birthday girl is quite a catch. The men in Florida were crazy about Phyllis," she said. "They couldn't get their wheelchairs over to her fast enough."

Monty laughed, though Sylvia was serious. "I have no need of a chair, you'll see. But I do have a need for Phyllis." He took Phyllis's arm, tucked it under his own and looked at the three Sibs. "There's a poem I'd like to recite," he began. Bruce visibly restrained Todd from getting up from their seat on Sig's white divan to take another photo. Monty stood and, like a schoolboy back in Glasgow, put his hands straight at his sides, ready to declaim to Phyllis. He began Andrew Marvell's poem, "To His Coy Mistress":

"Had we but world enough, and time,
This coyness, lady, were no crime."

"Oh, Jesus, Sig," Bruce whispered. "He called Mom a lady. Do you think she's going to go ballistic?"

"Shut up, I think this is the big moment," Sig told him.

Monty continued.

"I would
Love you ten years before the Flood,
And you should, if you please, refuse
Till the conversion of the Jews.
My vegetable love should grow
Vaster than empires, and more slow."

"What's he talking about?" Sharon whispered. "Does he want her to change her religion?"

"What's vegetable love?" Barney asked. "Is the guy drunk or perverted?"

"Shh." Sig silenced them.

*"But at my back I always hear
Time's winged chariot hurrying near;
And yonder all before us lie
Deserts of vast eternity."*

"Nice and cheerful," Bruce said. But Sig looked over and noticed that Phyllis looked enraptured.

*"Then worms shall try
That long preserved virginity,
And your quaint honor turn to dust,
And into ashes all my lust.
The grave's a fine and private place,
But none, I think, do there embrace."*

Monty ended with a flourish.

"Really cheerful," Todd commented. "Did he write that?"

"What did they teach you in high school?" Bruce asked Todd.

Todd shrugged. "I must have been out that day," he said.

Sylvia was wiping her eyes with a Kleenex. Monty turned to Phyllis and took her hand. Then he turned back to her children. "I'd like to ask for your permission to marry your mother," he said. "I won't do it if you have any objections—out of respect for your father and all. I'd understand, but I love Phyllis and at our age, we don't have time to waste. I have no family; I wasn't lucky enough to have children, but I've always felt family is the most important thing." He got misty-eyed. "I like you all and I'd be very gratified if you could think of me as part of this family."

"He wants dysfunction?" Bruce whispered, but Sig ignored him. She held her breath and looked at her mother.

"We would like that very much, Monty," Sig said. "But of course, it's up to Mom."

Monty turned back to Phyllis and pulled out a blue velvet box. He popped the lid and even from across the room the Sibs could see the sparkle of a huge centered diamond and large triangular baguettes at the side. Phyllis looked at the ring and looked back at Monty. For a moment, Sig's stomach lurched and she thought Phyllis was going to crack wise and reject Monty's offer. Then—miracle of miracles—Phyllis stood and began to recite herself.

"As my son, the compromiser, would put it:

"Roses are red,
Kids like a toy,
I'm saying, 'Yes.'
I'll marry the goy."

Sig let out her breath. Bruce, Todd, and Sharon cheered. Barney raised his glass and Paul Cushing clapped. Sylvia began, again, to cry. It was a beautiful thing, Sig thought—by tomorrow she might be able to tell the hotel that her mother was leaving.

Phyllis slid the ring onto her finger. It was enormous. She held her hand out and grinned. "It's bigger than my knuckles are," she said. "And they get bigger every year."

Monty kissed her and it was a real wet one. "I'll replace it as often as necessary with one even bigger," Monty told her. His affection was obvious. For some reasons tears welled up in Sig's eyes.

At that moment, she caught sight of Paul Cushing, who was looking at her from across the room. He nodded and smiled. And he lifted his glass to her. "May I propose a toast?" he asked. And everybody turned to him. "To Phyllis and Monty. When you love somebody, anything is possible." He winked at Sig, but in the moment before he did, Sig had seen something in Paul's blue eyes: sympathy, affection, or perhaps pity. Sig shuddered before she lifted her glass with all the others.

Sixteen

"D"o you think he'll want a prenup?" Sig asked her brother. She was on her headset phone from work, but it was just after four P.M.—when everyone on Wall Street turned into dinosaurs. She herself felt like chopped liver—but she had just enough energy left to discuss the possibility that her mother was actually going to marry a very wealthy man.

"You know, our plan worked," Bruce said, as if reading her mind. "I bet we could do anything if we worked together."

"Yeah, but it isn't going to happen overnight and we still have to survive." Because she was using her headset phone her hands were free. Sig stretched out her hand. She stared at her emerald ring. She thought of her mother's huge diamond, the new one that Monty had given her. Sig sighed. She'd feel naked and vulnerable without it, but it was her only valuable piece. It could pay for the Pierre and Mom's clothes and maybe even her back mortgage payments. "So? You think he'll want a prenup?" she repeated.

"I don't think Monty's that kind of guy," Bruce said. "He's old-fashioned. I mean, the Scots aren't known for their open-handed generosity, but they don't like to go to lawyers the way we do."

"We have to tell Mom not to sign anything."

"Oh yeah. Like she takes direction well!" Bruce laughed.

Sig laughed, or approximated one. She looked down at the comforting green depths of her ring. "Look, whatever happens that way, the whole thing is a miracle."

"Yeah," Bruce agreed. "Plus, I'm starting to get emergency reorders. The cards are selling. I was right. I feel so light I'm walking *en pointe*. I look like the goddamned sugar plum fairy."

"Well, you're *my* goddamned sugar plum fairy, and I love you," Sig told him, feeling a flood of affection for her kooky brother.

"Oh, I bet you say that to all your queer brothers," Bruce replied, but he sounded pleased. "Anyway, gotta go. I'm meeting with Bernard Krinz. I actually think he's going to invest some money in the business. I need it to deliver the new orders fast. Not to mention that Bernard's made Todd sit up and take notice of me. It's a beautiful thing. I figure I can be profitable again by gay Valentine's Day."

"Great," Sig told him. "Good luck with Bernard

and Todd," and disconnected the phone, but it rang again almost immediately and Sig, her headset still on, hit the connect button. It was probably the cage, confirming some of her sales. It had been a very busy day.

"So, you won't believe this," Sharon's voice brayed into Sig's ear. "I just got a call from Mr. Moneybags and he and Mom are planning to come up and spend the day."

"Oh, that's nice."

"Huh? It's a lot nicer than *nice*," Sharon said vehemently. "Monty suggested that we go over to tour Jessie's school. He said he'd heard I could use some help with the school fees. He says he wants to endow the place."

"That's wild," Sig said. The guy must *really* like her mother, she thought, then felt a pang. No one, no man, had tried to please her that way in a long, long time. "When you asked him, he just said yes?" she inquired.

"I didn't ask. He just offered." Sharon sounded wheezy with delight. "That's not all. He also says he wants to talk to Barney about a job in his company."

"This *is* a Christmas miracle," Sig breathed.

"Speaking of Christmas, are you going to come up here tonight for Jessie and Travis's Hanukkah party? It is the last night of Hanukkah. You know they'll want their Aunt Sig here. *And* I'm making latkes."

Sig nearly groaned aloud. Fried potato pancakes were just what Sharri needed more of, Sig thought. "Is Bruce coming?" she asked, hedging for time.

"Yeah. He's promised her the new Barbie."

"What Barbie is left?" Sig asked. "Bisexual Barbie? She comes with both Skipper and Ken?"

"Don't be disgusting," Sharon said. "I don't know, but Jessie's so excited she threw up this morning."

That's always the omen of a good time to come, Sig thought. At least the party wasn't going to be held on her carpet. "Okay," she said wearily, "I'll come."

"Great. Barney will pick you up at five."

Sig had just taken off her headset when the phone rang again. If it was an order, no matter what the size, she'd tell them to call back Monday. She placed the gear on her head and pressed the connect button. The voice on the other end was deep.

"Sigourney? Is that you?"

"Yes."

"This is Paul Cushing. I need to talk to you."

"Now is fine."

"No. I need to see you in person."

Sig thought of the latke party and her shopping. "How about Monday?" she asked.

"Why don't I drop by your apartment Monday night?" he said. "It's important." What was that about? she wondered, but she had too much to do.

Sig spent the rest of the time making calls to her mortgage broker, the co-op board, and the loan officer at Citibank. It took her more than three hours, but before she was done she had managed to talk everybody into believing she'd get current in her payments within two weeks. She'd made her decision:

she'd have to sell the ring, and then the apartment, but she'd do what she had to do and a Merry Christmas to all.

There was one more call she had to make, though she couldn't bear it. She lifted the phone and dialed Sotheby's and asked for Mr. Grenville. She was put on hold. The telephone music was playing "We Wish You a Merry Christmas" and it was just ending. Then, to Sig's despair, she heard the drum intro for "The Little Drummer Boy." Sig immediately covered the earpiece so she wouldn't have to be tortured any further. When Mr. Grenville was put through, Sig released her hand and began by reintroducing herself. Hesitantly, she said, "I think I would consider selling the emerald now."

"Ah. A fine stone. And our pre-Christmas sale would be the time to sell it. But you'll have to hurry. It's too late to be in the catalog."

Sig looked down at her finger. It's only a little piece of colored glass, she tried to tell herself, then sighed. No man had ever given her a ring, and now she had to give up the one she'd given herself. "I'd like to put it in the auction," Sig said.

With some money in sight she took a cab uptown to Takashimaya, the chic Japanese department store on Fifth Avenue. The tearoom on the lower ground floor was the only place Sig could go to during this season and have a guarantee she wouldn't be accosted with *any* version of "The Little Drummer Boy."

After a snack, Sig needed to focus on her holiday

gift shopping. She'd do it all there. She still had most of the cash she'd taken out, and she'd use her credit cards if she had to. She had decided on a beautifully packaged box of green teas for Barney, who, as far as she knew, didn't drink tea; an Italian silk scarf for Sharon, since scarves came in only one size; a long, hand-knit muffler for Bruce in an absolutely killing smoky color; and finally, resentfully, a cleverly designed pair of rubbers for Mrs. Katz. Sig hoped they would fit over the socks and sandals.

That left only her mother and, exhausted and fighting the holiday crowd, Sig made her way up Fifth Avenue, past Bendel's, Doubleday's, and Trump Tower. She easily passed up Tiffany's. After all, with that doorknob that Monty had given her mother, it looked like Phyllis wouldn't need any jewelry. Sig sighed, looked at her own ring, and got as far as Bergdorf Goodman. She decided to step in. There had to be *something* marvelous there for her mother, the woman who was about to have everything.

Sig entered through the Fifty-seventh Street revolving door but found herself awash in a tide of purposeful shoppers. She passed through the accessory department, passed the leather goods, and lingered only a moment in the perfume hall before taking the elevator upstairs. She walked around the third floor, where the crowd was thinned out by the prices and the intimidating help, until she found herself in the back corner, where luxe carpeting and two antique fauteuils sat invitingly. "Bridal Salon" said the sign, and Sig found herself walking into the hushed holy of holies. There, a mannequin stood in a satin and tulle fairy-tale creation. Sig stopped and stared, her breath caught, her eyes devouring the beautiful dress. She'd never worn one, but if she ever had, she wished it had been this one. "Can I help you?" the heavy, middle-aged saleswoman asked. Sig jumped and turned to face her. "Are you looking for a mother-of-the-bride dress?" the woman asked politely.

All at once Sig felt both a thousand years old and as vulnerable as an infant. "No," she said. "I'm the daughter of the bride," and then surprised herself and the saleswoman by bursting into noisy tears.

Phyllis and Sylvia, bundled up tightly against the December chill, were walking up Madison Avenue. "This," Phyllis said, "is where the really rich people shop."

"Not Fifth Avenue?" Sylvia asked.

"Nah," Phyllis told her as she took her friend's arm and helped her avoid a fast-strutting matron holding a Yorkie under her arm. "This is the place. And it's the last day of Hanukkah. I'm going to get myself a present—a trousseau."

Phyllis had always kept a little money aside. It had been her habit from the very earliest days of marriage to Ira. Though she'd worked with him all those years, he'd never paid her a salary. She had merely asked for the housekeeping money and managed to put a little bit of it away. Over forty-seven years it had added up. Of course she'd had to use it from time to time, but only bits, and only for things like gifts for the children or a surprise trip with Ira. She was frugal. Even now, when she had just a modest amount coming in, she managed always to put aside a little bit at the end of each month. She'd been afraid she might have to use the money for private nursing, or that the government would get it if she had some catastrophic illness. Now, instead of waiting for a rainy day Phyllis was going to spend it—well, maybe not all of it, but plenty, and she was going to spend it on a trousseau. She and Ira had gotten married right after the war when there was still a shortage of lots of things, especially money. She had never had a trousseau, but she was determined to come to Monty, her fiancé, her lover-to-be, with all the accoutrements a bride should have with her.

Sylvia looked around at the fur-clad holiday shoppers. "I think we could do better at the Saw Grass Mall."

Phyllis laughed. She'd learned a few things watching her son make her over. "Natural fabrics, Sylvia," she said. "And we're starting from the panties out. Monty's seen your underwear, but he hasn't seen mine."

"Bernard saw mine, too," Sylvia said with a dreamy smile.

When they passed the window full of negligees, Phyllis stopped in her tracks. Silk with the iridescence of butterfly wings was mated with lace as frothy as sea foam. Sylvia followed her friend's eyes. "Do you think it's machine washable?" she asked. But without even answering, Phyllis moved toward the door like a somnambulist.

She bought it all. All of it and a silk bathrobe in a pinky champagne color that made her look sixty again. She didn't question the outrageous prices, she didn't look at the sale rack. She did none of her usual moves. She merely pointed at the most beautiful things, had them wrapped, and paid for them. And the adventure of it all was heightened by the idea that only Monty would see her in this new garb.

"Spending money is exhausting," Sylvia Katz said as she took a booth seat at Three Guys coffee shop on Madison.

"How would *you* know?" Phyllis asked as she slid into the seat opposite.

Phyllis herself had bought three pairs of extraordinary lace undies, two matching bras, and the most beautiful nightgown she'd ever seen. They had cost her almost a thousand dollars, but she hadn't winced. Instead, she'd imagined the look on Monty's face when she stood before him. Her only regret was that she hadn't ever felt this way before, and that the body under the fabrics would not be nearly as silky as the garments themselves. She sighed.

"Phyllis, are you having regrets?" Sylvia asked, and then, before Phyllis could explain, ordered an egg salad sandwich from the harried waitress.

Phyllis herself ordered a BLT without mayo. "I'm going to get myself a new coat and a hat to match," she announced to her friend. "And maybe a bag." She looked across the table at the huge, battered, ugly purse that Sylvia, as always, was schlepping. "I'll buy one for you, too," Phyllis said. What the hell, she was spending this much, she might as well spend a little more.

"Oh, no," Sylvia protested. "When Sid left me, this is all he left me with." Sylvia paused. "Do you think this Monty will be nice to you? I mean, really nice?"

"I think so," Phyllis said. "It's very odd. It seems to me like Ira loved me, and put up with who I was because of it. But Monty loves me *because* of who I am. Does that make any sense to you?"

"No," Sylvia admitted and reached for the egg salad sandwich plate that the waitress was handing off.

For a moment, Phyllis was flooded with pity for her friend. Loving Monty had given her more compassion and more generosity. "Hey, you want some dessert?" she asked. "Lunch is on me. I'll blow ya."

"Delicious," Monty exclaimed, and gave a pat to his mustache where singed bits of potato pancake still hung. The holiday meal had been hideous, the latkes inedible and the salad sandy, and all of the embarrassment complicated by the fabulous gifts Monty had dispensed to the whole company, putting Sig's in the shade. Then there was the endless stream of apologies from Sharon, who absolutely demanded insincere but constant reassuring response.

"I think I'll slit my throat," Sig whispered to Bruce.

"Before you wear that Hermés scarf?" Bruce asked. He was distractedly stroking the suede jacket he'd been given.

"All right. I'll wear it tonight going home. *Then* I'll slit my throat."

Bruce nodded. "When *I* go home, I'm going to have seventeen hysterical messages from Todd, who is convinced that I'm having an affair with Bernard."

"Well, are you?"

"Don't be ridiculous. I'm not that kind of a boy. I always go for looks over money. It's my curse."

"Speaking of looks over money, I think things are looking good between Monty and Mom."

"I sure hope so. I wouldn't eat one of Sharon's latkes for less than the opportunity to inherit a million dollars."

At that moment, Monty cleared his throat. "Well," he said. "It was a wonderful meal." He rose from the table. "Thank you, mine host." He smiled at Barney. "And now, if you'll step into the living room, I have a little proposal I'd like to discuss with you, son. I think you need to keep busy."

Bruce and Sig exchanged looks. "Son?" Bruce asked.

"Oh my God," Sig said. "He is going to offer Barney a job."

"Pur-rump-a-pum-pum," Bruce said.

Seventeen

When Monty arrived at the Pierre after the
latke party, he was dressed in his evening
wear, except for the Murray's Space Shoes
on his feet. "Well, you look snazzy," Phyllis said, and
realized how out of date the word was. For the first
time in close to fifty years she felt as self-conscious as
an adolescent. "Have you got special plans?" she
asked.

"I do," Monty told her and leered at her in a most
attractive way. Though he was bald, and more over-
weight than he should be for his health, Monty
exuded a kind of self-possession that made him
attractive, even sexy.

There was a knock at the suite door, though
Phyllis wasn't expecting anyone. "May I?" Monty
asked and went through the foyer and opened the
door to reveal Bernard Krinz.

The architect actually entered the room smiling,

then scanned it. For once his handshake didn't feel like that of a used car salesman hoping to close a deal. He seemed, instead, enthusiastic—even impatient. For a panicky moment Phyllis thought Bernie was looking for her, but then Mrs. Katz came out of the bedroom, out of her lumpy sweater and in a beaded dress. Monty put his hand on Krinz's shoulder and gave it a hearty squeeze.

"Well," he said, "Metropolitan Opera opening night, the best box in the house, and a lovely woman to enjoy it with. Wagner isn't my favorite, but I'm sure you'll enjoy it."

Phyllis turned to Sylvia in complete bewilderment, but Sylvia seemed dressed and ready, as if she knew all about it. Bernard helped her on with her voluminous coat and her ever-present purse. It wasn't until they had gone that Monty turned to Phyllis and smiled. "More costly than buying off my little brother with a chocolate bar, but it is a guaranteed five hours of absence and privacy." Then he leaned toward Phyllis and put one hand over her shoulder and against the wall, so she was imprisoned between his bulk and the window at her right. She knew he was about to kiss her—a real kiss, a kiss that mattered and might lead to other things, and she felt a flutter in her chest that wasn't angina. It had been a long time since she'd been really kissed, and she wasn't sure how she would react.

At that moment the suite bell rang again. Monty raised his brows, smiled, and answered it. This time three waiters, one with a wheeled table, one with champagne (two bottles) and ice buckets, and the last with a tray of savories paraded into the room. "I thought we might dine in," Monty said. The head-waiter set up the table and, with a flourish, was about to lay the pink linen napkin on Phyllis's lap when Monty stopped him. "Thank you, but no. I'll take care of her," he said, dismissing all the staff. "If we need you, we'll call."

Monty had ordered everything. Oysters for himself, her favorite melon for starters. The fruit tasted wonderful with the champagne Monty fed her. Phyllis had never been babied in this way. When there was any taking care of to be done, she took care of it. She took care of the children when they were little, she took care of the business and Ira when he was sick, and she took care of all the extended family members when they were grieving. Now there was someone who had ordered her dinner, down to her favorite salad, and had even noticed the salad dressing she preferred. Monty was a man who paid attention. "I'm not used to this," Phyllis admitted.

"Well, you better get used to it," Monty said and spooned the last one of his oysters into her mouth. "It's fun to treat you really well." He smiled a wicked grin. "I have an idea." He stood up, leaving the rest of dinner and the unused cups and the silver coffeepot which was being kept warm by a Sterno can. "I don't think we need more food now," he said. "I think all we need is time."

He took her hand and Phyllis felt a tingle, a buzz so electric that she almost giggled aloud. The man was seventy-four years old and totally mad, but she responded. Yet at the same time as she felt his heat for her rising and being matched by her own, she felt a certain reluctance. It was shyness, and even a little fear.

As if he sensed her hanging back, Monty encircled her in his arms. " 'We are old, Father William,' " he said, misquoting some ancient poem Phyllis could barely remember. "I don't want to rush you, but I *do* want you."

"You do?" Phyllis asked, both shy and coy. She liked to hear him say it. She liked everything about this old man.

"I want you to sleep with me," Monty said, nuzzling her ear. "My performance may not be what it once was, but every now and then . . ." His voice was husky. "I don't believe in long engagements, do you?" Phyllis nodded and let Monty lead her slowly into the bedroom.

He kissed her at the threshold and then led her to the bed, laid her down, and gently took off her shoes. "I'm a little nervous," Phyllis admitted.

"Only a little?" Monty asked and laughed. "At our ages the tables have turned. You can't lose your virginity, but I can easily lose my pride." He bent over and kissed Phyllis, just a brief kiss, but he still tasted of oysters, champagne, and something else. Then, matter-of-factly, he sat down on the side of the bed.

He took Phyllis's hand in his own. "Do you know what I've learned in the last five decades about sex?" he asked. Phyllis, still self-conscious, shook her head.

"What I've learned is that there's a lot that goes into loving a woman that most men are too impatient to bother with. Age has stolen a lot from me, Phyllis my dear. But it's granted me patience." He bent over and kissed her again, this time deeply. "I can promise you two things: that you have nothing to be embarrassed about and that, in the end, you're going to have a very, very good time with me."

And he was right.

It was only two mornings later that Sig was awakened by wild knocking on her door, interspersed with equally wild buzzing of her buzzer. No one gets up this early on Sundays in New York. "What? What?" she mumbled grumpily and managed to wrap a mohair shawl around herself to get to the relentless noise of the door. Only nine shopping days 'til Christmas and she had to be bothered with this?

Sharon, panting, her face red, stood beside Bruce, who was as deadly pale as an Irishman's ass. "What's going on?" she asked. "Is Mom all right?"

"No," Sharon said.

"Oh my God, is she . . ."

"It's not that," Bruce rapped out. "She hasn't had a stroke. *I'm* going to. Monty's checks have bounced, both for my business *and* for the school contribution."

"What?" Sig croaked. "That's impossible. What about Montana? What about the airline? What about the Guinness heiress?"

"Fake. All fake," Bruce told her. "Except the heiress. He married her and bled her dry. He's a fortune hunter. He met Mom on the flight from Florida in first class. He must have been trolling for a rich widow."

"Mom flew first class?" Sig asked. She put her hand up to her head. The three of them were still standing in her doorway. Sig bent down to pick up the Sunday *Times* from the doorstep. She'd have to check to be sure her ad for the apartment was listed. "Come in," she said. "Come in." Bruce and Sharon filed past her, Sharon's shoulders hunched. They sat down in the living room. "Okay," Sig said, feeling more tired than she ever had in her life. "Start from the beginning."

"The statistical genius over here got it wrong. Her data, as they say in the market research business, was severely compromised," Bruce grimaced. "Monty is penniless. He invested his wife's money in his airline. It went bankrupt more than a decade ago. He's been living on credit and loans ever since. Copernicus, here, had the numbers wrong."

"But it wasn't my fault," Sharon cried. "Mom picked him out, not me."

"Where *is* Mom?" Sig asked and she felt both a

fluttering in her stomach and the beginning of that feeling she got when her throat closed.

"I guess she's still at the Pierre," Bruce said.

Sig groaned and visibly shuddered. What was the bill there going to be? She'd dropped off her ring for auction, but now, even with its sale, her prospects of keeping her home and straightening out her life were worse than ever. She couldn't stave off the despair. "Okay," she said with a studied air of calmness she didn't feel. "I have a plan: first we kill Monty. Then Bruce, you kill Sharon while I kill myself."

"And nobody kills Mom? What kind of plan is that?" Sharon bleated. "It was *her* fault. This Monty was *hers*," Sharon said.

Bruce ignored his suburban sister. "It just might work," Bruce told Sig, then patted her now bare hand comfortably. "Sharon, if you want to, you can kill Mom before I kill you."

Sharon began to cry. "It wasn't my fault," she repeated.

"Oh, shut up," Bruce told her. "Everything's always been your fault."

"It is not. It wasn't my fault Barney turned down the job with Monty."

"He turned down the job?" Sig asked. "Is he crazy?" Bruce looked at her. "Rhetorical question," she assured him. "Did he really turn down the job?"

"He said it was beneath him. It was only middle management, something in the marketing department.

He said he wouldn't lower himself to less than vice president."

"My God! He's been downsized and out of work for close to two years and he turns *anything* down?" Sigourney asked.

Bruce shrugged. "Just as well. It was a fake, I'm sure."

Before this grousing degenerated into a full frontal attack, Sig pulled herself up. "Enough," she said. "I'll be dressed in four and a half minutes."

"What are we doing?" Sharon asked.

"We're going to the Pierre to have a little heart-to-heart with Mom."

The dark, glossy door to the Pierre suite looked solid as a castle portcullis. They'd rung the bell three times and now banged on the door. "I feel like Westley rescuing Buttercup in *The Princess Bride*," Bruce said.

Sig looked at him grimly. "You're the only princess around here," she snapped. "No time for your movieolas now. And Westley would have had the door down by now."

"*We'll* have to call security." Bruce shrugged.

"Excellent plan. I need some security," Sig murmured. Then they heard a rustling, and the peephole eye was filled. The door swung open and Mrs. Katz stood there, clad in a fluffy Pierre robe. "So early?" Mrs. Katz asked. She cleared her throat. "Maybe you should come back later."

Sig pushed the door open all the way and strode past Mrs. Katz, the useless freeloader. How much had her visit cost Sig? The other two Sibs followed. Sig got as far as the living room, which was disordered by newspapers, a blanket on the sofa, and the remains of a small room service repast, when Mrs. Katz caught up with her. "Where are you going?" she asked.

Sig gave her one of her looks and walked on to the bedroom door. Her hand was on the doorknob. "Don't you believe in privacy?" Mrs. Katz asked protectively.

"Don't *you*?" Sig retorted. "You came up here and moved in on my mother. You've stuck to her like glue. What privacy did you give her?"

Mrs. Katz raised her brows in hurt surprise. Then, "Plenty," she said, shrugged and turned her back. "*You'll* see."

Sig threw the bedroom door open. Bruce and Sharri were right behind her. Before her their mother, her hair disordered but her face composed, lay in the crook of Montague Dunleathe's hairy old arm. "Oh my God!" Sharri said and threw her hands up over her eyes.

Monty, his bald head shining but his side hair awry, opened his own eyes and sat up. His chest was as hairy as his arm. His breasts sagged onto his belly. Sig almost closed her own eyes. Somehow she hadn't imagined this. "Oh my God!" was all she could say, a hollow echo of her sister.

"What are you doing to my mother?" Bruce demanded.

"I think it's known as 'the traditional.' Or do you in the States call it 'the missionary'?" Monty asked.

Phyllis opened her eyes. "Well, that's what you started with . . ." she began.

Sharon threw both her hands up as if to ward off a blow. "More information than we require," she cried out and shuddered.

"So who asked you to ask?" Phyllis wanted to know. She started to sit up until it became clear that she, too, was naked. Sig couldn't help but notice the pile of frothy silk thrown on the floor beside the bed.

Bruce averted his eyes and made a strangled noise. "God! Who would think Mom was . . . was . . . like Louise Brooks in *Pandora's Box*!" Sig snatched up a terry robe from the bedside chair and threw it at Monty while her mother fumbled to pull the sheet up under her armpits. Sig actually felt sick, but she had to persevere. She walked across the Axminster rug to the nightstand. She picked up the engagement ring that was lying there and held it up to her eye. It sparkled, without doubt, but now, looking closely she could easily see the colors were wrong—instead of the white brilliance of a perfect stone, the marquis cut reflected all the colors of the room. "Cubic zirconium," she yelled and flung the ring as hard as she could toward the window. "You fake," she cried. "You total fake!"

"Susan, get control of yourself," Phyllis rapped out. "What do you think you're doing?"

"What do *you* think you're doing?" Sigourney asked. "You just met this guy. You don't even know him, and you're in bed with him?"

"I'm engaged to him, Susan. And you *wanted* me engaged to him." Phyllis shrugged. "Me, I figure marriage, schmarriage. But Monty is old-fashioned." She looked up at him with a look on her face that Sig had never seen there before. It confused and upset her. It made her feel excluded, and even . . . resentful. She looked at Monty.

He was not just old-fashioned but *old*. Sig couldn't help but stare at the mound of aged flesh that confronted her, his mottled skin and the hair thrusting itself out of his ears, matched by the horrible web of wrinkles across the top of her mother's sagging chest. It was bad enough, Sig thought, that she'd had to suck in her stomach whenever she'd slept with Phillip Norman. At least she was toned, while Phillip's flesh was firm and smooth and tanned. He'd known how it pleased her in bed, and he was athletic in showing it. Why, then, did she have the feeling that Monty gave her mother something else, something more? She put the thought from her mind. "Get out!" she told him. "Leave my mother alone."

Monty raised his bushy brow, then shook his head. "You forget. We're betrothed."

Sig could barely contain her rage. Her hands were shaking and she felt the trembling go up her arms and into her body. Everything had gone wrong. There wasn't going to be any rescue, not for her, not for her mother. Her ring—her real one—was gone now and forever, and so was her mother's. This fake, this charlatan, had ruined everything. She'd lose her co-op, she'd give up on her job, and she'd wind up in Forest Hills, or Park Slope, or Riverdale, in some crummy rental apartment with her mother in the guest room—if there *was* a guest room. They'd split the rent, using some of Phyllis's Social Security check to make ends meet. It was she, Sig, the unmarried daughter, who would wind up taking care of their mother until her own breasts were down to her waist. "Get out!" she yelled again, but this time her voice was very close to tears.

"Excuse me?" Phyllis said. "Exactly who do you think you are?" She looked from Sig to Bruce and Sharon. "What are the three of you doing here, anyway? This is my life and you have no right to interfere like this."

Sig rolled her eyes. If she'd had a gun . . .

"Mom," Bruce began to explain, "the man is a liar. He's a con artist. He's . . . he's like Eli Kotch in *Dead Heat on a Merry-Go-Round*. Except not as good-looking as James Coburn. The guy is broke."

"Hey," Phyllis yelled, "I wasn't going to marry him for his *money*. Monty's seventy-four years old and he can still get a boner. Plus, he knows what to do with it!"

"And this from a woman who swore off genitalia," Monty said proudly, reaching with one arm to embrace her and with the other for the cigar at the side of the bed.

"Mom, get out of that bed," Sig snarled. Phyllis shrugged and obeyed, naked though she was. All three of her children screamed simultaneously and turned away in horror. Sig managed to pick up the lacy silk gown from off the floor and throw it at her mother, who calmly started to put it on.

"What's the problem here?" Phyllis asked as she smoothed the crumpled gossamer around her thickened waist. "He had money. Now he doesn't have money. Maybe he'll have some money again. Anyway, in the meantime, I promise you he's not stealing your inheritance." She paused and smiled wickedly. "And he wasn't stealing my virtue, either." Phyllis looked over at Sig. "If we're in the truth-telling mode, you don't have anything to be so proud about, Susan. If you think he was trying to con you, you were trying to con him with all of this." She gestured at the room, the new clothes, the fresh flowers.

Sigourney stared at Monty. "She has no money. Do you understand? She doesn't have a dime, except her pension check. There is no portfolio. The jewelry was costume. She has no prospects of getting any more money, either, unless you consider the pathetic cost-of-living adjustment to her Social Security payments. There is no house in Palm Beach. I'm paying for this suite. And I've run out of money. You're bankrupt, and I'm about to go under, too."

There, she'd said it. Now they'd finally under-stand—know all about the foreclosure, her failure, everything. But she'd still protect her mother. "You picked the wrong horse," she told Monty. "Get up and go away and leave my mother alone. You were in it for the money and there is none."

"It's time to beat it," Bruce said angrily.

"That," Monty said, "has become abundantly clear." And he calmly got out of bed, slipped his trousers on, and did so.

Eighteen

*Y*ou're *not* seeing him. Forget about it."

"What does that mean? What does that mean, 'forget about it'?" Phyllis asked.

"It means what I said," Sig repeated. "He doesn't like you. He wanted your money. Which, I might remind you, you have none of. Mom, he married an heiress before and squandered all her money. He just thought he was doing it again." It was black Monday, and what with the Monty fiasco and work about to begin, Sig was morose.

"Don't be ridiculous. How could I be an heiress?" Phyllis asked her daughter, who was tearing into her clothes.

"The portfolio. First-class flying. The clothes," Bruce explained. Sig had asked him over to keep all eyes on their mother while she was at work.

"The guy is a con man," Sig repeated. "Probably a thief. Didn't you ever hear of Sunny von Bulow? No way you're going to see him again."

They had stayed at the Pierre yesterday only long enough to morosely pack up Phyllis's belongings and for Sig to hyperventilate and sign the American Express bill. Now they'd adjourned, along with the adhesive Mrs. Katz, to Sig's apartment.

"I can't believe the tuition check bounced," Sharon whined. Sig had called her in to also guard their mom. "I'm so embarrassed. How can I show my face at Jessie's school?"

"Nothing stopped you before," Bruce spat. "Barney's checks used to bounce like a spaldeen." He paused. "What about me, Sharon? I just put in an emergency reprinting order that I can't pay for. I could have had a deal with Bernard, but Monty offered me an interest-free loan. I can't believe I was so stupid. This is the most important season of the year in my business. I was operating on paper, but at least I was on *good* paper. Now I've sent *bad* checks to my suppliers. How am I going to explain *that*? I was hanging on by a thread, but Monty's ruined it all. I'd like to strangle the Scottish son of a bitch."

"A nice way to talk in front of your mother," Phyllis said, crossing her arms. She paused, thinking it over. "He *did* like me. I know he did. And I don't care if he doesn't have any money."

There was a flutter at the other side of the room.

Sig couldn't help but notice Mrs. Katz, sitting prim
and proper on the edge of the chair clutching her
purse with both hands. What is it with her, Sig
thought? Mrs. Katz shook her head, as if she had
palsy, or wanted attention. Probably both, Sig
decided. She took a deep breath. It was either out of
annoyance or to calm herself. "That's not the point,
Mom. He's clearly a sociopath. I know. I've dated a
dozen of them. No normal man throws checks around
like that. Not when he knows they're going to bounce
like rubber. Forget about Monty," Sig told her, exasperated. "No more Montague nonsense."

"Who are you? Mrs. Fucking Capulet?" Phyllis
asked.

Sig took a deep breath. "Mom, we need you to
marry a rich man. If you don't, the two of you will be
living in the Bronx on food stamps faster than I can
say 'cost of living cut,' " Sig warned. "Anyway, Monty
thinks you're rich. He got out of your bed and walked
away. Once he found out you weren't, he left you.
You wouldn't have had enough money left over each
month to buy a subway token to visit us with."

Phyllis shook her head. "You know what's wrong
with you, Susan? You're too responsible. What's all
this to you? So I'll live in the Bronx. That's where I
came from. You're not my mother."

"Mom, I don't want to hurt your feelings, but you
were hustled."

"Hustled? Me! Monty couldn't even beat me at
canasta!"

"Or he didn't want to," Sig told her. "That's the way a hustle works."

"Well, I'm not even going to *touch* just any old geezer," Phyllis told her. "Florida was full of *them*. That's why I got out."

Phyllis sat very still for a moment. Sig wondered if she saw her mother's lips tremble. Sig lowered her voice and put her hand on her mother's shoulder. "I'm sorry, Mom. You deserve better. You really do."

Phyllis looked up at Sig. "So do you, Susan." She shook her head and lowered herself into a chair. "So. What next?" she asked.

Sig sat down next to Sharon on the sofa, distracted again by Mrs. Katz, who was holding her purse by the strap and methodically spinning it 180 degrees. Sig snapped herself out of the trance. "Well, next is bankruptcy for me. And I guess I leave Wall Street. And I suppose I have to find another job—which is really easy for a woman my age at my level," Sig snorted. "I'm completely tapped out."

"Oh, come on, Sig," Bruce shrugged. "You're always poor-mouthing. You did that last routine to unload Monty, right? I'm the one about to lose my business, and I've got nothing else. What's the portfolio really like? It ain't as light as Mom's," Bruce said.

Sig stared at him. It was always easy, she thought bitterly, for her family to think she could do anything, that she could pay for anything, and that she had everything under control. "I'm sorry to disillusion you, Bruce, but I'm not talking poor. I'm not even acting poor. I'm broke. There is no portfolio anymore. I've been selling off stock for the last two years. And taking a loss. Have you ever heard of downsizing, Mr. Entrepreneur? Mr. Economic Miracle?" She shot a look at Sharon. "Even Barney has heard of downsizing."

"We're going to have to take the kids out of private school," Sharon mourned. "They told us they couldn't come back after the Christmas break if we didn't pay up."

"Swell. So we're all sunk," Sig said. "I'm a senior broker who isn't delivering. All my corporate lawyer and marketing and real estate clients have dried up. They've been downsized. I have no commissions coming in. How much longer do you think they'll allow me that big corner office? I've been warned twice, so it's not much longer. And I'm not going back to the bull pen." She shook her head. "I'd rather wait tables."

"You mean it, Sig?" Sharon asked with disbelief. "Fired? Like Barney? You really mean it?"

Sig, tears of humiliation choking her throat, merely waved her hand and nodded. Her sister's empathy touched her.

"Oh my God," Sharon said and began to cry. "You're going to lose the apartment? This will be so hard for Jessie and Travis."

"Yeah. And it might be a little tough for Sig herself," Bruce added. "Same old Sharon." He went over to Sig and took her hand. "Why didn't you tell me?" he asked.

She shrugged. "What good would it have done?" she asked. "*You* couldn't help me."

Bruce squeezed her hand, looked down at it for a long time, and then nodded. "So I guess a small no-interest loan is out of the question right now?" he asked.

"Always with the jokes," Phyllis said. She stood up. "Sig, I have a little money put aside. You think it would be enough . . . ?"

Sig just shook her head. "Mom, my mortgage payment is thirty-eight hundred dollars a month. My maintenance is twenty-two hundred and I haven't made a payment on either for almost nine months." She paused, letting the numbers sink in. "This place is now owned by the bank. They'll probably foreclose in the next month or so."

"You're really going to lose the apartment?" Bruce asked.

"Unless someone buys it fast and I get out some equity," Sig sighed. "I waited too long. I've put an ad in the *Times* and I've gotten a few calls and I've also sent around the particulars to residential real estate agents, but I've only had a nibble or two and neither of them were serious." Now tears rose in Sig's own eyes. "An agent is coming this afternoon with the first prospect. Maybe something will happen. Other than that, I'm lost."

She sat down, exhausted. "And even if I get a

quick sale, once I pay the mortgage, the second mortgage, back maintenance, the commission to the broker, and all the rest of it, I may have just enough money for a studio apartment in Bensonhurst." Sig was heartbroken to have to give up her home. What had she worked so hard for all her life? What else did she have? Now what would she have to show for it? "Something went wrong with this country," Sig said. "Nobody has any money."

"I do," said Sylvia Katz. "I have plenty. You want some?"

The three siblings looked at her with impatience, while Phyllis took the time to move next to her friend and pat her on the arm. "Thank you, Sylvia. But we're not talking about small change. Sig needs close to a hundred thousand dollars."

"I got that," Mrs. Katz said calmly. "I got a lot more than that." Phyllis rolled her eyes and patted Sylvia's shoulder again, though she felt like she wanted to strangle her instead. Her daughter's life had completely fallen apart—no husband, no children, no money, no job, and no home. Meanwhile, her best friend had finally gone *meshuga*.

"Sha. Sha, Sylvia," Phyllis said dismissively.

"I have it right here in my purse," Mrs. Katz said, and finally opened the huge black patent leather monstrosity on her lap.

Phyllis, standing beside her seated friend, couldn't help but see that the large purse was indeed stuffed with neatly stacked and freshly strapped parcels of money. Each bundle—and there seemed to be scores of them—said $10,000. "Oh my God," was all she could say.

Bruce also looked down at the purse. He made a noise like the one old Jews made at the synagogue before they began to pray—a sort of half sigh, half groan. "Where did you get all that?" he asked, his voice hushed.

"Is it real?" Sharon breathed, looking over his shoulder.

"I got it when my husband left me. He had to pay a lot. A lot. My lawyer, Diana LaGravennes, was very good. She made Sid pay. I didn't know what to do with it, so I kept it. I didn't like to spend it."

Bruce whistled. "What has four legs and runs after cats?" he said. No one responded. "Mrs. Katz and her lawyer," he said, but no one laughed.

"You've carried that around with you all this time?" Phyllis asked, utterly astonished. It didn't matter if she lived another seventy years, she realized, she would never know the boundaries of human peculiarities or the interior of human hearts.

"Well, I didn't know what else to do with it," Sylvia admitted. "Sid took care of the banks and other things. Before he left me he'd always paid the utility and phone bills. I never even had a checking account. Anyway, what should I do with so much money? I never even wrote a check. I'm always reading about old women getting swindled by banks and brokers." She looked up at Sig. "Nothing personal, darling. Present company excluded." She shrugged. "So I just kept it. It seemed safest."

"It seemed *safest*?" Phyllis asked, her voice rising. "You walked The Broadwalk with a hundred thousand dollars in your purse?"

"No," Sylvia explained. "It's two million two hundred thousand."

"Two million two hundred thousand dollars?!" Sharon and Bruce echoed at once.

"Well, plus my change purse. I keep my change and my Social Security money in this." She pulled out a silver mesh bag.

Phyllis began to laugh. Once she began she couldn't stop until tears rose in her eyes. "You wouldn't spring for a motel when you flew up here! You had over two million dollars in your purse and you sat up all night at La Guardia? For six years in Florida you had to get up at four A.M. so you could breakfast by five so you could eat lunch by ten so you could eat dinner at three-thirty and save four dollars on early bird specials. You took home the extra rolls. You stole the Sweet'n Low packets from every diner we ever went to. You slept on my sofa here in New York. And the whole time you had more than two million dollars in your purse? In your purse! *In your purse?* Are you crazy? Did you ever hear of purse snatchers?"

"I hold on very tight," Sylvia said.

Phyllis laughed again until it hurt and then just shook her head. "You betcha," she said. Then the fatigue swept over her and she had to sit down. What now? For the first time in her life she was speechless.

Sig, who had been very quiet watching the two older women friends, came to join her siblings to peek into the money bag.

"So how much do you need, Susan?" Mrs. Katz asked, and pulled out a packet of bills. It was a big packet, all fresh, with a $10,000 unbroken brown band around it. Mrs. Katz began to take out more of them, stacking them like children's bricks on the table.

"Oh, I couldn't . . ." Sig said. "I don't know when I could repay—"

"Borrow the money," Phyllis rapped out at Sig. She turned to Sylvia. "Thank you, Sylvia," she said. "I never loved you for your money, but it doesn't hurt." She looked back at Sig. "I didn't realize how things were with you. I came up here to be a good mother to you, not to be selfish. I want to help. Call one of your other candidates. I'll see him." Then, with dignity she sat herself down, alone, at the other end of the room.

Meanwhile, like a snake fighting a snake charmer, Sharon managed to tear her eyes away from the contents of Mrs. Katz's purse. "I'll go back through the files," she said. "We made a mistake with the first, but we'll do it right this time. I can find the right guy."

Bruce looked over at Sharon. "Not a bad idea," he said. He looked over at Mrs. Katz. "Maybe you could help us with this project," he said. *"Then* we'll pay you back."

Sig crossed the room to her mother. She thought of how content her mother had looked in Monty's arms, though the man was a liar and crook. "You mean it, Mom?" Sig asked, her voice low.

Phyllis merely sat there, her head down. "If that's what I have to do, I'll do it."

Sig was back home from work, exhausted and drained. Her mother, Mrs. Katz, and all their possessions had been transplanted from the Pierre to Sig's library, which now looked like some bizarre cross between a college dorm and a convalescent home. Sig had taken one look at the pill and medicine bottles, Mrs. Katz's denture holder, the damp socks over the radiator, the prunes in a plastic jar on the bureau, along with all the other detritus of the two old women's lives and simply closed the folding doors on the whole thing.

Sig's buzzer rang. She shut the door on the room with the intention of not showing it at all. Sharon had gone home to her still unemployed husband, promising to dig out the files for new marital candidates, and Bruce had dropped her at the train on his way to Chelsea. Sig was on watch. Their mother and Mrs. Katz were lying down in her spare bedroom, but Sig was still awake, finishing the little touches to the apartment that she'd been told would help make it sell quickly. She had straightened the pillows, put out flowers, and scented the air with two bowls of Floris potpourri. If she knew how, she'd bake a cake, just so that the welcoming smell of sweet batter rising would entice a buyer. She was still in shock over Mrs. Katz and her incredible bag. It couldn't save her, but it could buy her some time so she could save herself. For the first time in weeks Sig found herself humming: when she realized she was humming the theme to *Felix the Cat* she had to smile. "Whenever he got in a fix, he reaches into his bag of tricks."

Sig went to the door to meet Cornelia, the agent from Stirling & Ross, the primo residential brokers in New York. She knew it was best not to be in when people came to look, but since there was no place else to stash her mother and Mrs. Katz, this time there really was no alternative. She may as well be here, sitting nonchalantly in the library, while some witch who'd married money criticized her bathroom wallpaper. Sig took a deep breath and opened the door. Cornelia was there, another one of those residential-broker-ladies-of-a-certain-age who invariably wore important earrings and a belt with a gold-tone buckle. Cornelia swept in, her smile tight. "Well, hello," she said, simultaneously raising her brows, looking around, and immediately flicking on the lamp in the foyer. "You've done a lovely job with this place," Cornelia said. "It'll sell quickly." Goddamn it, Sig thought, she'd forgotten to turn on the lamps, which was the number one broker trick. But the rest of her rooms were really light, it was only the foyer that was windowless.

She looked up over Cornelia's shoulder and started with surprise.

"Paul Cushing," Sig said and put her hand out to him. She experienced that moment of dislocation when she met someone she knew from another setting—like the time she bumped into her gynecologist's nurse in Bloomingdale's. She had completely forgotten about his promised visit and the news he couldn't tell her over the phone.

"Is this a bad time?" he asked.

"No. Not really. I'm just letting this broker take a look at my place. I'm thinking of buying another one . . ." Sig tried not to blush. How embarrassing, for Paul Cushing to show up when Cornelia did and to know she was selling her apartment. Sig was acquainted with Cornelia well enough to know that to make a sale Cornelia would definitely tell a prospect—or even a stranger—when a property was distressed.

He smiled warmly. "It's so nice to see you again, Sigourney. I had no idea you were even considering selling your place." He looked around. "So many of these New York apartments don't seem very warm. But you've made a home here." He looked directly at her. His eyes were very blue. "Why don't you show us both around? I didn't get a complete tour when I was here for your mother's birthday."

Cornelia smiled brightly. It was clear to Sig that

the woman wasn't going to lose an opportunity here. "Well, let me begin by pointing out the two foyer closets . . ."

"Oh, don't bother," Paul Cushing told her politely but firmly, and Cornelia wilted. "Sig knows what I like. *She'll* show me around." Then, to take out the sting, Paul Cushing smiled at Cornelia. His smile was really devastating for an old guy's, Sig thought. Cornelia, an old babe, recovered and actually fluttered her lashes at him. So *that's* how it is, Sig thought, as Paul took her elbow and allowed her to lead him into the living room.

"I know you've been here, but I don't think you saw the view, Cornelia." Sig took them to the window and pulled aside the Scalamandre curtains. She looked out at the view she loved. "You can see three bridges from here," she told them, staring at the river. "The bridges themselves are easier to see at night, but the park is best in the daytime." She looked up—he was tall—to find that he wasn't looking at the view.

"How's your mother, Sig?" Paul asked. "I have something I want to tell her."

"Oh, she's just fine," Sig said brightly. Maybe he'd do for Mom, she thought. "Actually she's here. She got tired of the hotel. She's resting now." Sig pictured what her mother looked like without three hours of Bruce's prep time and thought it best that she and Paul didn't run into each other. Not right now. She'd show him the guest room later—on another visit. She'd make sure there was another visit. Was this more than some kind of coincidence? Was it some kind of holiday gift? Sig looked at Paul. He was much better looking than Monty, and Sig knew that he was legitimate—how many millions had Sharon said he was worth? Maybe Sharon didn't have to go back to the files after all. Perhaps they had somebody right here.

"What is it that you need to tell my mother?" Sig asked.

"I looked up background information on Montague Dunleathe as I told you I could. I hate to say anything bad about a man, but he might not be as he seems." He paused. "I say this to protect you and your mother. Like I protect Wendy."

"That's very considerate of you. I appreciate it." His timing couldn't have been better, Sig thought. He didn't know the half of it.

"I wouldn't like to see your mother hurt."

Sig smiled up at Paul Cushing. "Step into my parlor," she told him.

Nineteen

"The Rainbow Room? On Christmas week? It will be a mob scene, nobody goes to the Rainbow Room," Sig was saying to her mother.

"How can it be a mob scene if nobody goes there?" Phyllis asked.

"Nobody who's anybody," Sigourney said.

"Well, we are. For dinner. All four of us," Phyllis told her daughter. Sig shrugged.

"Look, you don't have to go if you don't want to," Phyllis told Sig. "I don't want to go."

Sig narrowed her eyes. "No. You're going. You're going and you're going to enjoy it. If you could like Monty, you'll love Paul Cushing."

"Nah. He's not *my* type. He's more . . ."

"More what? More classy? More rich? More sincere? He's certainly more attractive. He's very, very attractive."

"Oh, you think so?" Phyllis asked. She half closed

her already hooded eyes. "What do *you* think, Sylvia?"

Sylvia, sitting in the club chair as usual, shrugged. "I prefer Monty," she said in a dreamy voice. "But maybe that's because he played canasta with me."

Sig shook her head. She was surrounded by senile dementia. Well, she supposed things could be worse. Sylvia Katz could be her mother.

So far, Sig the big Wall Street investment broker hadn't been able to convince Mrs. Katz even to put her money in a bank, much less invest in even the most secure stocks and bonds. Mrs. Katz, plain and simple, was having none of it. Sig had even given up trying to explain about interest. Mrs. Katz didn't care about interest. "I know from interest. When you have money everyone has interest in you." All Sylvia Katz wanted was to keep hold of the contents of her patent leather purse, which she would never spend, not even to save her modesty in a game of strip canasta. "Don't be mad, Susan," Mrs. Katz said now. "Mr. Cushing is very nice, but I'm like your mother. Except for the S, E, X part. I prefer Monty."

"Montague Dunleathe is a crook," Sig said, totally exasperated.

"He played a good game of canasta," Mrs. Katz said nostalgically. Then she pulled herself together and looked back at Sig. "He didn't try a thing," she assured her. "Not with me, anyway. It was just a friendly game."

Sig merely rolled her eyes. The junk from their

room had spread into the living room and was now threatening even her foyer. Mrs. Katz's shapeless sweater hung over a doorknob in the hall. Someone's reading glasses, the earpiece held onto the frame by a safety pin, were lying on the lowboy. The Halls Mentho-lyptus lozenges (which Mrs. Katz perpetually sucked on) were on one sofa table. On the other was an equally fetid collection of objects: Phyllis's brand of lozenges—billed as "curiously strong peppermints"—were spread beside their tin box. There was also an old Chap Stick, a stack of dimes—which Phyllis still collected, though telephones no longer used dimes—some coupons torn out of a magazine or newspaper or both, a pencil stub, a half-filled-in crossword puzzle, and two more pairs of reading glasses, one with a neck chain and one without.

Sig thought she might go mad, but with some luck Paul Cushing would take Mom off her hands, while Mrs. Katz would eventually be weaned into a place of her own—or at least make a home with Phyllis.

It seemed to Sig that—God knows why—Paul had been doing his best to woo Phyllis. He had taken both her mom and Mrs. Katz out for dinner yesterday, then he'd taken Sig, Wendy, and Phyllis to the Radio City Christmas show today. Sig had called in sick, and, anyway, nothing was happening these days right before the holiday.

Of course, Phyllis had almost blown that for them by talking throughout the entire picture, but her comments were a lot funnier than the film, anyway.

And it seemed that Paul Cushing could live with it because he'd given them this invitation. At least that's what Mrs. Katz had told them after she took the call. Paul Cushing didn't seem to Sig like the Rainbow Room type. He was much smoother, more sophisticated than that. Still, Sig had called up Bruce to do a job on Mom and now they were ready to go.

"Paul's very nice," Sig said to her mom, fishing.

"Very nice," Phyllis agreed. "But he doesn't like me."

"Of course he does. He likes you very much."

"Not in that way," Phyllis said. She looked Sig over. "Very nice," she said approvingly. "But you should wear a shorter skirt."

Bruce stood over Mom, spraying in the last few touches to her hairstyle with a fixative strong enough to bond frogs to steel girders. "There," he said, and gave the front of her hair a tug. "One final fillip."

"Speaking of Phillips . . ." Sig began and took a look in the mirror. "He should be here any moment." She'd lowered herself again, but she had to. "I won't see him after this," she said aloud.

"Well, thank God. Progress is being made," Phyllis said. "Now, if you'd only open your eyes and date a real man, not a corporate clone too scared to commit or have kids."

"Mother, most men don't want me. They say I'm too much to handle."

Phyllis smiled nostalgically. "Your father used to

say that to me." She lowered her eyes and her voice. "Monty said it, too," she murmured.

The Rainbow Room was crowded, but when they got off the private elevator and were greeted by the obsequious maître d' they were immediately ushered to a desirable table for four right beside the dance floor. Paul Cushing obviously had clout. And they'd arrived just in the nick of time, because as they took their seats the lights dimmed, the small orchestra played an anticipatory drum riff, and then, one by one, Rockettes appeared at the top of the curved miniature staircase. The women tap-danced symmetrically and beautifully down the stairs, one more perfect than the next, one leg more shapely than the one beside it, until they were all on the dance floor and moved into high gear. They dazzled the crowd, not only with their tapping and kicks but with the mechanical perfection they performed in.

Sig, however, was bored. She looked across the table. Phillip was looking on, also blasé and certainly bland, but Paul's eyes sparkled and he led the applause. There was something about Paul—even though he was so old—that seemed always to find new pleasure in life. When he bent to his left and said something to her mother that Sig couldn't hear, she wished she knew what it was.

After the performance, once the applause calmed down, the band began to play "Night and Day." When

Phillip asked her to dance, Sig was surprised but pleased, at least until she got onto the dance floor. Sig could dance, but not with Phillip. He made her feel awkward. He couldn't lead, and she actually found herself stepping on his foot. Each time she did, he apologized. Phillip was, without a doubt, the worst dancer north of the Mason-Dixon line. Probably south, too. Sig was very grateful when Paul Cushing tapped Phillip on the shoulder and cut in.

"Thank God," she breathed. Phillip relinquished her with only a slightly hurt backward glance.

"It looked like you needed rescuing," Paul said, "but I wasn't sure." Then he took command. He stepped back from her a bit and looked at her. "Nice dress. Very festive. Red is your color." Sig blushed. "Did you like the flowers?" he asked.

"They were lovely," Sig said warmly. Then Paul pulled her closer. His hand on the small of her back, asserting a gentle pressure, felt delicious. "My mother was very touched." Sig found it effortless to match her steps to his, to anticipate his moves and to relax. She hadn't done that the first time they danced, at the Winter Wonderland Ball. Younger men didn't know how to dance, but dancing became almost a participatory sport with Paul. They moved through the rest of "Night and Day," and they continued moving together to "I've Got You Under My Skin." Sigourney relaxed, and leaned a little closer to him. Then she remembered her mother, and the whole point of the exercise.

This is bizarre, Sig thought. I'm having a better time with Paul than I am with my date. Then again, Phillip was only nominally Sig's date, or anything to Sig. "We have to go back to the table," Sig said reluctantly as the band began to play "Just in Time." "This has been fun, though."

Paul smiled at her, took her elbow, and began to lead her off the floor. It felt good to have him take charge and move them between the dancing couples. But the good time evaporated right at that second. Because just before they reached their table, Sig looked up and saw her mother dancing with Monty—Montague Dunleathe—halfway across the room. "Oh my God!" Sig said and dropped Paul's hand, stepping away from him.

"What is it?"

Sig could say nothing. She merely pointed. He followed her gaze and raised his eyebrows.

"Your mother?" Paul asked. "Is she all right?"

Sig shook her head. Then she got very, very angry. What was going on here? She'd been duped. Surely this wasn't merely coincidence! "How did he know we were going to be here?" she demanded of Paul.

"I haven't a clue," he admitted.

Sig didn't know whether she should believe him or not. She was filled with a furious energy. She'd been had, and she knew it. Paul Cushing had, most likely, been dancing with her merely to distract her. He must be plotting on Mom's behalf, along with her other friends. "You picked this place," Sig said accusingly.

"*Me*? I didn't pick it. I thought it was for you. Why would *I* want to come here?"

"So *that* could happen," she said, pointing. "Otherwise it's because you like the Rockettes and enjoy being surrounded by people with bad haircuts. I don't know. I just know that Mrs. Katz said that *you* had made the reservations. Did Monty ask you to do it?"

"Mrs. Katz told me your mother wanted to come." He paused. "Wait a second." Paul's face, when he concentrated, looked all of his seventy-one years. "No, actually, I think she said *you* wanted to come." He grinned. "Frankly, I was surprised. Then I hoped it was for the dancing. You're a great dancer, Sig."

Sig didn't have time for any more talk. She had to figure out what the hell was going on with her mother. She strode across the dance floor and reached Monty and her mom. They had just executed a complicated-looking but graceful dip. Monty looked up. "Oh, cheerio," he said, as if being there in his ratty old dinner jacket, her mother wrapped in his arms, was the most natural thing in the world.

"What do you think you're doing?" Sig asked, outraged. The last time she'd seen them together they were in bed, naked. Somehow, in public and clothed, this looked almost as intimate. Montague Dunleathe, still holding her mother, stopped and looked up at Sigourney.

"You look very elegant tonight," Montague said.

"Stop with the con, Monty. It doesn't work on me.

And let go of my mother." Sig looked down at her mom. "It's time to go," she said stiffly.

"But we just got here," Phyllis almost whined. Ah, Sig thought, that's where Sharri got the whine from.

"Just in Time" was about to end. Monty pulled Phyllis out of her dance swoon and they stared into each other's eyes. They were standing altogether too close.

"Excuse me," Sig said. "I'd like to cut in." She tapped Montague Dunleathe on the shoulder.

"I'm not leaving," Phyllis said.

Sig looked at her mother. "You promised not to do this," she reminded her.

Phyllis shrugged. "I didn't do anything."

"I believe the expression here is 'It's a free country,' " Monty said to Sig.

"Only for people who don't pay their taxes," Sig spat.

Sig reached out her hand and took her mother's. "Who helped you? You should be ashamed of yourself. What did you do, make secret phone calls?"

"No. Sylvia made the calls," Phyllis pointed out.

"Oh, great. You've turned Mrs. Katz into the nurse in *Romeo and Juliet*. She's your go-between now?" Sig stepped between them and looked at Montague boldly. "Stay away from my mother," she said. "I don't want to see or hear from you. I don't want you to speak to me, my mother, or Mrs. Katz. You're a user, and a fortune hunter, a hurtful cad, and worse than all of that together. If you have any further questions about your character, you can reach me at my office."

By now, quite a little crowd had gathered around them. Paul Cushing stood to the side, as did the useless Phillip, but Sig didn't care. She took Phyllis by the arm and, turning her back on all the people in the room, led her mother to the elevator.

In it, on the way down sixty-six floors, the elevator music played five verses of "The Little Drummer Boy."

Mrs. Katz confessed. It wasn't hard to wring the truth out of her: Monty had secretly been calling for days and Mrs. Katz, who thought it was romantic, had passed messages on to Phyllis.

"What do you think you were doing, Mom?" Sig asked furiously.

"How could you do this?" Sharon wheezed at her mother.

Bruce just glared at his mother. No words were needed.

Phyllis sat up in the chair. "Okay, I see where you're going with this line of questioning. I'll do it your way."

"Good," the Sibs chimed in unison.

Sig called Paul Cushing and did a lot of apologizing about the Rainbow Room fiasco. He seemed perfectly comfortable with everything she said and proposed. He came over and took her mother and

Wendy out on a carriage ride through Central Park on Wednesday night. Had dinner with Sig, Phyllis, and Mrs. Katz on Thursday. Then the four of them went to see *Showboat* on Friday and Paul even got an extra ticket for Mrs. Katz. Things had progressed so well that they actually spent Saturday evening with Sharon, Barney, Jessie, and Travis. They took a stretch limo down Fifth Avenue so that the kids could look at all the Christmas lights in the store windows. Wendy loved Jessie, and the feeling seemed mutual. Things were moving quickly and Sig felt as if her plan was working. So why did she feel so unhappy? It was an odd sensation, almost dreamlike, as if everything she cared about was slipping from her grasp.

Twenty

ig wriggled out of the red slacks and decided
she'd wear a black skirt and dark pantyhose
instead. It was only once she had dressed that
she remembered that Paul had admired the red dress
she'd worn earlier in the week at the Rainbow Room.
Oh well. It wasn't she who had to please him. She
didn't want to look too dressed up, so she put on
boots rather than shoes. She threw open the door to
her beautifully designed closet and picked not the
short black boots nor the knee-high black boots but
the ankle-high black ones with the turnover cuff. She
actually had four pairs of black boots, she realized, as
well as three pairs of brown, six pairs of brown
shoes, eleven pairs of black ones, and then, of course,
there were all the other, less basic colored shoes. My
God, Sig thought, looking at it all. There wasn't a
pair that cost less than $200. How much money have
I wasted over the years?

She sighed. Even with the temporary loan from Mrs. Katz there would be no more shoe buying, no more custom closets. Sig pushed the door shut with a bang and surveyed herself in the three-way mirror, though why she cared she couldn't fathom. It was just another date night for Mom, and all Sig was doing was serving eggnog and Christmas cookies before seeing Mom off at the door. She gave a last look over her shoulder at the fit of her skirt. Was it a little tight across the back? She'd have to double up on her sessions at the gym after the holidays were over—at least until her membership ran out. There would be no more private workouts at David Barton's, the best gym with the best personal trainers in town. Sig sighed again and went out to the living room.

There Mrs. Katz was glued to the love seat. It irritated Sig to see that lately she always selected that spot, when it would fit her mother and Paul cozily. Instead, they'd be forced to sit on a larger sofa, or even across from each other. Mrs. Katz was so out of it. Sig immediately felt guilty for thinking that way, especially after Mrs. Katz's generosity. But the woman was human Super Glue, and Sig literally had to tell her to vacate the room so that Paul Cushing had some privacy when he escorted Mom home. Not that he lingered.

It was an odd thing, and it worried Sig, but Paul Cushing didn't seem to be at all physical with Phyllis. In some way she hated to admit, Sig was also relieved by that, perhaps because of the incident with Monty.

Or maybe she was uncomfortable with her mother's sexuality. Or in the sexuality of anyone old. It was just that otherwise Paul seemed so warm. Sig worried that perhaps it meant he wasn't as serious about Phyllis as she and Bruce and Sharri hoped he was. Well, she should be grateful. At least with Paul, she wouldn't have to worry about barging into a bedroom and finding him naked and in bed with her mother. Sig shuddered at the thought.

"Are you cold, darling?" Mrs. Katz asked. "Maybe you should put on a sweater."

"I'm fine," Sig said. She looked over at the placid Mrs. Katz, sitting there with her black bag on her knees. In a way, Sig was envious of her. She didn't read anything. She didn't knit or do crosswords. She didn't even watch TV. She just *sat*. She simply was, and it seemed enough for perfect contentment, if not a perfect house guest.

"Are you going out tonight?" Sig asked hopefully.

"It's possible. Bernard is coming by."

"Bernard? Bernard Krinz?" Sig repeated.

"Yes. We were going to talk more about my investments."

"Investments?" Sig asked. "What do you mean? The only thing you put money into is your purse."

"Oh no. Bernard has called up almost every day. He tells me about his market positions. I love his putz and calls."

"That's 'puts,' " Sig corrected. "*Puts* and calls."

Now what was up? Was *Krinz* pulling a con? No.

He was a reputable world-respected architect. Still, if anyone was going to invest Mrs. Katz's money Sig would be dipped in yogurt before she'd let it be anyone but her! She was about to investigate further when she was interrupted by the doorbell. She checked her makeup on the way past the foyer mirror and took a moment to refresh her lipstick with the tube she kept in the hall console drawer.

She opened the door. Paul Cushing was standing there. A sprinkling of snow, complementing the white hair at his temples, nestled on the broad shoulders of his blue cashmere overcoat. Despite his age he was still a very handsome man. He looked down at her. "Oh, black is your color, too," he said, as if he remembered his compliment from the Rainbow Room.

She began to help him off with his coat when she got an almost irresistible desire to brush the snow from his hair. She put her hand up, only to pull it away in time. *What am I thinking of?* "Is the snow sticking?" she managed to ask.

He turned and smiled at her, nodded and then looked down her legs. "You might need boots more practical than those," he said, and grinned the lop-sided way that he had when he was teasing. "Though it would be a pity to take those off since they look so nice on you," he added.

Sig looked down and actually felt herself blush. Maybe her mother was right—she *did* need a father, even at this late date, to notice and approve of her.

Paul's compliment made her feel girlish and squirmy, as if she was about to toe the floor with one boot, her hands twisting behind her back. Instead, she forced herself to calmly hang up his coat. Then she noticed he was carrying a small, light blue bag—Sig's favorite color and the color of her kitchen ceiling glaze: Tiffany blue. Her heart began to beat faster in her chest. Had he brought a ring for Mom? Was he ready to propose? It was odd, Sig thought, how her relief was mixed with something else. What was it? Regret? Disappointment? Envy?

God, she really was getting crazy! It must be the holidays. All the sappy music, all the Capra movies on TV. She was glad she wasn't going to see Phillip, but she'd have to try to start seeing somebody as soon as she could, before her Electra complex got the better of her. If she could afford it, she'd start up some sessions with Dr. Lefer, her old shrink.

"My mother is not quite ready," she said. "Why don't you come into the living room?"

Paul grinned. "Is the duenna there?" he asked.

"Mrs. Katz?" Sig grinned back. " 'Fraid so."

"Who sleeps with cats?" Paul asked.

"Mrs. Katz. And sometimes Mrs. Nussbaum," Sig told him, echoing Monty's old joke. They entered the living room and Paul, to her dismay, took a seat not on the sofa but on one of the leather Barcelona chairs. Sig was about to sit down on the sofa herself when the doorbell rang again.

This time it was Bruce and Todd, again along with

Bernard Krinz. "Happy holidays," Bruce said. The three men were coated with snow—the weather was getting worse. So was Todd. He looked absolutely mournful. What was it with Bruce? Was he going for an old geezer just for the money? It made Sig's skin crawl. What was it doing to Todd?

Whatever it was, they were very festive. Bernard had a sprig of holly pinned to his conservative lapel, Todd had on a red and green sweater, while Bruce was wearing the scarf that Sig had given him for Hanukkah and was carrying wrapped boxes. "Merry Christmas," he said. He kissed Sig on the cheek and she felt the coldness of the air outside still clinging to him.

"Bruce, you shouldn't have."

"I should and I did," Bruce said. "The orders have been rolling in. I'm having the best Christmas ever. Queer Santa came through for me in the end. Once I receive payments, I'll be in the black again. And Bernard gave me a bridge loan to tide me over!"

Bernard Krinz smiled. He looked at Sig and her brother. "Black's a very good color for both of you," he said. Sig tried to smile at the oily old toad, failed, and led the three of them into the living room. Bernard went directly over to Mrs. Katz and sat next to her on the love seat, while Bruce and Todd went to shake hands with Paul Cushing.

"Merry Christmas to all, and to all a good night," Bruce sang out and handed a wrapped box to Paul. Then he gave another to Mrs. Katz, this one a larger parcel. He gave a small gift to Bernard Krinz, another to Todd, and then handed the last box to Sig. "I've got something for Mom in my pocket," he added proudly, before throwing himself onto the sofa, disarranging all of Sig's carefully placed pillows. He grinned, clearly very satisfied with himself.

"Should we open them now?" Mrs. Katz asked.

"Why not?" Bruce responded. "Jews always open their Christmas gifts early."

Mrs. Katz went first and cheerfully pulled the paper off her large box, opened the glossy cover, and looked in.

"Oh, my goodness!" she said, and lifted out a beautiful Fendi leather bag.

"I thought you might like that one," Bruce smiled. "I think it's the right size. And the catch on *this* one works."

"Oh, my goodness," Mrs. Katz repeated. "I'm speechless."

"Just as well," Bruce murmured. Meanwhile, Bernard Krinz had carefully unwrapped the package he'd been given, saving both the ribbon and the gift wrap, to reveal a Rizzoli volume of immense proportion.

"Oh, Bruce, you shouldn't have," Bernard said.

"I should and I did," Bruce said again. He looked over at Sig and Paul. "It's the International Architecture Association's award-winning buildings. Todd took the photos. Bernard has three of his buildings in the book."

Bruce smiled over at Paul. "And yours?" he asked. Paul looked at Sig.

"Ladies first," he told her.

Sig picked up her small box and tore off the paper. Aside from her home and a job that made some money, she couldn't think of anything she wanted or needed, except, possibly . . . she looked up. "I haven't a clue," she said to Bruce. Then she opened the box and there lay her emerald ring, protected by the white cotton batting stuffed beneath it. "Oh, Bruce," she said. "Oh, Bruce." Her eyes filled with tears. "How did you get it?" she asked. "Oh, Bruce, you shouldn't have."

"I should and I did," Bruce repeated one more time, but this time he wasn't so flippant. "Don't get me wrong, I didn't buy it at the auction. I just stopped Sotheby's from selling it. I had to forge your name on the release, but . . . anyway, I also have a check for you, and it'll equal what the ring would have brought in, less commissions and tax. At least I think so. Consider it a loan."

"Oh, Bruce," Sig breathed, and ran to kiss her brother.

"Enough, enough," he said, standing up. "I better see what's keeping Mom. She probably needs me to put on her mascara."

"Well, wait a minute," Paul Cushing said and opened his little blue Tiffany bag. "I have something for you all as well." He handed Bruce a wrapped box, then handed one to Mrs. Katz. "I didn't know you would be here," he said apologetically to Bernard. "But I did get the Whetherall board to accept your proposal for the new headquarters."

"A very nice gift, indeed," Bernard said.

Then Paul turned to Sig. He took a small box out and handed it to her. Sig smiled at him. He was so kind, so generous. "This is for your mother," he said and Sig felt disappointment well up in her chest. It must be the engagement ring. Well, why feel badly? Wasn't this what she wanted?

Sig handed the package to Bruce. "How about you take it in to her?" Sig asked. Then, sotto voce, she added, "Ixfay her acefay while you're at it."

"Sure," Bruce said, winking at her. "You open your present, Paul, and I'll get Mom for hers."

Paul tore the paper off the box that Bruce had handed him and pulled out a silvery fringed scarf. It was beautiful, and when he slid it around his neck it set off his high color and the gray of his hair.

Sig, admiring it, saw Bruce come out of the bedroom and go into the kitchen. She watched out of the corner of her eyes as he came out of there and went into the powder room. Then, just a moment later, she saw him move through the hallway into the library. Sig got up and started to follow him, but she met up with him in the foyer. "What's going on?" she asked. "What are you doing?"

"Looking for Mom."

"What do you mean, looking for Mom? She's in my room."

"No she isn't. She isn't anywhere in this apartment."

"That's impossible, Bruce. I've been here all day and she didn't go out."

"Well then, Miss Smarty Pants, you find her."

Sig spun around and started toward her bedroom. As Sig passed the living room, Mrs. Katz asked, "Did you lose something, dear?"

Sig ignored her and continued through the room. She pushed open her bedroom door and stepped into the room. Nothing. She checked out the step-in closet and then walked into her bathroom. Nothing. As she turned to leave, she saw a paper taped onto the vanity mirror. Sig picked up the note and saw that it was in Phyllis's handwriting.

Dear Sigourney,

Sharon will always be a mess, but Bruce is finally settling down. Todd will appreciate him now and be perfect for him. I worry about you, though. You don't know what's important, Sig, or where to find it. Somehow, you thought you were responsible for me, for Daddy, for your brother and sister. Maybe you even think you're responsible for the hole in the ozone layer. Get a grip. You gotta stop bailing out your family— including me——and instead take care of yourself. Notice who your real friends are. We'll all be fine. Will you?

My advice is, be a little more patient and wear shorter skirts.

Meanwhile, I've left with Monty. Don't be angry or worried and don't look for me. I'll be fine, I promise. I love him, and he loves me. I'm happy, Sig. You should be so lucky.

Sig came out to the living room, opened her mouth to say something, then crumpled the note and began to cry.

"What is it?" Paul asked, rising and coming to her. "Sig, what's wrong?" She looked up at him.

"My mother ran off with Monty the fortune hunter. And she has no fortune." Sig sobbed. They were loud, embarrassing noises, but she kept sobbing as if her heart would break. Paul put his arms around her.

"What do you mean, she's gone?" Bruce asked. Sig handed him the crushed note. Bruce read it quickly. "Come on, Sylvia. She's probably just downstairs in the lobby, talking with Laslow the doorman. Let's go get her." Reluctantly, Mrs. Katz stood up and, with purse in hand, went out with Bruce.

Paul released Sig and she went into the kitchen to get a tissue to wipe her eyes and to collect herself. Maybe Mom had just been bluffing. Sig was leaning up against the counter, trying to get control of herself when Paul came in quietly and stood in front of her. "Are you okay?" he asked. He was very close. She could smell the scent of a mild soap, and something else equally good.

"I'll be fine," Sig told him, but then burst into tears again and, almost automatically, stepped forward and buried her face again into his shoulder. This time Paul put his arms around her more tightly and held her, patting her lightly on the back.

"This is all my fault," he said. "I told you I had heard some scuttlebutt about Dunleathe. I should have done more. I could have . . ."

"You knew what he was up to?"

"No. Certainly not. But I knew that she was having a hard time after he left. That's why I wanted to keep her busy."

Sig lifted her head from his shoulder and looked up at him. Paul bent to her face and started to kiss her, and—for a moment—the shock of electricity from his lips to hers overwhelmed her senses and blotted out thought. It had been a long time since she'd been kissed like this—or maybe she never had. Paul's lips were surprisingly soft, yet he kissed her with a firmness backed up by his left hand, with which he cupped her cheek and held her mouth to his. Without thinking, Sig raised her hand to his and covered his fingers with her own.

Then she realized what she was doing. She was kissing her mother's rejected boyfriend, and she was liking it! Sig pulled her mouth away, then pushed Paul back. Hard.

"What are you doing?" Sig asked.

"Seems obvious." Paul shrugged. He reached for her hand. "And I'd like to do it again. I think I could improve on the original."

"But . . ."

He took out a handkerchief and began carefully, tenderly, to wipe Sig's streaming eyes. "You're very beautiful, Sig," Paul said. "And you're very smart. But you're also a very dopey girl."

"I'm not a girl . . ."

"To me you are. Remember, I'm older. A lot older." Paul smiled, but there was a wistfulness around his eyes. "I hope I'm not too old. That's for you to judge." He finished wiping her eyes and cheeks and shook his head. "This wasn't in my plans. Not at all. Anyway, you're a very dopey girl, *and* a woman to me." He paused. "Lucky for you I like dopey girls. *And* real women." He reached for her shoulder, but, despite the flush of heat his touch sent down her neck and back, Sig pulled away.

"My mother," she croaked. "You're dating my mother."

"See what I mean?" Paul said, and smiled again. "Your mother was never interested in me. She told me all about this Monty guy and how much she liked him. I, on the other hand, was always interested in *you*."

"What?" Sig simultaneously heard the declaration and the past tense. One filled her with a strange yearning, the other with pain. "Were?" she repeated. "You *were* interested?"

Paul reached out to her again and pulled her gently

to his chest. This time she let him. "See how dopey you are?" he asked in an indulgent voice. "Remember those flowers I sent to the Pierre? They were for *you*. When you ignored them, I just figured you thought I was too old."

"You were interested in me?" she asked again, hardly daring to believe. "I mean, you are?"

"Yes, I *was* interested in you. And I *am* interested in you. And I *always will be* interested in you. Anyone could see that but you. So now the basic question that remains is: could you possibly be interested in a geezer like me?"

Sig colored yet again. Did Paul know about Operation Geezer Quest? He looked down at her. His eyes were very serious as well as very blue, his hair more white than pepper and salt. The soft suede of his jacket—very soft—felt so good under Sig's cheek. She rubbed against his shoulder until he lifted her face to his again. Then he kissed her, this time in a long, lingering way.

Totally shocked, she not only found that she liked it, but kissed him back. Deeply. At last, to her regret, Paul took his mouth off hers. "Sigourney, I've been coming around because of you. Since we met. I was at the Pierre that night with Wendy, but I was hoping to meet you. It's not that I didn't sincerely *like* your mother," he said. "I do. She's so much like you. Sharp, no bullshit, a real challenge. But I can't help it, Sig."

"Help what?" She felt as if she were melting, as if she was in some dream.

"I can't help wanting to love you. The first time I saw you, Sig, across that charity dinner table, I thought how absolutely open your face was. How smart, how mischievous, and how bold. Your face said, 'Hey, you'd be a real mensch if you could take me on.' I don't see that much. Not the fun, or your feisty joy." His face got very serious. "I've taken a lot of losses, Sig. Life doesn't play fair or last long. I'm in it for the joy, Sig. Not everyone is capable of it. Your mom is, and you are, too."

"Feisty joy?" Sig asked, but her own face had softened. She felt transformed by Paul's praise. Something had happened, something more than the kiss.

"I'm crazy about your mom, Sig. I'll help you find her, I promise. But it's you I love. No matter what length your skirts are." Sig found she couldn't breathe. "I'm an old-fashioned guy, Sig. Old, and old-fashioned. But all my parts still work. I don't have much time, so I'm impatient. And I don't sleep around. So you don't have to decide now, but do you think that you might marry me, Sigourney?"

Sig *did* feel flooded with joy. "I don't know," Sig said. "I mean . . ." She paused. "I think so. Uh . . . yes. I think so." She paused again. "But first you have to do something for me."

"Anything. Slay a dragon? Kill Monty Dunleathe? Engineer a hostile takeover?"

"No. Nothing like that. First I want you to kiss me again a few times."

Paul smiled his devastating smile. "It would be my pleasure," he said. "And yours too, if I do it right." He paused. "What else?"

Sig stopped smiling. "Help me find my mother. That's what I want for Christmas."

Twenty-one

*P*hyllis stretched and opened her eyes. One of the disadvantages of old age was that she had become a very light sleeper. But now she had found an advantage even to that: she and Monty had spent the night dozing and each time one of them shifted or woke, the other would also rise and they would hug and change positions before falling back to sleep.

Phyllis smiled. It had been a wonderful night. She was no spring chicken, but she was proud of herself.

Monty wasn't much to look at, and his belly sagged almost as much as her breasts did, but he was a true romantic. Once they had met at the airport he had taken her hand and he hadn't let go. The whole flight to the Caymans and the taxi ride to the hotel he had kept hold of her. "I'm not going to take a chance on losing you again," he said. "They didn't make two of you."

Phyllis couldn't argue with that.

The Cayman Islands, though tropical and in the Gulf Stream, were certainly not Florida. Nothing like it. This was a place she could *like*, Phyllis thought. The beaches were perfect white windswept sand and dozens and dozens of waving, clacking palm trees. There wasn't a Broadwalk in sight, and while there were plenty of older people, there were young people too and they all seemed to be active and more alive than the parade that had dragged themselves along the Florida Broadwalk every morning. There were young and old playing tennis on the lit courts, riding bicycles, and playing on the many golf courses. The kids would like this place.

When they pulled up to the hotel—a gorgeous white building decorated only with flowering plants at each balcony—Phyllis was impressed. It didn't look like Dania, Florida. And there were no French Canadians.

"You like it?" Monty asked.

"It's very nice," Phyllis said. "Do we have a room or a suite?" she teased. Now that she had stayed at the Pierre suite, she knew the difference between the two. And though Monty had explained a great deal about his financial position to her on the flight—about how his competitors had used illegal means to force him out of business and discredit him, how he wasn't as rich as he'd once been nor as poor as she'd thought—Phyllis didn't care. She wanted to see not how much he had, but how much he spent.

"You can have whatever kind of room you want," Monty told her. "I own the hotel."

Phyllis laughed. Then she realized that, for once, he wasn't joking. "I used to think that life could use a little embellishment," she said. "Somehow I think I'm changing my mind."

That wasn't the only surprise: there was a Hanukkah menorah and a Christmas tree, both decorated with bougainvillea, and then more surprises within the hotel: his real engagement ring, this one a huge sapphire, and a necklace to match. Then they were served a candlelit dinner on the balcony, overlooking the pool and the ocean, and then bed.

It amazed Phyllis, in a way, that she felt so much passion. She smiled again this morning, pulling the sheet up over her shoulder. It had been so long that she *had* forgotten. It was *not* like riding a bicycle. And, to be honest, Ira had never been, well, an artist. He'd been a meat-and-potatoes kind of man when it came to bed. But Monty! Monty was caviar and peaches. She was proud of herself. You *could* teach an old dog some new tricks, because Monty had already taught her a couple.

And then there was the cuddling. Ira used to fall right to sleep, but Monty . . . he seemed to actually enjoy hugging. She turned her head on the pillow to look at him. Well, he was nothing special to look at. Ira had been a good-looking man. Monty was not, and it didn't help that he was sleeping with his mouth slightly open. And could he snore! But then, he said she did too.

Monty slept on, but Phyllis wanted his company. She elbowed him in his breadbasket. After all, how much time did they have? The knowledge that this relationship could not last for forty years gave Phyllis a bittersweet feeling. Every moment must be lived, used, remembered. "Monty," she whispered. "Wake up."

He didn't open his eyes, but he smiled. "So it wasn't a dream," he said. "You're here, my love." And, eyes closed, he reached out and pulled Phyllis to him.

Sig stretched and opened her eyes. For a moment, she became frightened. What if it wasn't true? What if she turned her head and Paul *wasn't* there? Sigourney had been through a lot—some bad relationships, a difficult fight to the top at her brokerage firm, her brother's near-bankruptcy, her father's death, her sister's . . . everything—and she had survived it all. But, after last night, after the tenderness and heat of last night, she didn't think she could bear it if Paul wasn't there beside her. It would truly break her heart if she'd dreamed it or if he really wasn't going to stay with her. Because, despite his age, despite both of their imperfections, it had never been like that, it had never been like last night.

There was an advantage to older men, Sig found. They took their time, they knew their moves, and they seemed to know what worked for women. At least Paul did. He was sure of himself and he wasn't afraid to show what he felt. That was more erotic than the flattest abs could ever be. Phillip had been so clinical. Sig knew that, but hadn't known men could be so emotional. Paul had actually had tears in his eyes and she liked it. While he had been holding her, loving her, he had looked at her with such a melting passion that when she thought of Phillip Norman and their athletic but empty nights she was embarrassed and almost ashamed. *This* was the way it was supposed to be: she'd realized that and would not forget.

Now that she'd experienced it, Sig knew she'd never settle for less. No more Phillip Normans. She wanted Paul Cushing, she wanted him for the rest of her life, and she'd do anything to ensure that. But when she opened her eyes and turned over she found that Paul was gone. The bed was empty.

"I didn't know how you take your coffee, but I hope it's black. You don't have any milk," Paul said from the doorway.

She spun around, tangling her legs in the blankets. He was wearing her chenille robe, which looked adorably peculiar on him, but Sig was so happy to see him that she wasn't going to waste feelings on details. Paul was carrying a tray with two cups of coffee, two glasses of juice, and a plate covered with a napkin. He walked to her side of the bed, put the tray on her lap

285

and then walked around to the other side. "Do you like my peignoir?" he asked, and slipped out of it. Despite the age spots on his hands, his grizzled chest hair, and the rest of the signs of living, he was long and lean and beautiful to Sig. "Mrs. Katz seemed impressed by it. I bumped into her in the kitchen. She didn't have her glasses on and she thought I was you until I spoke."

Sig laughed, jostling the coffee. "Hey," Paul said. "Be careful with that! I don't cook breakfast that often." His face got serious for a moment. Sig could always tell because the parentheses deepened on either side of his mouth. "Not cooking is one of my shortcomings. Although for you I could try." He kissed her, then paused. "I've been thinking of other things, though. I already called my office. They traced your mother to the airport. She met Monty there. She didn't take a flight to a U.S. destination. We think she left the country with Monty, but it's going to take me a little while beyond there. Sometimes the FAA can be difficult." He took her hand.

Sig nodded.

"We'll find her, Sig."

She had no doubt Paul would. He'd deal with all that later. But right now, all she wanted to do was kiss him over and over for the rest of her life. He was right: she was dopey. Instead of kisses, she handed him his cup of coffee. "Sorry about the milk," she said. "Is that the way *you* drink it?"

Paul shook his head. "I like it with cream, Sig.

Cream and no sugar," he smiled. "Why does that remind me of you?" He reached out and rubbed the back of her neck. She wanted to purr. "Probably because everything does." He put down the coffee mug on her bedside table. "Move that tray over," he told her. "I have something I want to share with you."

Sig giggled and put the tray on the floor.

"Will you marry me today?" Paul asked as he wrapped his arms and legs around her. "I'm an old-fashioned guy, Sig. None of these tawdry affairs. I want to marry you. I want you to be my wife. I want you to have my ring on your finger and my name at the end of your name. I'm sure it's politically incorrect, but it's a strong urge, Sig. One of two strong urges I'm having right now." He pulled her to him more closely and Sig found it difficult to catch her breath.

"I want to keep my own name," Sig said. She paused. "And I want something else."

"Okay," Paul breathed in her ear. "Anything you want. But I want you."

Sig felt her toes curl. She also never knew there was such a direct connection between the inside of her ear and her other canal. Her breath became even more difficult to catch until she heard herself begin to pant. "Oh, Paul," she moaned. She felt his tongue just touch her ear and at almost the same time his teeth gently bit her earlobe. The dress—the wedding dress at Bergdorf's had popped into her mind. She pulled away. She had to tell him. "I saw a special gown. It's silly, but I want to be a bride for you."

"It isn't silly," he told her. "It's sweet. It's the way it should be. Of course you'll have a gown. And a veil, if you want it," Paul said. "Marry me," he whispered, "or I'll never lick your ear again. Will you?"

"Yes," Sig said. "Yes, yes, yes."

"We're in the Caymans. The Islands. We were married two days ago," Phyllis was shouting into the phone, as if she had to physically bridge the gap between the Caribbean and New York. "Monty is really very wealthy, but he didn't want to be loved for his money. When he lost everything, back in 1984, he learned who his real friends were. And who they weren't—which was almost everyone. Then he made another fortune, starting from scratch," Phyllis yelled proudly. "He just tested us with that bounced-check stuff. I told him it wasn't nice to test people and he's apologized. He won't do it again. He has a nice little gift for you and Bruce and Sharon to make up for it."

"Mom, I'm getting married."

"No, Susan, I'm *already* married," Phyllis shouted. "Monty and I already got married."

"Congratulations. But I'm not talking about you! I'm talking about me! I'm marrying Paul Cushing on Christmas Eve Day."

For a moment, only silence and static hummed along the line. Then Phyllis began talking again, this time in a normal volume. "Thank God. So you finally woke up and smelled the orange blossoms," she told her daughter approvingly.

"You're not surprised?"

"Don't be ridiculous. He was interested in you from the beginning."

"You knew?"

"Knew? I tried to tell you, but you couldn't see it. *Mazel tov*. Now we both will have mixed marriages." Phyllis laughed. "Well, better than no marriages at all."

"Mom, I really love him. I mean . . . I mean, I *really* love him," Sig said.

"I knew that, too. I was just waiting for your brain to catch up with your heart. So, did he give you a ring? Is it a sapphire like mine?"

"No," Sigourney admitted.

"Well, don't worry, he will." And then either Phyllis laughed or there was a burst of static, but whatever the noise was, when it was over the phone lines were dead.

"I heard from Mom," Sig announced to Sharon and Bruce after plugging them into a conference call from her office. Might as well talk. Sig hadn't been able to do any work; her head was too full of plans and her heart too full of hope. Corny Sigourney, she thought to herself.

"Where is she?" Sharon asked.

"Where's Monty?" Bruce wanted to know. "I'm going to find him and choke him."

"Forget about it," Sig said, "he's your stepfather now and he's loaded. Offshore accounts on the Cayman Islands. His reputation may be no good here, but apparently he's a really wealthy man." Sig giggled. "Anyway, that's not the important news."

"*That's* not the important news?" Bruce asked.

"So what is?" Sharri wanted to know.

"Well, I'm inviting you to a little gathering tomorrow."

"Oh no. Is this the C-list brunch? Another goddamned Christmas party," Bruce moaned.

"No. It's just my wedding."

Sharon laughed. "I thought you said 'just your wedding,' " she giggled.

"She did," Bruce said calmly. "So Paul Cushing got up his nerve and asked you and you said yes?"

"How did you know?" Sig and Sharri asked simultaneously.

"Because I'm truly sensitive to nuance," Bruce said. "Marriage must be in the air, along with Taiwan flu virus. Anyway, Todd and I have been thinking about it, too."

"You're kidding!" Sharri and Sig exclaimed together.

"No, it seems to be the season for it. You know what the song says: ' 'Tis the Season to Be Married.' "

"Not for me," Sharon said darkly.

"Well," Sig said. "I'm happy for Mom and I'm

happy for Monty. I'm happy for you and Todd. So will you come tomorrow? Paul and I are just going to do the ceremony at City Hall."

"Fabu," Bruce said.

"I'll be there," Sharri responded. "With the kids. A flower girl and a ring-bearer. Did he give you a big ring?"

"God! You sound just like Mom!" Sig told her sister.

"Nah. Could never happen. Not with any of us," Bruce told them. "Oh, and Sig? Do you need any help with your hair?"

Sig laughed and put the phone down. There was so much to do: paperwork, phone calls, and the wedding preparations. While all of this had been happening she also had seen an almost overnight turnaround in her business. Monty had asked her to manage some investments for him, while, oddly, both Bernard Krinz and Mrs. Katz had decided to put their money in her hands. As if that wasn't enough, Paul had put Wendy's very significant trust fund under her supervision. But that would all have to wait until the new year. Sig stood up and turned off her Quotron. She was leaving early to prepare for her wedding and then she and Paul would spend the next week together on their honeymoon.

Twenty-two

For a change, Bruce was not hovering around Phyllis. Instead he was hovering around Sigourney, and as he took a step backwards he breathed a sigh of complete contentment. "God! This is just like *Peau d'Âne* when Jean Marais has to find a woman more beautiful than his dead wife. And the only one he can find is his daughter!" Bruce was a little hyper, but Sig loved him and knew he was happy for her. Instead of dissing him she kissed her eccentric brother. "Are we in a French movie?" he continued. "Sig, are you Catherine Deneuve?" He didn't pause for breath. "You *are* absolutely ravishing," he said, and Sig smiled, believing him. "But let me fix your lipstick. And don't kiss anyone else."

Sig was wearing the Bergdorf's satin wedding gown and strangely enough didn't feel the slightest bit ridiculous. That was because she was wearing it for Paul, and as he had said to her, "When you love someone, anything is possible."

Sig had even opted for the veil. She definitely didn't feel like the mother of the bride now. Paul—older, more experienced, and so loving—made her feel young. She didn't feel too old, too overdressed, too dramatic, or too anything. What she felt was beautiful—her most beautiful self.

So she wasn't surprised that when she looked into the mirror she saw that Bruce was right. Her eyes sparkled, her hair was lustrous, and the satin of the dress glimmered. She didn't care that they were only marrying at City Hall, or that they had no guests other than Bruce, Todd, Sharon, Barney, her niece and nephew, Wendy, and Mrs. Katz. When she thought about it, those were the people she needed to have around her—them and Paul.

And her mother, of course. She would like it if her mother and Monty could have been there. But now she understood: if her mother had felt like this, *did* feel this way about Monty, Sig had been very, very wrong to stand in her way. Sig truly believed that if Paul didn't have a penny she'd still be on her way downtown. She looked forward to all of the small things in their future life together—cooking dinner, helping to raise Wendy, seeing movies together, and just talking. Corny Sigourney. Corny or not, she hoped her mother felt half as besotted with Monty as she did with Paul. And she hoped that her mother's honeymoon in the Caymans would be half as nice as their honeymoon, which they were going to spend here, in Sig's apartment, which Paul had bought and put in both of their names. Sig was about to have her cake and eat it too, and she only hoped that her mother was enjoying more than just crumbs.

It was getting late. Paul was not, of course, supposed to see her arrayed like this, so he would meet them downtown. But he was sending a limo for them. Anyway, Sig felt that if he did see her it wouldn't bring bad luck. She'd already had all of that that she'd ever need. Now she had nothing to worry about. If anyone was willing, had experience or the knowledge of how to make a marriage work, it was Paul. He'd loved his late wife, he'd loved their son, and he loved his granddaughter. He knew how to be married, and in case she didn't, he'd show her.

The buzzer rang, and the doorman announced that the limo was waiting. Bruce and Sig took the elevator down to the street level, where they were greeted by Jessie and her brother, both in white velvet outfits trimmed with bunny fur. As Sig and Bruce stepped out through the door, the children threw handfuls of spangles, rice, and confetti at her. "Not yet, not yet!" Sharon yelled. "You throw it *after* Auntie Sig gets married."

"That's right," Uncle Bruce told them. "Don't mess up her outfit." He brushed some of the sparkles off Sig's shoulder, then turned and looked at Sharon, who was wearing a shapeless blue velvet shift. "Where's Barney?" he asked.

"I've left him," Sharon said.

Sig and Bruce stood there in the cold, stock-still. "You're kidding!" Sig finally exclaimed.

"Hey, one out of every three American marriages ends in divorce," Sharon said, always ready with research. "I figured I'd carry the brunt of it and let you off the hook. It leaves you safe with Paul and Mom fine with Monty."

"Come on, Sharri. Seriously. What's up?"

"Get in the car, kids," Sharon told the children, who did. Then she exploded. "Oh, Sig, Barney's not just a failure. I could take that. It's that he's so comfortable failing. It was too much! Imagine turning down a job when Jessie and Travis have no lunch money! When *you* were paying his kids' tuition. It was enough."

"Another Christmas miracle," Bruce exclaimed, looking up to the ominous sky. It looked like a white Christmas was on its way. He put his hand on Sharon's arm. "I'll support you any way I can," he said, his voice solemn. "Except, of course, financially." They all laughed.

"Congratulations," Sig said in a serious voice. "You deserve better, Sharri."

"Hey, even alone is better than Barney," Sharon said.

"Time to go," Mrs. Katz called from the car. "You don't want to make a man wait. The groom could get cold feet." She actually sounded nervous.

"You could get cold everything out here," Bruce said.

Sharon, Bruce, and, lastly, Sig got into the long black stretch limo. A word to the driver and they moved off toward City Hall.

Downtown, despite the tacky surroundings, Sig didn't mind that she'd spent so much on her wedding dress. She swanned through the long, high-ceilinged corridor, as near to perfection as she would ever be. "To the Marriage Bureau," said an ancient sign painted in gilt. It looked as if it was older than City Hall itself. How many brides-to-be had looked at it? Had they all been as happy, as hopeful as she was? Sig wondered. They trailed down the long hallway of the huge municipal building, following the faded signs until they at last reached the right office. A none-too-clean waiting room with assorted odd chairs and even odder people awaited them. The holidays clearly made for some strange bedfellows. Mrs. Katz held open the door as Sig, in her forty-eight-hundred-dollar gown, swept into the room. With her entrance, the dirt, the very, very pregnant bride-to-be sitting beside her nervous groom, the couple getting married with their two children along with them, the bored clerk at the desk—all of it—seemed to fade away. All Sig saw was Paul Cushing, who was standing beside Wendy, his granddaughter. With him there the room was transformed: the pregnant girl in her cheap polyester gown was beautiful. When Paul turned and looked at Sig, when she saw the joy and affection—

the love—in his eyes, the room became beautiful, just
as she did. The rest of the room felt it too, and it
seemed as if there was a deep breath, a collective
sigh. Today Sig was a princess, not a businesswoman:
a princess, and beautiful enough so that all of them
were transformed. Paul Cushing smiled and walked
across the room toward her.

"The judge will be ready to see us in a minute," he
said, taking her arm.

"Hey, hold on there," Bruce said. "This part is my
job. I'm giving her away." Bruce appropriated his sister. "She's not quite yours yet."

"Smile pretty," Todd told them as he focused the
lens and took a picture.

Mrs. Katz held out the box she was carrying.
"Don't forget this," she said, and Sig opened it. She
found two beautiful bouquets. In the frenzy of planning, she'd left out flowers! "Oh. Thank you," she
said. "But why two?" Then she looked at what else
was included. There was a blue handkerchief and a
tiny locket.

"Something old, something new. You know . . ."
Mrs. Katz said. Sig smiled and reached into the box.
"And then you'll lend them to me. Okay?" Mrs. Katz
asked. "That will be the borrowed part. The locket is
old, the flowers are new, and the handkerchief . . ."

"But why the two bouquets?" Sig repeated.

"One's for me," Mrs. Katz admitted. "I'm going to
be like your mother." She lowered her voice. "Except
for the S, E, X."

"Don't tell me *you're* running off with Monty," Bruce joked.

"No, no. Don't be silly," Mrs. Katz said, the joke going right over her badly permed hair. "I'm getting married here after you do. I hope you don't mind."

Sig couldn't imagine what delusion this was, or who on earth Mrs. Katz could think she was getting married *to*. She never left the apartment, and when she did, she'd always been with Phyllis. The only male other than Monty, Todd, or Bruce that Sig had ever seen Mrs. Katz talking with was—"Bernard! You're marrying Bernard?" Sig quickly looked around the room. And there he was, sitting in a chair in the corner. "Don't you know that he's . . ."

"He's perfect for me," Mrs. Katz said. She lowered her voice again. "I don't have to change the monogram on my towels. Plus he promised to take care of my money. And no . . ."

"I know. No S, E, X." Sig laughed and then bent down and hugged Mrs. Katz. Oh, why not? Krinz was no crook. He'd been married before. And a lot stranger marriages had worked.

"Hold that pose," Todd exclaimed, tearing up. "This is so beautiful."

"Get out of here with that thing, will you?" Bruce told him. "We've got to get this show on the road." He paused. "It's not a show. It's a Frank Capra movie. *It's a Wonderful Life*. God, how did this happen? It's the holidays and *I'm* in a Frank Capra movie!"

Sig had to agree, finally, with Bruce's endless movie references. It *was* a wonderful life, or she expected it to be. The ceremony was both enormously quick and exceedingly slow to Sig. She felt her hands actually shaking under the flowers she clutched. It happened so quickly, and she had waited so long. Had she made a mistake? All the time that the judge spoke words over them she looked only at Paul's face. He was not a young man and she hadn't known him more than a month, but already he was very, very dear to her. How would it feel, now that she had found him, to have to live life without him? How many years did he have left with her?

At that moment, the judge asked for the ring. Bernard, serving as Paul's best man, collected it from Travis and handed it over. How morbid I am, Sig thought. Nobody knows what's going to happen, ever. At any minute something could go wrong, something could happen; a test result could come back positive, or a random incident of violence could strike.

As if in response to that thought, the door was thrown open and Montague Dunleathe stuck his head into the room. "We're not too late! We're not too late!" he exulted and stepped aside so that Phyllis could walk in. She looked exactly the same as always, except that she was tanned, well dressed, and for some reason Sig immediately focused on the fingers of her left hand. There *was* an enormous sapphire solitaire, along with a diamond-studded wedding band. So it was all true.

"I couldn't let my eldest daughter get married without me," Phyllis said, smiling at the crowd. "So . . ." she paused, obviously pleased with her dramatic entrance. "Don't let me interrupt anything."

Sig looked at Bruce. They both rolled their eyes. Their mother was an act of God, a freak of nature, a pain in the ass. But they loved her.

They began Sigourney and Paul's wedding all over again.

It didn't take long for the ceremony to end and then they all waited while Mrs. Katz—now Mrs. Krinz—married Bernard. "My dress wasn't as nice as yours," Phyllis whispered to Sig during the second wedding, "but Monty gave me a lovely gift for a wedding present." She leaned closer to Sig. "A million dollars. It's in my name in a bank in the Caymans. And *that* check didn't bounce." She looked down at her sapphire ring, not quite as big as the perfect diamond that Paul had just given Sig, but quite big enough.

"He's got a condo in the Caymans as a present for you two."

"We don't need any gifts," Sig said.

"Speak for yourself," Bruce told her. "Todd and I could use it."

"Yeah," Sharon added. "I got a job, but I'll take all the help I can get."

"*You* got a job?" Sig asked, taken aback. Todd clicked his camera; Sig could imagine the look on her face.

"On your own?" Bruce added. Todd took his picture, too.

"Shut up, Bruce," Phyllis admonished. "Be nice." She looked at Sharon. "*You* got a job, on your own?" she asked. Todd completed the trio with a shot of Phyllis.

"Just a little something for the wedding album," Todd chimed in and went on to his next victims, the newlywed Krinzes.

"I'm going to be research librarian at Stirling Corporate Headquarters," she admitted, shyly.

Bruce, Sig, and Phyllis burst into applause. "Well done," Monty said. "Have you heard the one about . . ."

"Well," Paul said, interrupting the family conference. "We have quite a bit to celebrate. Let's go." They got into the waiting cars, drove past the busy last-minute Christmas shoppers and finally reached the Carlyle, where Paul had kept a pied-à-terre for years. He had a light dinner waiting and he was about to break out the Veuve Clicquot. "Here's to all the newlyweds—all six of us."

"Well, eight actually," Bruce added. He turned and looked at Todd. "We've gotten married," he said. "Or its equivalent in this state." Shyly, he held up a beringed hand.

"Oh, Bruce!" Phyllis cried. "I'm so proud of you." She turned to Todd. "I couldn't like you better, even if you were a doctor." She kissed him on the cheek. Todd actually blushed, then raised his camera and took a picture of them all.

"Congratulations, or best wishes, or whatever," Sig said to Todd and hugged him. Then she turned to Bruce. "Best wishes to you," she said and the two of them embraced.

"Love is a beautiful thing," Mrs. Krinz told them all, Bernard Krinz at her elbow.

I guess she's not Mrs. Katz anymore, Sig thought with a pang. No more cats jokes. But, she thought, there'd be plenty of Krinz jokes. As if he heard her thought, Bruce leaned over to her. "Doesn't she make you Krinz?" he asked.

"No, he made *her* Krinz," Paul said. "But I couldn't make your sister into a Cushing." Sigourney had kept her own name.

"No," Bruce agreed. "You could only make her into a really happy woman." He looked around the room. "What a long strange trip it's been," he said.

"Yes," Mrs. Krinz agreed. "The municipal building was way downtown."

Sig laughed, and Phyllis joined her. Paul filled all of their glasses. Sig looked at him in that way that couples exchange glances. Meanwhile, Phyllis winked at Monty and Bruce and Todd both cracked up.

"Happy holidays to everyone," Phyllis said, raising her glass.

"*And* a dysfunctional new year," Bruce added.

"It's a sure thing," Sig told him and smiled at her family.

THE SWITCH
Olivia Goldsmith

The following pages contain an extract from Olivia Goldsmith's new novel THE SWITCH, also available from HarperCollins.

CHAPTER ONE

Sylvie stood for a moment in the cool dark hallway. It was the only dim place in the house and though Sylvie loved the light—in fact had fallen in love with the house for its light—she always found the comparative darkness of the hall a welcome contrast. She really had too much to do to be standing here, one hand on the simple carved mahogany of the banister. She put her thumb on the comforting place where the curve of the wood had been worn flat by years of other thumbs. You don't have time to linger here, she told herself sternly. But despite her admonishment now, just for a moment, she would enjoy this quiet. She listened to the wall clock tick and then picked up the cup of tea she'd poured herself. The jasmine smell filled her head.

Sylvie began to walk down the hall but glanced first

into the dining room, then the living room opposite, before moving down the hall toward the music room. Oh, she loved her house. It wasn't large by Shaker Heights standards—just a center hall colonial with only three bedrooms. But visitors, once in it, were always surprised by the grand dimensions and dignity of the house. Each of the four rooms downstairs was exactly the same size: all of them were large, light, airy rooms with ten-foot ceilings and long, high windows. Bob, at one time, had suggested they sell the house and buy a bigger one but Sylvie had been shocked and steadfastly refused. She didn't need a guest room—guests stayed next door at her mother's or camped out on the music room sofa. She didn't need a family room: all the rooms downstairs were for the family.

Sylvie knew how lucky she was. And she didn't take it for granted. Bob sometimes laughed at her for her little habit of checking each room. "Do you think they're going away?" he'd ask. Or "Are you looking for something?" he'd inquire. "Not for, at," she'd told him. She was looking at her home, a place she had created slowly over time with Bob. Sylvie knew she'd been right to never consider selling the house. Perhaps they'd been the smallest bit cramped, but what would they do now with a larger place? Without the twins at home, the two bedrooms upstairs stood empty, but the rest of the house seemed to enfold her and protect her. It was not a house too big for a couple and perhaps someday she could turn one of the children's rooms upstairs into a guest room. Maybe she'd make a den for Bob out of the other. Then he wouldn't have to leave his paperwork all over the desk in the corner of the dining room.

Sylvie moved down the hall to the music room, carrying her cup of tea before her as if the luminous white china could light her way like a lamp. She had only a few minutes before her first lesson and turned into the music room to see the usual organized clutter of sheet music. Schirmer's Piano for New Students, piled beside A Hundred Simple Piano Tunes and Chopin's Sonatas. Her gray sweater lay across the bench of the Steinway, but nothing sat on its beautiful lacquered top. Sylvie felt a little shiver of pleasure as she walked into the room. There was a touch of autumn in the air and she closed one of the long windows. It was too early for a fire but with the approach of autumn she knew that soon would be the time she liked best in this room, when she would give lessons and play while apple wood burned in the grate behind her. Though she missed the twins, this season was always a good time: September, when the children had begun school and she'd gone back to her full routine of piano lessons. It felt like the year was beginning. Students were returning from their summer holidays. Sylvie remembered that Jewish people celebrated their New Year about now. It made sense to her.

No reason to be sad, she told herself, no empty nest syndrome here, just because the twins were no longer at Shaker Heights Elementary or Grover

Cleveland High. Irene—Reenie to the family—would settle in at Bennington and Kenny already seemed perfectly happy at Northwestern. So Sylvie told herself she should settle in and be happy, too. And she was planning a treat. Bob had asked what she wanted for her birthday and she'd finally decided. She wanted romance. She had everything else.

Sylvie had always felt sorry for women who had to work outside of their homes. She had been so very lucky. Lucky to meet Bob as early as she had, lucky that he came back to Shaker Heights and had seamlessly become part of her family. She was lucky that the twins were both so healthy, so smart, and had never been in any real trouble. The family had no financial problems. Bob had given up his music to become a partner in her father's car dealership, and that had provided well for them, though it always caused Sylvie some regret. Still, Bob seemed to have done it willingly, though there was no doubt in her mind that he was the more talented musician. Perhaps his talent had actually made it easier for him to give up music as a profession; Sylvie didn't mind teaching and wasn't troubled by the knowledge that she was almost, but not quite, good enough to tour. Her talents had been exaggerated by a loving family. Julliard, at first a startling comeuppance, had been a pleasure once she realized she didn't really have the stuff it took to be a concert pianist.

But she had become a good teacher, and she enjoyed teaching. For her it was not a fall-back, the boring trap that serious musicians were so reluctantly forced into. She loved bringing music into people's lives and she found that she also enjoyed the glimpses into their lives that the lessons afforded her. She was a woman who enjoyed process and for that she was grateful. She actually enjoyed teaching scales, just as she enjoyed playing them. She liked the orderliness of building one week's lessons upon the next, and the slow construction of a musician, week-by-week, as people mastered fingering, timing, and sight reading until the moment came when music burst out in apparent effortlessness. Sylvie treasured those moments when students looked up from the Steinway keyboard, dazzled by their own ability to bring forth a waterfall of sound, to recreate the ordered noise that Handel, Chopin, or Beethoven had first composed.

Oh, she was lucky all right. Lucky with her material possessions, with her family, and with her ability to be satisfied. She had, thank goodness, none of her brother's constant dissatisfaction, or Bob's restlessness, which Reenie seemed to have inherited. She was more like Kenny, her son. But then, she had never had to give anything up, to sacrifice anything as Bob had. She had gotten to keep her music and her family. She'd gotten to have it all: a good marriage, good kids, a house she loved, a career she cared about.

Honey, her student, was late. Typical. She heard a noise in the hall and stepped out there again. The mail came sliding through the post slot in the front door. Maybe there was a letter from one of the children.

Kenny would be bad about writing but Reenie might. Sylvie knelt to pick up the pile. The usual bills, some catalogues (soon the pre-Christmas deluge would begin), and a card from her sister. Irene was always early with her birthday greetings. Sylvie opened it.

"Forty and fabulous" it said on the front, with a photo of a wizened old woman in frightened make-up. Thank you, Irene. And there was a postcard from Reenie. Sylvie read it quickly.

It was the Sun Holidays brochure that excited her. Bob had been so busy and distracted lately that Sylvie was feeling a little, well, ignored. No, that was too strong a word, she told herself. But she felt as if she and Bob needed to rekindle the lamp, the light that had always been at the center of their relationship. And now, with the children gone, there would be time.

The phone rang and Sylvie quickly took the mail with her to the hall table.

"Are you in a lesson?" Mildred, Sylvie's mother, began almost every phone conversation that way.

"No. But Harriet Blank is due over any minute."

"Lucky you. The only woman in the Greater Shaker Heights–Cleveland area with no boundaries whatsoever. After her, do you and Bob want to come over for dinner?"

"No thanks. I've defrosted chicken." Bob loved Mildred. But he got enough of Jim, Sylvie's father, on the car lot most days. Sylvie finished sorting through the mail. There was an envelope from Sun Holidays.

"Your father is barbecuing."

"Well, that is an inducement. I haven't eaten charcoal since July Fourth. You know, Kenny says Grandpa's burgers are carcinogens. Something about free radicals."

"The only free radical I know about is Patty Hearst," Mildred snapped. Sylvie opened the holiday envelope. It was the glossy brochure she's written away for. She unfolded it, her heart beating a little faster. The photos were like gems, glowing deep sapphire and emerald in the dimness.

"I thought I'd do your birthday dinner on Thursday. In case Bob was taking you out someplace fancy on Friday."

"He hasn't mentioned it. I'll ask him."

"Maybe it's a surprise."

"No surprise parties, Mom. I mean it. It's bad enough being forty. I don't need the whole cul-de-sac gloating. Not to mention Rosalie." Sylvie held the brochure up. There was a picture of a guest room with a canopy bed hung in white. She and Bob, tanned, lying under the canopy . . .

"Sylvie, are you moping? Not that I'd blame you. It's hard that both children had to leave at once. For me, I had six years to get used to Irene, William, and then you leaving. . . ."

"I'm not moping. I'm happy." Sylvie clutched the brochure and dropped the other mail into the basket. "I've got to get ready for my lesson."

"All right, dear. Call if you change your mind."

There was a tapping on the glass of the French door. Mrs. Harriet Blank—Honey to her friends—was standing at the back entrance. "You have a lot of leaves in the pool," she said as she stepped into the room. "You should get that automatic pool sweeper."

"Nice to see you, too," Sylvie said mildly. "It's been a long summer."

"I practiced every day," Honey assured her, defensive. The lazy students always told her that. Honey took off her sweater and lay her bag on the armchair. She moved toward the bench. "I saw you at L'Etoile, out by the lake, last week with Bob. You did something great to your face. . ."—Honey took a good look at Sylvie—". . . that night anyway. I thought maybe you had a face-lift over the summer. You know, Carol Meyers did. She looks awful. Stretched. I hear she went all the way to Los Angeles for it. Anyway, you looked great at L'Etoile."

"Bob and I haven't been out to dinner for months," Sylvie said mildly. "Not since Bob started campaigning for Chamber of Commerce."

Honey made a face of disbelief. "Are you lying or did you forget?" she asked.

"I wouldn't lie about being with my husband," Sylvie laughed. "Or a getting face-lift." She touched the part of her neck that had just begun to go crepey.

"Come on. You were there. The two of you were flirting like crazy. That's why I didn't even say hello. You guys looked so romantic."

"That proves I wasn't there. In Shaker Heights, husbands don't flirt with wives—at least not with their own."

"It was you." Honey paused. "Only your face was somehow. . . up. And you had only one chin." Honey examined Sylvie's face more closely. "You didn't seem to have a wrinkle. And you were tan."

"Honey, I never tan. Not since I was born. I turn red, crack and peel. My mother can verify that." Honey was a pain. "Shall we?" Sylvie asked, gesturing to the keyboard.

Honey leaned closer to Sylvie, examining her face. "Well, you were tan two weeks ago. Did you buy that thing on QVC with the tape and the rubber bands? That temporary face-lift thing?"

"No, but I once did get the Thighmaster. It's still under my bed. Want it?" Sylvie smacked her right leg and gestured Honey to sit at the bench. "Obviously, I never used it."

Honey seemed miffed by Sylvie's response. They settled down to some finger exercises. It was clear that Honey hadn't been practicing. Slowly they moved through the lesson. Somewhere near the end Sylvie thought she heard Bob's car. She glanced over at the brochure, propped at the edge of the music holder. Sylvie smiled.

At last the hour was up. Sylvie gave Honey a new assignment and walked her to the French doors. They said good-bye. Then Honey looked up at her. "If a person is going to look that good, even for one night, I think it's really mean not to share how you did it with a friend," Honey said.

"I share all my musical tips with you, Honey," Sylvie said. "Here's my best one: practice." Gently she pushed the door closed and turned to join her husband.

CHAPTER TWO

Bob wasn't at his desk or in the living room. Sylvie checked the kitchen, flipped the chicken that was sitting in its marinade and sighed. Bob must already have slipped upstairs.

Sylvie was halfway up the stairs herself before she realized that she had left the travel brochure in the music room. She turned around, bounded down the stairs, got the brochure and doubled back. Now she could hear the sound of the shower in the master bath. That was what she was afraid of. It meant that Bob was probably going out again this evening. The chicken would be wasted. Damn it! Sylvie didn't want to have to put off this conversation, but she didn't want to be forced to sandwich it in between Bob's ablutions and departure.

Since Bob had begun to talk about running for

Chamber of Commerce president he'd been so busy. Why did he even want the position? It didn't pay anything and it couldn't really be any fun. And why he needed to shave, change, and dress up for a smoke-filled room was also beyond her. It seemed as if he'd become more vain lately—she didn't remember him bothering to shower and shave before Rotary, even when he was the president of that. Sylvie got to the bedroom door, smoothed her hair and the brochure in her hand. It was time for a change for both of them. Charm and quirkiness worked with Bob. She smiled to herself as she walked through the bedroom. She stopped for a moment at her nightside table and took out a roll of adhesive tape. She'd get his attention.

She went into the bathroom. The steam pushed up against the door, up against her body with a wet force. She couldn't stop herself from looking at the place on the wall where the paint had begun to peel. She wished, for the hundredth time, that Bob would remember not to turn the water up quite so high, but he never did. Acceptance was just a part of marriage. Sylvie shrugged and walked over to the glass shower wall.

Through the mottled texture of the glass she could see Bob's body, but the effect the glass gave was to turn him into what looked like animated blots of color, kind of like the way technicians scrambled people's faces electronically on television when they were being interviewed against their will. She stared.

Pointillistic Bob. She picked up a hand towel and wiped down the glass. Jauntily, Sylvie pushed the brochure up against the shower wall and used the adhesive tape to secure it there, despite the moisture.

"Hi, honey. I have a surprise."

"Your lesson over?"

Sylvie could see that the white dots topping the pink dots of Bob's head had just about been washed off the animated figure that was her husband. That meant that the shampoo was over and that he could safely open his eyes. She tapped the glass. "See what I brought you," she said. She watched as he moved closer to the glass. He bent, suddenly almost against the textured partition and his face clearly emerged. Very wet, but recognizably Bob's nice-looking face. Close to the glass the wavering images didn't blur. She knew from the inside he could see the brochure.

"Show and tell?" he asked casually.

"Show and go," she said.

But then, to her disappointment, his head disappeared again. He became a Seurat painting: Tuesday in the shower with Bob.

No. He had to pay attention. She tapped the shower stall again. "Bob! Look! There haven't been colors like this since the seventies."

He was fumbling for something. "Beautiful. What is that? Something like Hawaii?"

"Good, Bob. It is Hawaii." For a moment she felt more hopeful, but then she realized he wasn't even looking. "You see those two people snorkeling? Isn't it weird how they look just like us? They could be us, Bob." Sylvie paused for his reaction. Then, to her dismay, she saw more white, animated dots appearing at the top of her husband's wavering form. He was shampooing twice. That was unusual. Bob never read the directions on any product or appliance, not since she met him. When did he ever read the instructions on the shampoo bottle? Since when did he soap up twice?

Sylvie quickly took the brochure down. Already its crisp new feel had begun to be transformed by the bathroom steam. The pictures now sagged across the double-page spreads. For a moment the sag was echoed by the sag of Bob's little belly, which emerged first from the stall, followed by the rest of him, only to be quickly wrapped in the special bath sheet he liked to use. Then, swaddled, he turned and inserted his arm into the shower, shutting off the water at last. The silence seemed startling to Sylvie, who felt more than a little bit forlorn for the moment. Perhaps Bob noticed, because he turned and gave her one of the big bear hugs that he was famous for. Just as she started to relax into it, he dropped his arms, turned to the sink, and took down his razor and the can of foam.

"You hear from the kids?" he asked casually.

"Nothing from Kenny, but Reenie sent a card. She says she wants to change her major again."

"No more French poetry?" Bob asked, spreading the foam along his right cheek and stretching his neck

320

up in that way men did before they patted the cream on their jowls.

"She feels she has to major in post-communist Russian studies."

"Has to? That seems like something no one has to do." He pulled the razor down his cheek.

As always, Sylvie felt she had to spring to the defense of their mercurial daughter. Temperamentally, Reenie and Bob were so similar that sometimes Sylvie had to run interference. "She's been thinking about it a lot. I admit she's a little at sea right now."

"Well, she better move up to an A, or a B-plus at the very least," Bob punned. He flashed her a quick smile. His teeth seemed yellow against the unusually white white of his foamy bubble beard. It gave him an almost unpleasant wolfish look. Sylvie thought of the phrase "long in the tooth." "She has to get a scholarship by next year is what she has to do," Bob continued. The razor sliced another path through the foam. "First she had to pick the most expensive school in America. Now she has to study irrelevant recent history. You can't even make a living in irrelevant ancient history."

"The two of us felt we had to major in music," Sylvie said quietly.

"Yeah. It sure helped me in my career. When I'm giving a test drive I know all the classical radio stations."

Sylvie didn't like the tone of this conversation. Bob seemed distracted and cranky. Normally, he was an indulgent father, a loving husband. Feeling a little desperate Sylvie leaned forward and taped the buckling brochure to the mirror beside the reflection of his now almost-shaved face. It was hard to get the tape to stick to the wet glass.

Bob ignored the thing and rinsed the razor. "It's not the seventies or eighties any more," he said. "Reenie has to begin thinking responsibly. Realistically. Do you realize the kids are older now than we were when we first met?"

"They're too short to be that old," Sylvie told him.

He laughed and used one hand to pinch the nape of her neck, giving her the tug that connected deep inside her. Sylvie smiled into the mirror at him and started to gesture to the brochure, but he pulled his hand away and bent over, rooting around in the cabinet under the sink.

"When we finished Julliard, we were going to travel around the country in a painted bus. And play music wherever we felt like it. Why didn't we do that?" Sylvie asked. Her voice, she realized, sounded plaintive. Where was quirky? Where was charm? Bob was slapping his face with an aftershave.

"Two reasons," he said. "We were a decade too late and we had a life instead."

"Bob. About Hawaii. For my birthday I'd really like to . . ."

"Oh no! A trip? Now? Come on, baby. That's out of the question. We have the new models just jamming the lot. Your father's talking about an advertising push, and I'm flirting with the idea of this political thing. Anyway, with tuitions . . . we just can't."

"It's not expensive," Sylvie protested. "Not at this time of year. The season hasn't begun yet. There's a package deal. And I have money saved from lessons."

"Hey! Pay for your own fortieth birthday present? I don't think so." He bent to her cheek and kissed her. His aftershave smelled unfamiliar. "Anyway, I already got your present for you. I brought it home tonight. Want to see it?" He pulled on his briefs, stepped into his slacks and looked around for his belt. Sylvie handed it to him. As he threaded it through his belt loops, Sylvie watched the brochure slide slowly down the wet mirror and crumple onto the vanity.

Bob, his shirt on, gave her another bear hug. "Hey! Come downstairs. Don't worry. I haven't forgotten your upcoming big day. Four decades! And you don't look a day over forty." She smiled weakly at him. He took her hand. "So, come on down and see your reward."

Sylvie slowly followed Bob as he led her downstairs, through the kitchen, out the back door, past the rose bed and her row of double peonies over to the driveway. The light was beginning to fade, and his car—his obsession—was parked in front of the garage.

"You're giving me Beautiful Baby for my birthday?" Sylvie joked mildly. If Bob had a choice between losing his car or his prostate, he'd probably keep the two seater. It was a perfectly restored 1971 XS200. But what in the world had he gotten for her? Her heart fluttered for a moment. Bob's car was tiny, but there was enough room in the glove compartment for a jewelry box.

"You know, my birthday isn't until Thursday. Shouldn't we wait until then?"

"Come on! You seem a little down. I want you to enjoy this as soon as possible. Use it on your birthday." Bob pressed the remote to open the garage doors. As they swung up, he turned on the lights.

There, illuminated by the overhead fluorescent, was a new BMW convertible. Across the hood a huge red bow was stretched. Bob put his arm around her. "Happy birthday, honey," he said. "Kids are gone. Time for a fun car. Enjoy yourself."

Sylvie looked at the sparkling silvery paint and shiny chrome object. "You took away my sedan?" she asked weakly.

"Don't worry about a thing. Already detailed and in the previously owned section." He gestured to the convertible. "Isn't she a beauty? Isn't that better than a trip to Hawaii?"

Sylvie reluctantly nodded. She should feel grateful and excited. Even if the family did own a BMW dealership and she got a new car as a matter of course. This one was special. She knew Bob couldn't keep the new convertibles on the lot. So why did she feel so . . . disappointed? She looked up at Bob. "Thank you," she said, trying to muster some enthusiasm. She failed. "It's great," she said, and she heard the flatness in her voice. God, she didn't want to hurt Bob's feelings.

But Bob didn't seem to notice. He patted the leather of the seat. "You'll love it as much as I love mine," he told her. Sylvie doubted that, but she managed a smile. "Look, I've got to go." He continued, "We'll take the car out for your birthday, okay? Maybe we'll drive up to the lake. Eat at L'Etoile. We haven't been there in a long time."

"Sure. Okay." Sylvia paused. "That's funny, because when Honey Blank came over today . . ."

Bob had pulled out his car keys. "Honey Blank? Can you tell me in four words or less?" he asked. "Or save it for later. I really have to go."

"Never mind. I'll tell you when you get home," Sylvie agreed. What difference did it make?

"I might be late. I won't wake you." Bob got into Beautiful Baby and started her up. For a moment Sylvie saw him there as a stranger: a middle-aged man with a bit of a paunch sitting in a very young sportscar.

"I wouldn't mind if you did wake me," she told him, but he had already begun backing out of the driveway. He waved as he pulled into the cul-de-sac and then accelerated. Sylvie watched him go.

She stood for a moment in the twilight, the ugly fluorescent shining out of the garage behind her making the macadam under her feet look slick with oil.

"Well. That's impressive."

Sylvie looked up. God! It was Rosalie the Bitter, her ex–sister-in-law. It wasn't that Sylvie didn't love Rosalie and feel sorry for her. She even took her side over her brother's, but Rosalie was difficult.

"A new car?" Rosalie asked. "I can't even get Phil to fix my transmission. And he's in charge of the service department."

There was no way to have a conversation with Rosalie. Everything was a complaint or an attack. Though she'd wound up with the house, alimony, and healthy child support, Rosalie still felt cheated. Of course, Sylvie had to admit she had been cheated on.

"Have you been jogging?" Sylvie asked, to change the subject and to say something. Rosalie was in shorts and the kind of industrial Nikes that cost in the three figures. Sylvie pressed the garage button to close the door.

Rosalie ignored the question. It seemed to Sylvie that she'd displaced most of the energy Rosalie used to use nagging Phil and now used it to exercise with. Rosalie jogged, lifted weights, taught aerobics, and even attended a yoga class in downtown Cleveland. Maybe, Sylvie thought, she should give Rosalie her Thighmaster. "You know how lucky you are?" Rosalie demanded. "Do you know?" Rosalie looked around at the flower beds, the lawn, the house. "A new car in your garage, two kids in college, and a husband in your bed." Rosalie shook her dark head.

Sylvie turned away and started for the back door.

She felt sorry for Rosalie—her three children were out of school and out of work. But she never stopped complaining. Rosalie followed her across the slate patio. Rosalie the Stuck.

"Forty isn't easy for any woman. But if anyone has it easy, you do," Rosalie was saying. "You're lucky. You've always been lucky."

Sylvie got to the screen door and opened it. Then, from the inside, she locked the button. "You're right, Rosalie," Sylvie said through the screen. "I'm lucky. My life is a paradise."

Then she shut the back door.

CHAPTER THREE

Sylvie had put the top down, although there was a chill in the air. It was wasteful to drive the new convertible with the heat pumping and the top off but she was doing it. What the hell. She'd be self-indulgent. She was forty. Live a little!

The groceries she'd just bought were arranged neatly in four bags across the backseat and as she took a sharp turn she glimpsed them in the mirror. They shifted but didn't spill. Before the children had left she used to have to fill the trunk of the sedan with groceries—Kenny ate like a horse. Now four bags and a dollar tip to the box boy was all it took to fill the back seat and the larder at home.

The wind whipped at her hair. It was odd there was so much air, but she couldn't seem to breathe.

Somehow all she could manage were shallow breaths. Maybe she should take a yoga class.

Last night after choking down a dinner of over-done chicken alone she'd waited for Bob. He'd come in after midnight and he hadn't wanted to talk. Sylvie didn't push it. Instead she'd lain awake most of the night, sleepless and confused.

Out of nowhere a car pulled out of an almost hidden driveway on her right. Sylvie moved the wheel and the convertible swerved. A van was in the oncoming lane. The slightest touch brought her car back, long before the van was a danger to her. She had to admit that the convertible was beautiful to drive, but she didn't want it. It was wrong somehow. It felt wrong.

What's wrong with me? Sylvie thought. Most women would give up their husbands for a car like this. Or give up their cars for a husband like mine. And I have both. Rosalie is right. I'm very lucky. I should be grateful. I'm healthy, I love Bob, he loves me, the kids are fine. It's a beautiful sunny day and the leaves are just starting to turn colors. The unease she felt, the sense of dissatisfaction wasn't like her. Sylvie felt ashamed at her unhappiness, but it was there right under her breast bone. She stopped for a red light, the car gliding smoothly and effortlessly to a stop.

The steering wheel under her hands became wet with sweat. The feeling of unease that had been building in her, lodging in her chest, now moved into her throat and blocked it. She tried to swallow and couldn't do it. It didn't matter anyway—her mouth was so dry there was nothing to swallow. Either I'm going crazy or something is really wrong, she thought as the light turned green. A horn blared behind her. The driver hadn't even given her a minute. She accelerated. All at once she was swept with a surge of anger—of rage—so complete that she had trouble seeing the road. She looked in the rearview mirror at the old man in the big Buick behind her and flipped him the bird.

God! She'd never done that before in her life. What was going on?

She didn't want this car. Bob hadn't thought of her when he took it off the lot. He took her for granted. He hadn't listened about Hawaii, either. When was the last time he had listened? She didn't want automatic gifts, no matter how luxurious. She didn't want to be taken for granted. She didn't want to be ignored by Bob. There were so many things that she had that she didn't want, she felt almost dizzy and nearly missed the left-hand turn into the cul-de-sac. She burned rubber making the turn. She drove slowly on Harris Place, the street she lived on, where her mother had the big house with the white columns and where her brother had lived before he divorced Rosalie. The few other houses there were all traditional, well-designed and maintained. She drove past the beds of vinca in front of the Williamsons and the row of gold chrysanthemums unimaginatively lined along Rosalie's fence. Everything appeared so right, but this foreboding, this sense that it was wrong, became insupportable. It was as if the open top of the car let the weight of the universe in to crush her. Her house, the house she loved, loomed up.

Sylvie made a sharp right and felt the wheels of the BMW effortlessly move over the curb. Calmly, she drove the car across her own side lawn and, when she reached it, through the perennial border, right over the delphiniums and peonies. She felt an icy calm as she proceeded onto the back lawn and engineered a carefully calculated right turn, avoiding the slate patio. The aqua rectangle of the pool was right before her and, without slowing down, she headed for it, the car like a homing device moving toward the concrete edge of the eight foot diving drop. As the front wheels spun out into empty space just before they took the plunge into the turquoise water, Sylvie was able to take the first deep breath she had taken all day.

Bestseller

Olivia Goldsmith

'Told with such brio . . . there is plenty to savour'
Mail on Sunday

It's autumn in New York, and in the anything but gentle-
manly world of books the knives are out as the new
season's list is launched. Stars and wannabees, hustlers
and has-beens all scramble for the prizes, the profits and
the prestige – not least at big-time publishing house Davis
& Dash where success depends on a handful of authors:

Susann Baker Edmonds: the face-lifted megastar whose
blockbusters have topped the charts for longer than
anyone can remember.

Gerald Ochs Davis: novelist and publishing supremeo –
known to his minions as G.O.D. Is his latest offering worth
the million dollars he paid himself?

Camilla Clapfish: a demure English rose. A chance
romantic encounter brought her elegant little novel to
Davis & Dash.

Behind the books and the writers, and the people who
make and break them, is a whole world of passion, politics
and intrigue. Who will survive in the race to the top?

0 00 649673 3

Olivia Goldsmith

Fashionably Late

'A bittersweet tale brimming with excitement'
Company

Wherever she goes, forty-year-old Karen Kahn is fashionably late. She can afford to be: the star of the New York
fashion scene, with her own company, a handsome husband
and a deal that could make her millions, she is the apple –
and the envy - of everyone's eye.

But she is too late for the ultimate in creation: a baby.
Motherhood is proving to be elusive – as elusive as her own
parentage, and as difficult as the cut-throat business of
couture. Yet Karen is not one to take no for an answer, and
late is better than never . . .

'Full of wisecracks, and gossip . . . this is a book for the beach.
Olivia Goldsmith can keep you reading'   *Cosmopolitan*

0 00 647972 3

£4.99 net

Sisters & Lovers

Connie Briscoe

'A frank and funny tale about the everyday lives of three black women' *Essence*

Beverly, Charmaine and Evelyn are three sisters living in the same Maryland town outside Washington D.C., each wishing her life were just a little different.

Beverly is twenty-nine and single, a successful magazine editor who would love to be in love. The problem is, no man can meet her high standards. Charmaine longs to finish her degree, but meanwhile she has to juggle a thankless job, a beautiful child, and an irresponsible husband she doesn't quite have the nerve to leave. Evelyn has her own psychology practice and her husband is a partner in a prestigious law firm. She seems to have it made - but there's trouble in paradise, and Evelyn is refusing to face the facts.

Warm and bittersweet, believable and real, *Sisters & Lovers* is a novel of families and love, heartache and hope, and above all, the triumph of sisterhood.

'In *Sisters & Lovers*, Connie Briscoe has drawn a vivid and dramatic portrait that will make readers laugh out loud and nod their heads in recognition' *Los Angeles Bay News Observer*

0 00 649804 3